JACK BLOODFIST: FIXER

JAMES JAKINS

To whoever gave me that first book.

PROLOGUE

The texture is of fresh-cut grass. Not at all what I expected.

The whole experience, if eyes were closed, might be confused for rolling down a steep hill.

Beneath me, below this invisible grass, I can see the countless lights of the universe. The swirling, infinite expanse stands in stark contrast to the rest of my surroundings.

With each rotation in my spinning descent around the perimeter of time and space I am forced to look out into the darkness.

The darkness outside creation. The darkness that creeps into the spaces between things, between worlds. Hiding within that never-ending nothing is all that God has rejected.

When He saw the Light and called it good, He rejected this space. Or perhaps He just hasn't seen it yet. Maybe it has escaped His notice, and now hides here, at the end of infinity, outside any realms of light.

It is sobering, to find yourself on this precipice between life and the absence of living. To have, on one side, the infinite, lonely beauty of stars and suns and life, and on the other to have an absolute nothing.

Darkness that cannot even rightly be called darkness. Because to call it darkness, you have to first accept that at some point there was, or will be, light.

I roll further down the hill that is life, until, after what feels a million lifetimes-and maybe it is-the bottom comes into view.

Beneath the invisible structure that separates everything from nothing is the Great Plain.

As far as my eyes can see is the dull brown-green of rough grass. Here and there small hills break the endless expanse.

One half of the plain is lit by the dim light of countless, distant stars. The other seems to be an endless expanse of darkest night. In the lack of light, no grass grows, and the dirt glows with an inner light, somehow making it seem that much more barren.

The more I consider this place, the more I think that maybe this dead or dying world that spreads beneath the infinite and the nonexistent is Hell.

I think, when the stories are told of the fallen being cast down, this is where they went. I think it's from this place that war is waged against any righteous that might exist out there.

I don't know, though. Honestly, in this moment, all I do know is that for a little while, I had been a god.

But right now, as I end my descent around the needle-point of the universe, where it stabs into pale, red dirt, I know that life is over.

Sound rushes in. The gentle rustle of stale wind through dead grass. After so long in the complete silence of my fall, it is loud enough that I must cover my ears.

The countless rotations of my descent make themselves known.

I fall to my knees and empty anything my stomach has. It isn't much, and the thirsty dirt drinks greedily.

I push myself up, and spare a glance at the dual skies above.

I roar with a voice known for its volume, "I'm coming back for you, you son of a bitch!"

Neither of the skies bothers to answer. Just as well. I probably wouldn't like any answer given.

And now, you want to know everything. You want to know who I am, and how I came to this place.

The answer can be given simply. I lived. I fought and killed. I loved a woman. I became a hero. Then a god. I was betrayed and sent here in place of another.

But you want the full story. You want specifics.

Fine. I'll tell you.

ONE

From the outside the building looks like any of the other skyscrapers in the city.

Maybe a little more modern, definitely more expensive. But still, the world headquarters of the Dongli Conglomerate mostly just looks like any other office building belonging to a billion-dollar company.

Because that's what it is. It houses the offices of some of the most powerful people on the planet.

What it also has, that very few other building in New York have, are cells.

Cells containing some of the most dangerous men and women in this world and others.

About halfway up the generous floor count, the cells start.

In one of these cells a man is kneeling. The spartan chamber holds him, a cot, a stainless steel toilet, and a camera that watches his every movement.

This is where, for the purposes of this story, we start.

His name is Arthur Shield. A long time ago, in a whole

other world, he was a high-ranking servant to a very powerful deity.

You might not believe it now, looking at him. A thick unkempt beard scrapes the worn concrete floor of his cell as he bows his body in prayer to his god.

He has done this almost everyday since being put in this cell.

He is a dangerous man, but without the blessings given him by his god, he is only as dangerous as any well-trained mortal can be.

That is why he prays. He has faith that if his prayers are long and loud enough, his lord Saban will hear him, and grant him the power he needs to escape his prison and seek revenge on those responsible for his crisis.

It turns out, that all you really need to get something you want is to pray for twenty years straight.

The camera that watches the small, round chamber catches everything.

The guards on duty watch the video feed, slightly confused at Shield's sudden change in behavior.

The man stands up, a grateful smile on his usually menacing face. They are more concerned, however, with the glowing eyes.

"Thank you," Arthur Shield says as he raises an open palm to the ceiling.

For an instant the same ethereal light that comes from his eyes glows around his upraised hand.

The camera dies and every alarm in the building begins to scream.

On every floor that houses prisoners, there is a room full of guards. Mostly they just play pool and watch whichever sporting event they can find on the TV that hangs above their mini fridge, but they are all trained killers.

Some of them used to reside in the very cells they now guard, but good behavior has its rewards.

Now, as alarms blare and radios scream out the floor and cell number, they all rush to arm themselves.

"It's Shield," a floor commander yells as he strap a vest and slings a rifle over his shoulder.

"He's a norm, right?" One of his men ask. There has been no precedent for them to expect anything from Shield.

"Thought so. Either way, shoot to kill."

There is a chorus of agreement right before they all march out of the combined break room/armory and into the hallway.

The lights of this floor have gone out. One florescent bulb flickers, trying to cling to life, before dropping the hall into darkness.

The guards click on lights attached to their vests and make their way to the cell of Arthur Shield.

There are no windows on the cells inside the Dongli Conglomerate building. There are prisoners in there that can kill with a look.

These prisoners are not even given cameras. It's just assumed they are alive. Or they're not. No one really seems to care enough to even consider Schrodinger or his cat.

The guard captain approaches the door, holding a hand up for silence. He places an ear to the thick steel door, in the vain hope that maybe he can hear something.

There is a snicker from one of his fellows and he casts a baleful eye toward the sound.

"Guns ready," he says.

There is the quiet clatter of rifles being shouldered.

He sidles over to the console next to the door, his rifle held with one hand, aiming with the rest of them.

There is the beep of a code being entered into a touch

screen, then he scans a card that hangs on a lanyard from his neck.

The door slides open, the sound of well-oiled gears moving in the walls.

Their lights reveal nothing but the settling of dust from the destroyed ceiling. There is also a steady dripping sound.

A curious guard aims his light toward the sound. Hanging from the hole in the ceiling is a hand, the body attached to the hand still hidden in darkness.

Blood travels the length of the arm, dripping off one of the fingers.

The captain, at this sight, grabs at the radio on his shoulder.

This is when Arthur Shield attacks.

He drops from the hole in the ceiling, his body engulfed in a blue fire. The occupant of the cell above held firmly in burning fists.

None of the guards wait for orders. They open fire.

The bullets tear through the dead man Arthur is using as his defense, but none seem to hit him.

The corpse in his hands erupts in flame and he throws the burning figure into the nearest guard.

They all leap back, recovering quickly and raising guns again to fire on Shield.

He moves faster than any looking at him would expect. His speed and strength seem too much for a man of his age.

The first guard he touches begins to scream in pain as the fire around Arthur's hands spreads. Soon the guard lies on the floor, the dancing blue of fire his only movement.

The other guards stand in shocked silence, though only for a moment. They are trained for these contingencies. For many of them, this is not the first time they have seen something like this.

Again, rifles are shouldered and the hallway erupts with the sound of gunfire.

The air around the prisoner shimmers with the same blue that fills his eyes and fuels the flames that cover him.

The bullets bounce of the shield of light that surrounds him, and the walls crack and shatter at the countless impacts.

Shield does not wait for the magazines to empty. He doesn't need to.

His eyes burn brighter as he jumps forward, the around him alive with the fire of his god's power and the sparks of ricocheting led.

His hand darts toward the nearest guard. He grabs the forearm and wrenches the rifle from the man's grasp.

He spins, leg flashing out, kicking the man in the chest.

The guard flies across the hallway, crumpling into a useless pile after connecting with a wall.

Shield faces the remaining guards and holds up his new weapon.

The guard captain has time to consider that maybe they shouldn't have trained this man to use a gun

A small area in the air in front of Arthur opens, allowing him to fire his rifle through his shield.

The rounds tear through the standing guards, painting the floor and walls with a handful of lives.

In the end, only the captain is alive. He sits on the floor, his back against the broken, blood-stained wall, gasping for breath.

"Stop," he wheezes, aiming his empty weapon with a shaky hand.

Arthur Shield turns to consider the man.

"No. If I stay, I'll be forced to kill more of you. It's really for the best that I leave." His voice is deep, commanding. It is the voice of a man that knows power.

"They'll stop you," the guard says.

"No, they won't." The prisoner steps back to the guard and places a blazing hand to his vest.

The guard manages a pained whine as the flames engulf his body.

Arthur does not stay to watch the man burn down to ash.

He walks calmly down the length of the corridor to where he knows elevators wait.

He flicks the security card he has stolen from a fallen guard over a security console.

The doors slide open with a soft "ding," and gentle, nondescript piano music filters into the silent hallway.

Arthur reaches inside the elevator, without stepping inside, and touches the card to a second security console.

After it acknowledges the card with another electronic tone he pushes the button for the top floor.

He steps back into the hallway and waits patiently as the doors close and the elevator rises.

The power to the elevator is cut before it gets more than three floors up, but that is more than enough for Shield.

He works his fingers between the closed doors and pries them open.

Before him is a fifty-foot drop through darkness. With another prayer on his lips he steps into air.

The lobby of the building is filled with guards now. Any guests have either been asked to leave, or locked in one of the many panic rooms the company has prepared for just such an occasion.

More security personnel are positioned outside the building to discourage anyone from wandering inside.

Several of the company's more specialized guards wait in the lobby as well, men and women trained to either use magics of some kind, or to disable the gifts of others.

They stand, dispersed around the lobby, some with artifacts of their various arts held at the ready. Others hold hands open, or closed, or in fighting stances.

They all hear the sound from above them: The crash of glass as the windows of the story above them burst and rain down into the plaza below.

Their prey sails through the air, landing squarely on the upturned face of a suit-wearing guard.

The Italian silk of the suit bursts into flames along with its owner.

The flash is bright enough that all watching cover their eyes.

Many of them recover quickly, but the brief moment of distraction is all the escapee needs. Arthur Shield is gone.

For the rest of that day, and the following, they hunt him.

They do not find him. He hides in alleys and in stolen cars, walks through crowds that will never recognize him because his captors cannot afford to let the world know he exists.

He has no fear of them finding him. His god has returned to him. From a different world, with infinite chasms between them, Saban has found him and given him his power again.

Arthur Shield accepts this power and the mission that comes with it.

When he came to this world, he came seeking relics stolen from his temple. He will find them, and those that took them.

He will find the monsters, and he will kill them. Every. Last. One.

Now, the thing about goblin food is that it's greasy. I mean, shit-through-a-screen-door-at-thirty-paces greasy.

It pays to have family in the food service business. Free food, no matter how quickly it goes through me, is not something I would ever turn down.

And, for those in the know, goblin fry cooks are in very high demand. They mastered the American dining experience long before they ever set foot in the country.

It's an amazing heritage, let me tell you.

Luckily, if nothing else, it's a heritage that comes with a hole-in-the-wall diner.

Jack's Place is not named after me. The restaurant and I share a namesake. As do a couple dozen of my cousins, on both sides.

Our namesake, Jackson Smith, is a pretty popular guy. Comes with the territory, I suppose. He's a powerful wizard who also happens to be the savior of two large tribes. Every orc and goblin on the planet owes him their lives.

So, as a result, Jackson—and every variation of that name—will be the first choice every time a goblin or orc is born.

I know what you're thinking. What kind of wizard is named Jackson? Well, my understanding is that he was born in the Midwest United States somewhere, so Radagast probably wasn't a likely choice.

My real name is actually Garack. Good strong orc name. I did mention I was an orc right? No, I'm sure you caught that.

Garack was my father's name. He was the one responsible for uniting the tribes.

The one to blame for us having to move to Summervale, Virginia.

I was born in the old country, so when we came to the States my name was changed. Less likely to draw attention to the fact that we were not human, I guess.

Since the family settled, none of my cousins have even bothered with traditional names. All Jacks and Jills.

It's actually pretty amazing how quickly people can adapt to a new culture.

Sorry, probably too much info up front for you. Let me start over.

My name is Jack Bloodfist, and I'm an orc. Well, half-orc. Mom was a goblin. Love is blind, right?

I inherited more of the orcish looks, though, so I just say I'm an orc.

And despite what you might be picturing, I'm not some hideous, malformed mutant.

I'd be lying if I said there were websites dedicated to my beauty, but I'm definitely not the ugliest in the family. Not by human standards, at least. And those are the only ones that really count in this world.

Thanks to the small, slender frame of the goblin I'm not as much of a hulking brute as some of my full-blooded orc cousins. In fact, my size is pretty close to within the normal range for most humans.

There are other things I have to deal with that might give me away. The tusks, for one.

Like most of the other orcs in the area, I trim those. They grow back pretty fast, but a good grinding every two days or so keeps them from sticking up over the top lip.

I also grow a decent beard, which I let grow as much as possible to hopefully hide my fairly noticeable underbite.

My ears also point a little bit, but less than some of the elves I've met over the years. And not really enough that anyone's ever actually commented.

Hair? Well, unfortunately I inherited my mother's hair. Goblin hair is almost as greasy as their food, so I keep that dome bald.

Mostly I do everything I can to move around unnoticed.

I had to for my job back then.

As you might imagine, when you suddenly transplant a large horde of goblins and a decent-sized orc fist into suburban Virginia, problems arise.

Someone needs to play the part of middle-man. Fix any issues that may pop up. Smooth over that good old-fashioned tribal violence with the local PD. All that fun stuff.

That's what I did. My father did it until his death five years ago, then I took over.

At the time I felt pretty proud of it. Even had cards made. I thought I was an essential part of the community.

I even took my responsibilities pretty seriously. I had an old ratty suit I threw on anytime I had official business to take care of.

This usually led to an interrogation from my mother and her father, who ran Jack's Place.

The fact that I also wore the suit on any dates I happened to have, as rare as they were, meant they got excited.

Most goblins don't live to see their grandkids be born, so Ma wanted that, and Gramps wanted to be the first goblin to meet his great-grandkids.

Honestly, I felt no regret in disappointing them.

"Meeting lady friend tonight?" Gramps asked me in his

broken English from behind the counter. He stood on a custom ledge that ran the length of it so he almost stood eye level with me as I sat there.

I focused on the massive plate of greasy potatoes, meat, and eggs, mostly gone.

I had only one errand for the day. Just one of those little things the family liked me to take care of so they didn't have to.

"Maybe later," I answered truthfully. I never knew when the lady friend in question might be up for something, though I never had actually told Gramps there was only one. He assumed I was the town lady-killer. Which was ridiculous.

"Work then?" he asked.

It wasn't hard to hear the curiosity in his voice. My work always had the possibility of being a gold mine for gossip. Goblins love gossip.

"You remember Devin?" I asked.

He gave me a blank stare in response.

"Snaga?" I said, taking a minute to recall his name before the move.

"Ah, Shakill's oldest?"

"Karen, yeah." My father's sister had also changed her name. Gramps was really the only one in the families that had any problem remembering that we had to fit in.

None of us really tried to correct him. It's not that orcs or goblins have a traditional respect-your-elders philosophy. It's all about strength. As a result, most didn't live very long.

Gramps was almost eighty. That was practically unheard of for anyone that had grown up in the homeland. My generation might expect that to be almost normal, but not those that came before us. We didn't have to deal with any of the shit this old man had lived through.

So everyone in the community respected the old bastard. They also like his cooking. That helps.

"Yes, yes, Karen." He waved an annoyed hand at my correction. "What about the boy?"

I shoveled a pile of greasy potatoes into my mouth and spoke around the food. "Moving back into town, bringing his fiancée with."

Devin had been a few years older than me, so I had never known him very well.

Being a little more orc than me, he'd also taken up with the local street toughs, though Summervale didn't really have anything worthy of his time, so when he was older he moved to New York.

If I'm being honest, I think he just moved out there to become an actor. I mean, seriously, why else does anyone move to New York? Stand-up?

"So you, what? Set up house for them?" Gramps asked.

I nodded as I pulled some egg out of my beard. "Got a trailer ready for them, just need to hand them the keys."

This was something I did a lot. Whenever someone decided to move back home they had a place to stay until they got their feet underneath them.

My landlady always kept two or three of her units vacant for me. She's a nice lady, for a gnome.

"This fiancée," Gramps asked, "she pretty?"

"No idea. Never met her."

"If she pretty, you should steal her. He doesn't need a wife. You do."

"I'll take that into consideration."

"Good. How's the food today?" he asked.

"Good as always, sir." I shoveled more grease into my mouth.

"Damn right it's good. Fresh-laid eggs, boy. Much better than store-bought shit."

I nodded my somber agreement as I finished the last of the plate.

"So, I make lunch for the orc and your future wife?"

"Sounds good. I'll send them by."

"When they arrive?"

"I'm meeting them at my place in..." I pulled my phone out of my pocket and checked the time. "Shit, ten minutes. I'd better go."

I wiped egg yolk and grease out of my beard and tossed the napkin on my plate.

"Tell Ma I said hi," I shouted over my shoulder.

The old goblin waved a dismissive hand as he started to clean up my breakfast.

Once outside, the humid summer air hit me and I regretted my commitment to the suit.

Jack's Place is on the outskirts of Summervale, right off the freeway.

On one side is the main road that runs into town, lined with gas stations and run-down apartment buildings. Another is the rarely busy aforementioned freeway, and every other side is flanked by thick groves of Virginia pine. At least I think that's what they are. Could be maple. You know what, let's just say trees.

I crossed the parking lot, the sun-baked asphalt hot under the thin soles of my worn shoes, and unlocked my old Cadillac.

It wasn't the greatest car in the world, probably very far from it, but I loved it.

My phone vibrated as I climbed behind the wheel.

"Jack," I said as I answered without looking at the caller info.

"Bloodfist," a terse voice said, "got a body at the morgue. Need you to ID the bastard."

"Well, good morning to you too, Denny," I said to the woman on the other end.

"What did I say about that?" Her voice carried its normal aggression.

"Sorry. Good morning, Detective Halldorson." I tried my best to oversell the formality,

"When can you come in?" she asked, tone just as angry despite my etiquette. "Fresh orc corpse in the morgue."

"Ah, shit. Who is it? One of the Jacks?" I was more annoyed than anything.

I'm basically related to every orc on the planet. Not directly. There are three different clans in our fist, but they're all basically family.

All that really means is that anytime one of us bites it, it's a death in the family. Which would suck if we were more sentimental.

Still, it's kind of sad if you think about it too much. In just a few generations there won't be any real orcs left. That alone makes each death hurt a little more. Well, it should, anyway.

It also makes our natural tendencies to look for trouble seem a whole lot dumber than they might have in the homeland.

"If I knew who he was I wouldn't ask you to ID him. I'd ask you to find their next of kin. You do remember how this works, right?"

"So, no ID then?"

She let out a long sigh, "No. No ID. Farmer found the body in his field this morning. When can you come in?"

I checked the time on my car's clock. "I have an

appointment in a few minutes. Shouldn't take more than half an hour. That okay?"

"Yeah, that's fine. I'll keep him cold for you." She hung up before I could say anything else.

Denelle Halldorson is not the friendliest individual. I do still consider her a friend, even if she doesn't always share the opinion.

She's always been really good about keeping us informed about any situations that should probably be kept away from the general population. She's even willing to help if you need to cover something up. Really good at it too.

She's had plenty of practice. Living in the same city for two hundred years without anyone noticing takes some skill. I was just happy she was willing to use those skills to help me do my job.

I returned my phone to my pocket as I pulled into the trailer park.

I know. You were expecting me to have some smoky office downtown. I wish. I can barely afford the rent for my trailer. The families would never spring for an office.

An old sedan was parked in front of my trailer. I pulled into my tiny driveway and studied the woman standing on my front porch.

Tall, slender, and blond. Just missing the red dress.

I couldn't see her face, because her hands were cupped over it as she tried to see through the dirty window on my door.

TWO

"Can I help you?" I asked, slamming my car door.

She spun at the sudden sound, leaf-green eyes open wide in surprise.

"Are you Jack?" she asked. Her accent was European. Nordic, if I knew anything. Which, honestly, I don't.

"I am. You must be Devin's fiancée. Keelee, right?" I walked up the steps and extended my hand.

She accepted it and nodded shyly as her free hand pushed her bright hair behind her ear. Her pointed ear.

"You're an elf," I blurted out without thinking.

Her hand was still trapped in my grip, and my sudden grin must have scared her. It took two pulls before I realized she was trying to free her hand.

She spoke when I finally released her. "Half. My father's elven. Or was. I really don't know."

"Ah, sorry. Not really any of my business." I continued to be a creep and stared at her ear.

She moved her hair back over the ear and blushed slightly. Somehow the embarrassment made her more attractive.

I realized how much of an ass I probably looked and gave myself a quick lecture. I'd seen elves before. Detective Halldorson is an elf. Well, drow, but still. Elf.

The thing was, there are even fewer elves in the world than there are orcs. So you really don't see them often.

And I've always had a thing for elf chicks. Don't judge me.

"So, uh, where's Devin?" I asked after the awkward silence had grown to an unbearable volume.

"He had some business to take care of outside of town. He said I should come in ahead and get settled. He should be in tonight sometime."

"Alright. Well, let me just grab the keys and I'll show you the place."

She moved out of my way, quickly shuffling sideways, arms folded across her slender chest.

I pulled out my keys and unlocked the trailer.

The closest thing to the smoky office I could hope for at the time was the living room of that trailer.

It was definitely dingy enough. A messy desk sat directly across the narrow living room from the door.

I'd placed the keys for Devin and Keelee's trailer where I knew I'd remember to look. They sat on top of a pile of books I'd ordered online the week before, the latest rule books for a popular tabletop RPG. I don't play. Seriously, I don't. But I like to study the different mythologies that surround my heritage.

I'm occasionally pleased to find that they get stuff right. Sometimes.

Keelee stood in the doorway and anxiously studied the room.

It wasn't messy. It was never really messy. More of an organized clutter

I grabbed the keys and turned back to her.

She had stepped inside the trailer and was studying a shelf I had hanging next to the door.

"What are these?" she asked, indicating the rows of figurines that lined the shelf.

"Just some stuff I've collected over the years." I walked up to the shelf and readjusted a small brass camel so it was facing the same direction as the jade elephant next to it.

Those two were accompanied by a whole menagerie of animals. There were almost as many materials as there were animals.

The other half of the shelf was my orc army—figurines from different games and hobby shops.

I swear, I don't play with them. Anymore...

"This one looks different." Her finger gently probed my prize piece.

It was a small eagle, carved from a strange blue and white layered stone. Its wingspan was almost as wide as my palm.

It was the only one of its kind in the world, in any world, as far I knew.

"That belonged to my Pops," I said.

He had given it to me the day he died. It was a trophy from his last raid before Jackson had brought us to Summervale.

"I see." She seemed to sense my tone and offered me a consoling smile, though her eyes lingered on the shelf.

"Well," I jangled the keys, "let me show you your new place."

I led her outside and began to explain some of the rules of the park.

"Most of the residents are non-human," I said, "so you don't have to be too careful about hiding things, but common sense is always appreciated. I don't know if Devin told you, but Summervale actually has one of the highest non-human populations in the eastern United States."

She nodded her head and feigned interest as I played tour guide.

"The city was founded by gnomes, you know."

"Gnomes?" That apparently surprised her.

"Oh yeah. The history books will tell you it was the Irish. I guess they may have been Irish, but the point is, gnomes. They've got their fingers in just about every pie in town. Your new landlady is a gnome. Moira's a nice lady. I'll introduce you later."

I realized I was off topic and returned to the rules, "So there's a rule about loud noises after ten. And, let's see... no rituals, rites of passage, or sacrifices in the park. Since some of those can get pretty messy, we're all asked to keep those to whichever church, synagogue, or grove is meant for each activity."

She gave me a look that I had seen almost every time I brought up that rule, the half-disgusted, all-curious kind of look.

"The rule wouldn't exist if someone hadn't made it necessary," I said with a shrug. "I honestly don't know what happened, but Moira reminds me to emphasize that one every time. Other than that, it's mostly a do-whatever-you-want kind of place."

"Are there other elves in town?" she asked.

"I know of one. Denny. She's a drow."

Keelee's face twisted for just an instant before returning to normal.

"Elves are about the only race not really represented much. Though I guess that to be expected, huh?"

She nodded, her face sad.

"Everyone else is here though. About a dozen little communities like the park throughout town. Some a little more, ah, specialized? Than others. I'm sure you'll see Orc Town when Devin takes you to meet his family."

"Orc Town?" She asked.

I laughed. "It's not really orc town. More humans than orcs. But enough of us live there that I just call it that. Goblin Burrows? Now that's a real thing. Two whole apartment buildings on the edge of town. Every apartment stuffed with goblins. You'd really think people would notice a building full of little green men, but no one seems to have caught on yet."

"Humans are very good at not seeing what they don't want to," Keelee said, voice bitter.

"True," I agreed. "I don't mind. Keeps me employed. If they were more keen on seeing, I probably wouldn't be very successful, and would probably have to find a real job. Here we are." I stopped in front of the trailer I had reserved for her and Devin.

I unlocked the front door and pushed it open, then I stepped aside and handed Keelee the keys.

She walked past me and inspected the bare living room.

An old couch sat against one wall and an old, boxy television set sat on the floor in front of it. A stamp on the side of the ancient picture box proudly declared it the property of the Sunside Motel.

"This is..." She paused to consider her next word, and finally settled on, "nice."

She did not sound like she believed that one bit.

"No it's not," I said, "but it's free. First month's rent is paid and you have at least that long to find somewhere less..." I indicated the room with a wave of my hand, letting that be my adjective.

"Shitty?" she asked, looking at me over her shoulder.

I shrugged. "Yeah, pretty much. Sorry. Look I've gotta to run. I have another appointment this morning."

I fished around in my suit's breast pocket and pulled out a faded business card.

It was thin card stock, with my name in blocky letters on the top—"Jack Bloodfist"—and in slightly smaller letters below that, these in a charming blood red, the word "Fixer."

I'd ordered a couple hundred of the things years before, when I'd taken over for my father.

I rarely, if ever, had a reason to give them to people. Anyone that ever actually needed my help usually had me saved in their phones already. It wasn't really a business that demanded clients. I kinda just did crap for the same people.

So it always made me feel pretty great whenever I got to give one away.

"My number's on the back. Call me if you need anything."

I paused for a second, remembering something else. I dug around in another suit pocket and pulled out another slip of paper. It was a coupon for Jack's Place. In big letters on the front it read, "Free fries with any purchase."

I handed her the crumbled coupon. "I can show you the way later, if you like. Devin probably knows the way. My grandfather owns the place. Tell him I sent you."

"Thank you." She accepted the card and coupon, her voice not quite matching the gratitude of her words.

"And you know where I live if you can't reach me on the phone. My job is to make sure you and Devin are taken care of until you're settled.

She offered me an impatient smile as I backed out of the door. I turned my back on her and walked down the steps. It was not my most awkward visit with a woman. At least it was over.

I locked my own trailer and climbed inside my car.

It started with a cough and spewed out a column of black. I guided it out of the park and toward town.

It was time to see which of my cousins had gotten themselves killed.

———

It was Devin. I mean, of course it was. Why wouldn't it be?

"Know him?" Detective Halldorson asked.

I rolled my eyes at her. Of course I knew him. She knew I knew him. Hell, I know every orc on the planet. Maybe not by name, but I could probably figure it out in a few guesses.

"I actually need you to confirm that you know him, Bloodfist."

I sighed. "Yeah, I know him. His name's Devin Goretusk."

Denelle's dark face grew darker. "Karen's eldest?"

Denny and my aunt Karen were close. As close as either of them were capable of being with someone. They were both what some might call "bitches."

I like to think of it more as aloof and independent, but I may just be a bad judge of character.

"Do you know what happened?" I asked.

She shook her head; a strand of black hair fell over her face and she swept it away. Turns out drow do not have silver hair. You have no idea how upset I was to learn that.

"Nothing specific. Medical examiner has some preliminary stuff, but nothing solid. There was fire, we know that much."

I looked at Devin and grimaced. One look would have been enough to tell me that, but I just had to look again.

The right side of the orc's face was almost completely burned away. One shortened tusk stuck out at an odd angle through the charred skin.

A fear I couldn't explain chewed at the back of my mind. This wasn't the first time I'd been called in to identify a dead orc. Usually it's orc-on-orc violence. We're about the only ones dumb enough to mess with each other. We also have been known to have anger issues.

I'd never seen something like this though. It almost looked like someone had held Devin's face on a hotplate until it melted through the skin.

"So, is that what killed him?" I asked, indicating my own face with a waving finger.

"No." She flipped the sheet that covered his chest back.

Well, it covered most of his chest. There was a fist-sized hole where his heart would have been. The sides of the gaping hole showed more evidence of burning.

I made an embarrassing sound in my throat and Denny gave me a blank expression, one I'd learned meant she was laughing at me. On the inside.

"We're pretty sure he was dumped in the field. No blood, and no evidence of the heat source."

"What were you doing, you idiot?" I whispered to the body.

"You know if he's pissed anyone off lately?"

I shrugged. "He's been out of town for the past six or seven years. He was supposed to be moving back today. I just showed his fiancée their place."

"Fiancée?" she asked.

"Yeah."

"Where has he been living before today?"

"New York."

She pulled a notepad out of her SVPD blazer and scribbled my answers down.

"What do you think of the fiancée?"

"Seems nice enough."

"Think she might have a reason to do this?"

I considered carefully as I studied the dead orc. "No," I said finally. "I remember him being an asshole, but never really the kind that might convince a woman to kill him. Besides, why would she kill him here? Wouldn't it be just as easy to take care of him before leaving New York?"

She looked at me like I was an idiot. She does that a lot. "You really think leaving a body in New York is easier than on the side of the road in the middle of nowhere?"

"Okay, but why bother coming into town then? Telling everyone he's on his way?"

"They're called alibis, Bloodfist."

"Alright. I just don't think she did it." I looked at the gaping hole in Devin's chest again. I had a hard time seeing the slender elf do something like that.

I was pretty ignorant back then. Really had no idea what an elf was actually capable of, but no one has ever told me I'm a genius. Not without some sarcasm in there, at least.

She shrugged. "You're probably right. Still, she's our best lead at the moment. Will anyone take issue with us bringing her in for questioning?"

My father had convinced Denny years before that allowing the fist to govern itself was the best course of action. She always respected that.

In the twenty years since we'd settled in the city we'd slowly allowed her and the rest of the local police to play a more active role. But they still asked, which I always appreciated.

"No, go for it. God, that's gotta be a fun conversation, huh?"

She shrugged again. She'd seen enough dead bodies and grieving loved ones that I'd honestly be surprised if anything fazed her anymore.

"Can I get the address?" she asked.

"Sure. Or just follow me?"

Her lip curled in distaste. "I'd rather not get anywhere near that piece of shit you call a car. I'm always afraid something's going to fall off and hit me."

"Fine." I feigned offense as I gave her the trailer's lot number. "Should I let her know you're coming?"

"Nah. She might run." She turned her attention back to the dead orc.

"Do you know what he was doing in New York?" she asked.

"Acting?"

She gave me an emotionless glare.

"I don't know. We weren't that close before he left home."

"I thought you were really close with Karen's boys."

"Just the one." Devin's brother Luke, born Lukil, was the same age as me. The two of us had grown up together. Practically our entire childhoods took place sitting next to each other in front of one cheap TV or another.

Devin, on the other hand, hadn't been around much for those early years. Even before his move to New York he'd been largely absent from his family's home.

I told the detective as much.

She nodded her head, accepting the answer. "Alright,

you can go, Bloodfist. Keep your phone handy though. There'll be legal stuff to take care of."

"Should I—?" I started.

"No, I'll tell Karen. Go home. Change out of that suit. You look like an encyclopedia salesman."

"Gee, thanks. Unfortunately I probably need to keep the monkey suit on. Gotta look professional for all that shit about to hit the fan today."

"If you say so. Can you do me a favor, if you have to wear it?"

"Maybe."

"Just ask around for me. See if you can dig anything up on Devin here. I'm sure your cousins will be more likely to open up to you than me. I know how you orcs feel about your vigilante justice. But I'd really like to do this one the right way. For Karen."

"I'll see what I can do." I didn't say that Karen would probably prefer the vigilante justice, but I had a feeling Denny wanted me to keep her in the loop so she could dish it out herself.

I said goodbye and was rewarded with an absent head nod as the detective pulled out her phone, I assumed to call Karen.

I was halfway to my car, considering everything I had to do now, when my phone rang again. Busy day.

"Hey, Ma," I said.

"Jack boy, you need to get here. Quickly." She'd called me from her home phone—she doesn't own a cell, so the two options are her apartment or Jack's Place, so I knew "here" was Goblin Burrows.

"What's happening?" I asked. I was not in the mood to deal with goblin drama.

"Mr. Peck is threatening to evict us." She said the gnome's name like a curse.

Mr. Peck was the brother of my own landlady, Moira. The Peck family was an institution in Summervale. They did settle the town. And still owned most of it. Almost everyone I knew rented from, or relied on, someone in the Peck family.

The young Mr. Peck was not a fan of my mother's family.

I can't even blame him. Several hundred goblins crammed inside two apartment buildings? Even considering how small they are, it's not sanitary, or safe.

But they were my family. I'd have to help out.

"I'll be right there," I said with a sigh.

Maybe I could ask a few goblins about Devin while I was there. Goblins are almost as mean as orcs, and a helluva lot more vindictive. Always possible one of them did it.

It took a few coaxing tries before my car sputtered to life. I pulled onto the road and made my way to the city block that was home to every goblin in the world.

THREE

Goblin Burrows used to just be called "Tranquil Towers."

Most people still call the two apartment buildings that. Which they shouldn't, since it's a horrible name. One day my title for the area will catch on.

The problem Ma had called about became pretty obvious when I pulled into the parking lot.

Marty Peck, the owner of Tranquil Towers—ugh, horrible name—was standing at the entrance to one of the two buildings.

The one with a bonfire burning on the roof.

There was a wall of goblins preventing him from getting inside.

Since my car has no AC, I had the window rolled down and I could hear him shouting that they let him inside or he was going to call the cops. Honestly, I was surprised he hadn't already.

I hurried out of the car and rushed over to the milling mass of short creatures.

I realize now that I probably haven't really told you what goblins look like.

I'm sure you have a picture in your head. And you might be right on, but just for the hell of it I'll give you some details.

I'll start with my mother, then you can probably figure out the rest of the horde based on that image.

My mother is short, kind of round, with a long pointed nose. If you've ever seen Batman Returns, just think of Danny DeVito as the Penguin. That's basically my mother. Except, you know, darker skin.

The nose is a universal feature with goblins, as is the height. Most brush the bottom of the table at a whopping four-and-a-half feet, give or take an inch. Their builds beyond that are pretty varied, ranging from muscular to atrophied to fat.

So I quickly approached the horde of super-villain lookalikes and shouted over their own squawking protests against Marty. "What's going on here?"

They all fell silent and turned to consider me.

Marty's face dropped from a deep crimson to a light pink.

"Jack, thank God. Your goddamn uncle is going to burn the building down."

I nodded. "I kind of guessed that much." I turned to the goblins.

"Who and why?" I demanded of them.

Ma pushed her way through the crowd. "Jack boy, it's your uncle Terry. I don't know what got into him. Says he's casting a spell. Won't listen to any of us."

Some days I wished Marty would just call the cops on my family. Usually I just have to show up, throw my weight around and scare everyone back in line. Maybe a night behind bars would do them some good.

I waded through the goblins and opened the doors.

Marty probably could have done the same thing if he weren't the same size as the noisy menaces.

I took the stairs three at a time. I'd like to say I wasn't out of breath by the time I made it to the roof, four floors up, but I lived on a diet that was mostly grease with some eggs thrown in. I was blowing pretty hard by the time I made it to the top.

I practically knocked the door to the roof off its hinges as I stormed outside.

My uncle Terry sat in front of an impressive pyre.

To his credit, he'd built the fire on a platform a few feet above the roof. Still didn't make it a good idea.

"Terry, what the fuck?" I asked as I stalked across the distance between us.

His eyes opened from whatever meditation he'd been practicing and he jumped up to face me. His body language told me he was ready to fight if I pushed him.

"What are you doing here, pup?"

I bristled at the title "pup." It's not a term of endearment among goblins. He was basically telling me I was a worthless child, nothing but a drain on the resources of the horde.

"I'm here to stop you from burning down your home, you stupid jackass," I growled at him.

He shrunk a little at my tone, but otherwise didn't back down.

"I do important work, boy. Go away."

"Do you want to spend a night in jail? Because this is how you get to spend a night in jail. I can arrange it."

"What? Going to sick you elf bitch on me? It's a free country."

"Yes, and we're all free to face the consequences of the stupid shit we do. Now put out the fire and let's go."

Terry considered, his beady eyes darting from me to the fire. Finally, he shrugged.

"Fine. Spell's finished anyway."

"Good. What were you doing anyway? I didn't know you did magic."

"I was the horde magician, pup. Before your father dragged us here." He spat into the fire at the mention of my father.

My anger started to grow again, but I forced myself to calm. "Let's put out that fire, Terry."

I was lucky enough that Goblin Burrows had gardens on the roof. Chicken coops, too. The goblins grow most of their own food. Any time Gramps needed eggs for Jack's Place he just ran across the street and stocked up. When the hens were laying, anyway.

But with a garden, you have to have water.

I hosed down the fire as Terry watched with a sour expression on his face.

"So what was the spell, Terry? If it was a summoning of some kind, it worked."

Terry looked up sharply at my joke. "None of your business."

"Fine." I ignored him until the fire was out and I was confident it wasn't going to start up again.

"You can clean up the rest." I marched past him and found the doorway blocked by a mass of goblins.

"Fire out?" Ma asked me.

"Yes. How long have you been there?"

"Whole time," she answered.

"Couldn't help put out the fire, huh?"

"We can't interfere with a magician's work." Ma seemed offended that I didn't know that.

"Sorry." I wasn't.

"Look, guys," I addressed the group. "If something like this happens again, I can't stop Mr. Peck from kicking you out. You're kind of asking for it. Do you really think anywhere else in the city is going to let you in? I don't. So, shape up, okay?"

There was a half-hearted chorus of agreement. Better than nothing.

Marty was waiting for me in the building's lobby.

"And?" he asked.

"Fire's out, and I got them to promise it'll never happen again. I'm sorry, Marty."

"I like you, Jack. You've been a good tenant for my sister. You rush here whenever you're needed. But I don't think I can keep this up. Your family is just..." he paused reading my face. He apparently decided not to tell me what my family was. "I don't know. I need your assurance."

I sighed. I liked Marty. He could be an ass, but that might just be me being overly protective of my family.

"Let them stay, and I'll owe you."

"I think you already owe me."

"No, I don't mean the money for repairs to Ma's apartment. I mean I'll owe you a favor."

That did it. His right ear twitched. That was his tell.

"What kind of favor?"

Generally, I only worked for the orcs and the goblins. That had been my father's arrangement, and I hadn't seen any reason to change it. But I had connections within the community. I could make things happen. Marty knew that.

"Any kind. Just call this a foul instead of a strike."

He nodded slowly. "Okay. I'll let you know if I think of anything I need."

"Thanks, Marty." I stopped myself from patting him on the head as I walked outside.

I knew the rest of the day was going to be rough.

I'd have to visit Karen and Luke to figure out how they wanted to handle the funeral. Then the call to the funeral home. Orc funerals don't take much preparation, but I always let the mortician know beforehand.

So I figured before I did all that I'd head home and relax a little before my day was lost to me. As I drove back to the trailer park I did something stupid and sent a text. Don't text and drive, kids.

Hey. Big day. Might be late tonight.

A year before that text would have been filled with spelling mistakes and missing all punctuation, but dating a writer cures you of that.

Well, I guess dating might be a strong word for what we were doing. It was more we just met up occasionally and got dinner and spent a few hours talking about stupid crap.

I did really like the girl, though. Even if she refused to meet my family.

No problem. This have anything to do with the dead orc I keep hearing about?

I stared at my phone a little longer than is safe while driving and had to correct quickly to stay on the road.

Who told you that?

I know people.

I was actually a little hurt. She usually came to me first about stories like that.

I was in the process of composing my return text when I pulled into the park.

My trailer is the first one you see when you pull in, so I noticed pretty quickly that my screen door was swinging in the wind. I figured I'd just forgotten to close it properly. You actually have to make sure it clicks closed or it's just going to sit open all day.

For some reason it made me think of Keelee, and I wondered if Denny had stopped by to see her yet.

I slipped my phone back in my pocket without responding to the last text and walked down the lane, planning on checking on Keelee.

She hadn't moved her car from in front of my trailer yet, which meant she hadn't skipped town. One point in her favor. I decided I'd move it for her later.

I froze when I noticed an old pickup truck parked in the driveway to Keelee's trailer.

It wasn't a vehicle I recognized. I know that doesn't sound like anything special, but anyone that had a reason to visit the girl would have been in a car I recognized.

I studied the truck as a large man stepped out of it. He was older, I'd guess mid-fifties, maybe even a well-preserved sixty. Shoulder length white hair and a beard of the same color and length.

He was dressed in a dirty pair of jeans, a t-shirt and hoodie, and a pair of white running shoes. The outfit didn't match the man.

He held a phone to his ear as he closed the driver-side door of the truck and approached the trailer.

He lowered the phone when the front door opened and Keelee stepped out, holding her own phone in her hand.

I was close enough that I could see the fear in her eyes.

The man's beard moved as he spoke to the girl.

She shook her head at whatever he had said. I took that as my cue to introduce myself.

"Everything alright here?"

Both their heads snapped around at my voice.

Keelee's eyes opened even wider, her fear now directed at me.

The man turned to her and strode up the steps, shouting as he went, "Give it to me, girl!"

His accent was vaguely familiar, though I couldn't quite place it.

"Where's Devin?" she shouted back.

She took a step into the trailer and started to close the door.

At the mention of my cousin's name I went into motion. Reaching under my suit jacket I drew the old .38 I keep there and hurried toward the trailer.

The man stopped in front of the closing door and considered me as I charged toward him. He must have found me unworthy of his attention, because he just turned back to the door and casually raised a leg.

The door flew inward from his kick and I could hear Keelee's pained scream as she was thrown across her living room.

I heard the thud as she hit the wall.

By the time I made it to the top of the porch steps the man was already inside.

I aimed my gun inside the dim living room and shouted, "Hold it!"

The man ignored me as he stalked across the small living room.

Keelee huddled on the ground, shouting something in her native language. I couldn't understand her words, but the fear was easy enough to translate.

"I said, hold it!" I repeated, my gun trained on the old man.

Keelee gasped something unintelligible as the man

wrapped a single, wrinkled fist around her throat and raised her off the ground.

He turned with her so she was floating between us. I lowered my gun, but kept my finger close to the trigger.

"Where is it, girl?" he asked, his long hair plastered across a too serene expression.

Keelee gasped something, and I only understood one word: "Devin."

"Give it to me and you will see your orc lover again."

Keelee's hand shook as she stuck it in a pocket. She pulled it out with something in her grip.

I recognized the blue and white of my father's eagle instantly.

"Keelee, no!" I shouted.

The man must have loosened his grip, because I heard her clearly, "He has Snaga. He'll kill him if I don't."

Her hand moved toward the man as she spoke.

"He already did," I snarled, as I pulled my gun up and aimed at the man through the girl.

His expression grew sour as he considered me from around the choking girl. His free hand shot out and ripped the eagle from her grip. Then there was a soft crack and I found myself staring into Keelee's dead eyes.

Her head hung at an unnatural angle and a single tear ran down her cheek.

I froze when I realized what had happened, and then the girl was flying toward me.

The gray-haired man had thrown her hard enough that, as she hit me, we flew backward out the door.

I hit the walkway that led from the road to the porch and slid a few feet, all breath knocked from my lungs.

I pushed the dead girl off my chest as I struggled to my feet.

The man was moving already, stone eagle in his hand. He backhanded me without even acknowledging me.

I staggered back from the blow, my vision hazy and my legs like rubber. It took me a few seconds to recover and when I had enough sense to look for him I found the bastard climbing inside his truck.

I took a few shaky steps toward him, gun raised.

The truck's tires squealed as he took off toward the entrance to the park.

I took quick aim at his car and fired. I honestly have no idea if I hit anything.

Somehow I managed to make it to my car and climb inside before he was completely out of sight.

The old car sputtered to life on the first turn of the key and I slammed my foot down on the gas. A cloud of black exhaust coughed out after me as I followed the killer.

I let out a solid stream of curses as I followed. I ignored everything else as I tore out of the trailer park and turned onto the road after him, driving away from the city.

The road ran straight for several miles, and it turned out that his ride was even more of a piece of shit than mine, because I found myself gaining somehow.

I was considering trying to shoot out his tires when my phone rang. The sound shook me from my simmering rage for a brief instant.

"What?" I shouted as I answered.

"Bloodfist, what the fuck is going on?" Halldorson's voice demanded. "Gunshots at the park? What the hell are you doing?"

"Chasing Devin's killer," I snarled back.

"What?"

"Devin and Keelee," I said. "Some Jeff Bridges wannabee motherfucker." I said.

"Where are you? I'm almost at the park."

I spared a quick glance at a road sign, "Heading east on the 671," I said just as my prey turned a quick right. Didn't even signal, how messed up is that?

"Shit, make that south on the 80."

"I'm on my way. Don't—" I didn't hear the rest of it.

Instead I threw my phone into the passenger seat and used both hands as I turned. Just because it was a high speed chase didn't mean I wanted to have an accident. There are always insurance payments to consider.

We were far enough from town now that the majority of our surroundings were fields with the occasional stretch of trees and a random farm house or barn keeping it from being all wilderness.

I had begun chanting, "Yes, yes, yes," as my car slowly began to gain on the murderer.

I realized too late that he was actually slowing. I was right behind him, having just convinced myself that ramming him was the logical next step for this situation when he braked.

My car plowed right into the back of his truck and I was reminded that I was not wearing my seat belt before everything went black. Or red, now that I think about it; it might have gone red.

I woke up when my door was pulled off of the car.

I grunted an eloquent "thank you" as I turned to consider my rescuer.

The old man's large hands reached into the car and pulled me into open air.

I scratched feebly at the fists around my throat, but all my strength was gone.

"There is something familiar about you." He was

speaking to himself. I could tell because he didn't speak in English, but in a language I had almost forgotten I knew.

My oxygen-deprived brain didn't register that at the time, though.

"Definitely orc," he continued, his eyes harder as he considered me longer.

"Yeah, I'm an orc. What of it, asshole?" Normally I would have been concerned that a human had figured it out, but right then I had bigger problems.

"Are you a Bloodfist? Your eyes say you are."

"I am Garack Bloodfist," I tried to snarl. Staying defiant in the face of death is kind of an orc thing. Might as well go out with pride in my blood.

His eyes opened wide. I had never seen hate like that before. "You are his son?"

He pulled me close, his nose pressed against my own as he stared deep into my eyes, looking for his answer.

"What?" I asked, confused.

"You are, I see it." He let out a wordless roar as he turned and threw me away from the road.

I watched the tall grass of the field pass below me as I sailed through the air. I turned slowly in my flight until I was staring up at the sky.

I hit the ground on my back and slid, feeling the dirt breaking up beneath me as I moved.

All I could think of at that moment was the dry cleaning bill for my suit. Not the greatest of priorities.

When I stopped moving there was a long trench of freshly broken dirt to mark my path through the field.

Too dazed to say anything, I looked up to find him standing over me.

"Look at me, orc. Garack Bloodfist," he said, squaring his shoulders. His eyes were burning with an odd blue light.

"I am Arthur Shield, of the Order of Saban, Guardian of the Lawful Temple."

All of those words meant something to me, somewhere in the back of my mind. Part of me was screaming in fear at what they all meant. But the part of me that was conscious just stared dumbly.

"Had you been of innocent blood, I would have spared you today, but for the sins of your father, you must die. Now." He reached down and wrapped his hand around my throat again.

My eyes drifted to his own throat and I noticed a necklace fall out from under his sweater. Something about the blue and white of the stones that ran its length seemed familiar.

"Now I come one step closer to avenging the wrong that your father committed against my order."

The blue glow in his eyes grew brighter and a gentle heat began to burn at my throat.

My mind darted back to the image of Devin, naked on a steel tray in the morgue, face burned, broken teeth and tusks sticking through the skin.

I closed my eyes and began to hum to myself, a habit I had picked up as a kid.

My cousin Luke and I had been playing basketball outside a church in town, and I had heard the choir practicing for the Sunday service. *The Battle Hymn of the Republic.*

For some reason it had stuck with me, and I'd found whenever I was scared I could hum that tune to myself and I usually felt better.

The heat at my throat was replaced with an ice cold that hurt far more than any fire.

The unnatural fire blinked off, and Shield grunted in

surprise.

His fist tightened around my throat and I wheezed in one final pained breath before breathing was impossible.

I had just consigned myself to death by broken neck when the gunshot cracked in the air.

The hand released me and I fell back to the ground, coughing.

"Another time then, orc."

I opened my eyes to see Shield staring out across the field.

Denelle Halldorson, in all her strong, black-woman glory, was charging through the tall grass toward us, her sidearm aimed at the man.

Tolkien wasn't exaggerating when he described the grace of elves. I don't think she broke a single blade of grass; the field just sort of parted in front of her.

Arthur gave me a glare that left no confusion about his intentions as he turned and charged through the tall grass. He left a path of broken stalks behind him.

Denny stopped over me, her gun aimed at the man's back.

"You okay?" she asked.

"Yeah. Get him!"

"I don't think so." She gave me a look. "You saw the way his eye's glowed, right?"

"Yeah. So?" I coughed as I tried to sit up.

Denny pushed me back down. "As an elf, I like to think of myself as an expert of knowing when to not fuck with magic. At least not without backup."

"But you have him on the run," I insisted.

"I also got a good view of him. We'll have every uniform in the county looking for him within the hour. Right now, we're taking you to the hospital."

"I actually like that idea." I forced myself into a sitting position and brushed Denny's hand off my shoulder before she could push me down again.

"You mind driving? I don't think my car can make it."

"How—" she started before shaking her head. "Damn orcs. You look like shit. I just want you to know that," she told me as she helped me walk to her car.

I only almost fell once, maybe twice.

"Really?" I asked, "Cause I feel great."

I actually did feel much better than you might expect. I figured it had to do with the narrow escape from certain death.

FOUR

Denny threw me in the back seat of her car so I could lie down. She'd made me take off the layer of mud that was now my suit jacket first. She made no comment on the empty holster that rested under my arm.

I stared at the ceiling of the car as she drove me to the hospital. I kept humming to myself as we went. It made me feel better.

"Would you shut up back there?" Denny demanded. She rubbed a tired hand over her neck.

"Sorry," I said, sitting up.

"You know, Detective, I actually feel alright. You really don't need to take me to the hospital. You can just drop me off at Jack's Place. I'll borrow my mom's car."

She ignored me as she watched the road.

I probably should have taken the hint and stopped talking, but I get nervous around Denelle. I mean, she's like two-hundred-something years old and still looks like she just hit thirty. That's intimidating for some reason.

"So, uh, thanks for saving my ass back there. I really thought he had me."

She snorted. "He did. He was talking to you. What did he say?"

"Said his name is Arthur Shield. With the Order of Saban, or something like that. I think that's the guy who created the Power Rangers... And he's guardian of the lawful temple. Mean anything to you?"

She shook her head. "No. What else did he say?"

"Has something against my dad. Didn't really say what."

She glanced at me from the corner of her eye. "If my men don't find him, should we expect more deaths?"

I considered, and the more I thought about it, the tighter my chest seemed. "Probably."

She fished out her phone and passed it back to me. "Call your mother. She's the goblin boss, right?"

"What?" I was a little taken aback by the detective's... well, detective work. "How did you know that? The families try to keep that from anyone."

She gave me her trademark emotionless glance. "I didn't. Karen hinted at it. You just confirmed it for me."

"Damn." It wasn't really that big of a deal. It wasn't like the goblins or orcs had the same enemies in this country that we did in the old world. It was only tradition that kept us running things the same way we had before.

Mostly the same, anyway. Before, we hadn't needed anyone in my position—someone to go between the families and the local authorities. In the old world we had lived in caves and nomadic camps. If we needed something we just killed whoever had it and took it.

Jackson had taken us away from that life, though.

At least, I'd thought he had. This Arthur Shield was evidence that my father may not have gone as straight as he had claimed. I wasn't sure how I felt about that. I would worry about my father's sins later, though. For now I had to let my mother know.

I dialed the number for the diner and waited while it rang.

My mother's accented voice answered and I froze as she spoke. "Jack's Place. How can I help you?"

How had I missed the similarity between her accent and Shield's?

"Hey, Ma, It's Jack." I kept my voice level.

"Oh, Jack boy. How did it go with the pretty girl? Gramps says you're probably getting married soon. Why didn't you tell me?"

I could hear a few catcalls from those around her. The fry cooks were all privy to my personal life and felt obliged to remind me of that often. I imagine they were all incredibly bored with their lives if mine interested them at all.

"Sorry to disappoint, Ma." I glanced at Denny and was surprised to see a wry grin on her face. Damn, but elves have good hearing.

"Why not?" Ma demanded.

"Well, for one, she's dead."

"Dead?" she asked. The noise in the kitchen died down.

"So's Devin," I continued, "That's why I'm calling."

"What's happening?" she asked.

"There's someone in town who has his history with dad." I thought of Arthur and the title he had given himself. Guardian of the Lawful Temple, Order of Saban. That meant something to me, but I still couldn't place it. It hovered there, just out of reach of my conscious mind.

"Who would have history with your father? No one in this world..." She stopped and I could almost hear the wheels turning over the phone. "He have a name?"

"Arthur Shield," I said.

My mother can curse with the best of us, and she demonstrated that at the sound of the man's name.

"Do you know something?" I asked.

"Does Detective Halldorson know about this man? About your dead cousin and the girl?" she asked.

"Yeah, I'm with the detective right now. She has people looking. They'll find him.

"Good. Let the police handle it. You need to stay away from this man."

"Yeah, my thoughts exactly. Look, can you get the word out? Let everyone that needs to know, know? I'll be swinging by the diner later, I need to—"

Denelle ripped the phone from my ear and placed it over hers. "Pat? It's Detective Halldorson. Yeah, yeah, I'm good. Listen, I'm taking Jack to the hospital."

I couldn't hear what was being said on the other end but the tone of Ma's voice changed.

"Not sure. That's why I'm taking him. Mhm. Yeah. This Shield guy did a number on him. Yeah, he's a tough bastard, I'll give you that." She glanced at me again. "Yeah. Hey, once we're done at the hospital, do you mind if I come pay a visit? I'd like to learn everything I can about this guy." She waited for a response, nodding along to whatever my mother was saying.

"Sounds great. No, no, don't worry about feeding me anything. I'll just take a coffee. Just like me, Pat, dark and bitter. Thanks. See you soon."

She hung up the phone and stuck it in her shirt pocket.

"We really don't need to go to the hospital. I'm fine."

"Really? A car accident that launched you twenty feet into a field? How can you be fine? I don't care how tough you orcs are, once the adrenaline wears off, you're going to be hurting."

"The crash didn't launch me. It was Shield. Threw me."

"You must have hit your head really hard," she murmured.

"I'm being serious," I insisted.

She considered for a moment before nodding. "Okay, but that doesn't change anything. You're seeing a doctor."

I couldn't argue with the finality in her voice. "Fine. As long as it's quick. I have a job to do."

"What's that exactly? This is a little beyond running errands for lazy goblins and ungrateful orcs," she said. There was no malice in her tone. It was just a matter-of-fact statement.

I sat back in my seat. Holy shit, I was just a gopher.

I think the adrenaline wore off then, because I was suddenly in a lot of pain. Not so much my body, but when someone points out that your life might actually just be a steaming pile of donkey shit, it hurts.

Doctor Terzi is kind of an asshole. Mostly because he treats his patients like idiots. At least, he treats me like one.

Look, just because the rulebooks say we have a negative modifier on our intelligence score doesn't mean we're actually stupid.

So what if just one generation ago we were living in the woods? It was a choice, damn it.

Anyway, all I'm trying to say is that Doctor Dave Terzi is a dick. A short, fat, curly-haired, Greek penis.

He jokingly calls himself "the vet." In front of his patients. Who does that? Just because we're not human?

I really dislike the man. If this were the old country I'd tear his arm off and tell him to turn his head and cough. But it's not the old country, and Denny would do equally horrible things to me if I did that.

The worst part is that he's the only doctor in the surrounding area that knows about—or at least accepts—the existence of the non-human community. So that means when the good detective forced me to go to the hospital, she asked for Terzi.

Denny stood against the wall next to Terzi while the man reviewed my patient history. She quietly explained to him what had happened.

I sat on the end of a paper covered bench in a pair of boxer briefs and nothing else.

When I'd objected to her presence in the room the detective had snorted something about having sons and being old enough to be my great-grandmother.

"Is this going to take much longer?" I demanded of the doctor.

"Not much longer. Just finish filling out your form and we can get started." He didn't look up from my file.

I picked up the clipboard and grumbled to myself as I scribbled on it. Usually I would have had to fill out the form and then wait an hour or so before the doctor would see me, but Denny had rushed the process.

"Fine," I said, not at all belligerent.

The worst part about being non-human in the US is the constant deluge of paperwork. Every single one asks for race. And in case you're wondering; no, there is not a box marked ORC.

Some of the other races get lucky. Denny can just mark BLACK. Which is true, I guess.

My landlady and her brother can just claim WHITE. Also true.

Green skin? That's not an option. Now, it's not some

lime, St. Patrick's Day green. You really should stop assuming stuff like that. Makes us both look stupid.

No, it looks more gray, but the green is in there. The point is, my skin would never pass for black. Some of my cousins can pull it off. I can't. And I definitely can't pretend to be a white man.

After years of staring at the forms I finally settled on claiming Native American Heritage. They don't usually ask for a specific tribe, which is good, because I probably wouldn't know which one to use.

It does help that Bloodfist almost sounds like something from an old, racist western.

I finished up the form and set the clipboard on the table.

Terzi looked up at the sound and closed my file.

That file isn't as full as you might expect, considering how much time he'd spent staring at it. Before that morning I'd never been thrown across a field. Never had a broken bone. Never really been sick beyond the random virus I caught as a kid.

"Alright, Mr. Bloodfist. Looks like we can take a look at you."

"Thank you, Doctor," I growled from between clenched teeth.

"Detective Halldorson has explained a little bit. A car crash, right?"

"Yeah. I just need you to give the okay for me to get back to work." I glanced at Denny through narrowed eyes.

Screw her. I had a great job. Got to make my own hours. Had a collection of IOUs that anyone would envy.

"Work?" he asked. "For some reason I always assumed you were on welfare."

A deep growl escaped my chest. Strike one, Doctor.

A firm hand fell on my shoulder and I glanced over to find Denny giving me a hard look.

"Well, let's take a look at you," he said, oblivious to my anger.

He slid a stool next to the table and began his inspection.

He started with my torso. I had the start of a nice bruise where my chest had hit my steering wheel, and I imagined my back had a similar situation going on.

He poked me with two fingers and asked if it hurt.

I shrugged. "Not really."

He poked a few more spots on my chest and back with the same result.

"Looks like it wasn't nearly as bad as Detective Halldorson thought," He said, "nothing appears to be broken. Looks like the bruises are the worst of the little fender bender." He laughed as he turned away from me.

"Fender bender?" I asked, not quite sure how to take the implication.

Before I could let myself be angry at the man for his callous attitude toward my new, carless state he started to inspect the gash on my forehead.

My steering wheel had been just as cruel to my head as it had my chest when I'd crashed into Shield. Denny had wrapped it for me before we'd left for the hospital.

Terzi unwound the bandage and the fabric stuck to the dried blood, pulling the wound open again. He wiped my dark blood away with a cloth and inspected the wound.

"Shallow cut. Nothing serious. A few stitches and you'll be fine." He pulled out a needle from somewhere and poked it next to my head wound before I could object.

I swear, I did not flinch.

"Relax," he said, opening a little white envelope and

removing the threaded needle from inside. "it'll be over before you know it."

"Doctor?" Denny said.

"Hm." He looked up from his needlework.

"You're sure he's fine?"

He turned back to my injury and continued to sew it shut as he spoke. "As far as I can tell. If I'm being honest, I don't know that much about orcs. They were never mentioned in my father's books."

Terzi's father had been the one to get the good doctor into medicine. He'd also been the first human to have non-human patients. It made sense that we weren't mentioned in his records. We are fairly new to this world.

"So he might really be hurt?"

"I wouldn't say that. I don't believe he's big and dumb enough to completely ignore a serious injury."

"Gee, thanks," I mumbled.

"You're welcome," he continued. "He's put together close enough to a human that anything worth worrying about would be noticeable."

"So you think he's okay to leave?" she asked.

He shrugged. "I don't see why not."

"I'm not worth consulting in this?" I asked the two of them.

The doctor spared me a quick glance before returning his full attention to Denny, who didn't even acknowledge me.

"I can prescribe some pain killers, if you think he might need them."

Denny was at least considerate enough to let me answer that one for myself. She looked at me and I shook my head.

"No thanks," she said.

"Fair enough."

"Thank you, David."

"I'm right, here, Doctor, you could have asked me." I angrily shoved my arms through my shirt sleeves as I glared at the two of them.

"Let's go, Bloodfist," Denny said. "Put your pants back on."

FIVE

After our delightful visit to the emergency room, the good detective drove the two of us to Jack's Place. She waited, only sighing loudly twice, as I scraped the dry dirt off my suit jacket and put it back on.

The front door was locked and the closed sign prominently displayed through the dusty glass. Peering through the window we could see that every table, booth, and seat at the bar was occupied by goblins.

They were all older goblins. My aunts and uncles, whether biological or not. None of my cousins. This appeared to be a council of the old world. Those of us that had adapted to the new had apparently not been invited. I couldn't make out the specific words being spoken, and I could sense more than hear the general spirit of the packed dining room.

Uncle Terry was standing on his chair waving his arms animatedly. Others were responding with their own excited movements.

I tapped on the glass door and every face inside turned to consider us.

My mother's own round face popped up from behind the counter and lit up at the sight of me. She didn't bother going around the counter, but pulled herself up and over in a surprisingly graceful scramble.

Everyone else fell still as they watched her rush to the door with waddling gait, her smile at odds with the concern furrowing her brow.

The door clicked unlocked and opened.

"Jack boy," Ma said. "You okay?" She indicated I lean forward and she poked at the bandage on my forehead.

"Ah, Ma, come on. I'm fine."

"Good, good. Come in, quick. Much talking to do."

Her long-fingered hand darted out and grabbed my own brick like-fist.

She pulled me inside and waved a hand at Denny. "Come, come, Detective."

I was suddenly very aware of every eye in the diner studying the detective.

"Good afternoon, Pat. Everyone." She returned the looks with her trademark expressionless glance before returning her attention to my diminutive mother. "I was hoping we could have that talk you promised me?"

There was a moment of tense silence as my mother seemed to notice the anger and unease coming from every other goblin in the room.

My family has never been fond of cops. Probably a side effect of the generations living in the woods as bandits. They pretended to be civil with the detective, and at least cooperate with her, if only because it was better than the alternative.

Jackson had promised that first generation, the generation that currently occupied the diner, that the first time he was told they were a danger or hindrance to the authorities of this world he would personally take care of it. The two options for his taking care of it, as they understood it, was for him to return us to our homeland, a death sentence after what my father had done, or—and I was led to believe was more likely—he'd just kill us himself.

I was relieved to see that my mother, at least, remembered these conditions.

She closed the door behind Denny, and while the elf couldn't see her, she gave everyone in the room a look that reminded them she was in charge for a reason.

"So, who is going to get the detective her coffee? Black, if you don't mind."

When no one moved she shouted in harsh, high-pitched goblin. One of the fry cooks practically fell out of his seat and rushed to fill the order.

Denny approached the counter to accept her drink and one of the goblins seated there climbed down and offered the stool to the detective. She accepted the seat and the drink without a word.

After a loud, drawn-out sip from the mug of steaming blackness she pulled her notebook from a pocket of her jacket. She pointedly licked the tip of her pen and poised it over the paper.

"So, who wants to go first?" She looked around the room, an expectant eyebrow arched.

With the little I know of Denny, I knew she enjoying the awkward silence that dominated the dining room.

"Excuse me?" my uncle Terry said, tone matching the angry arm wave we'd interrupted with our arrival.

Detective Halldorson turned her attention to Terry. When she gets that look on her face, you never call her Denny. Never. Even if she can't hear you. She'll know.

"I am here to question all of you about possible connections with the fugitive Arthur Shield," she said calmly.

The room erupted with sound. Curses and accusations, most in ear-piercing goblin, were thrown back and forth. Gramps was standing on the counter, stomping his tiny feet as he raved about the inevitability of it all.

Denny took another sip from her coffee and waited for the chaos to subside.

I'm a little ashamed to admit that for the opening moments of this sudden twenty sided argument I just stood in the middle of the room. I was both too shocked and embarrassed to really understand any of what was being said or why it needed saying.

I did recover though, and after the deafening screeching had continued for longer than I could stand I took a deep breath and bellowed, "Shut the fuck up!"

The room fell silent. My father had always told me I had warcrier lungs. I hadn't always been sure what that meant, other than the fact that I could be really loud when needed.

"How dare you?" Terry said, his beady eyes narrowing in anger. He managed to make the high-pitched goblin sound dangerous. "You arrogant little pup. Coming in here with an outsider. Allowing her to learn of things *you* shouldn't even know."

I pulled myself up to my full height. That was twice in one day he had called me that. It was not something you want to call a full-grown goblin. He was calling me a child. Didn't matter that I was twice as tall as him, three times as wide.

"I think," I said, my deep voice making my goblin sound like some horrible demonic tongue, "that you should show some respect, Uncle. My job is to protect you. How can I do that without your help?"

Denny's eyes slowly moved from Terry to me. She didn't look worried, but she looked ready to shoot both of us if anything started. She couldn't understand what was being said, but I'm sure she could sense the tone.

Terry laughed, a mean, spite-filled sound. "Protect us? You pathetic orc. You don't protect shit. You jump when we say frog. So why don't you take your elf friend and remove your snout from business you have no talent in handling. Go on," he waved his hand toward the door, "frog."

My vision began to darken. I believe they call it, "seeing red." An orc temper is a dangerous thing, but I'd been living with it all my life and was able to calm myself down. After a few deep breaths I was able to replace the need to tear Terry's face off and feed it to him with a really strong desire to tear his face off and feed it to him. Big distinction.

"Jack boy," Ma said. "Listen to Terry. I think maybe you should leave." She held up her car keys.

My heart tightened in rage and hurt. "But I thought..." I trailed off. I'd thought Ma was in charge, but apparently there had been a change in the horde hierarchy recently.

Ma just shrugged before turning to Denny.

"I'm sorry, Detective," she said in English, "but it might be best if you not ask any questions right now. We know nothing of where this man might be. But trust me, we want him caught."

Denny remained seated, watching me. I gave her a small nod and she rose slowly. She placed a hand on the lip of her mug and tipped it over on the counter.

"Whoops," she said as she brushed past me and made her way out the door.

There were a few grumbles from the goblins responsible for cleaning the restaurant, but no one said anything.

I had turned to follow Denny out when Terry said, "That's right, frog. Hop away."

"Go fuck yourself, pynwid."

Pynwid means pine cone. It's about the worst thing you can call a goblin. You see, goblins have different classes of warriors, stoneslingers being some of the most respected. They throw stones. Pretty straightforward.

The story goes that once, a stoneslinger did something stupid and ran out of stones. So he threw a pine cone. All this managed to do was piss off the troll. So now the troll knows where he and all his friends are, and kills them.

A stoneslinger has to be able to brain an opponent with one stone. That's the difference between life and death for a goblin. So when you call a goblin a pynwid you're telling him that he is just stupid enough to get everyone around him killed.

It's a huge insult. Just trust me.

Which is probably why Terry jumped from his stool at the counter and, clearing the distance between us, latched onto my back. His arms wrapped around my neck and his teeth sunk into the meat of my shoulder.

Goblins have sharp teeth, if you didn't know.

I let out a pained cry as my hand instinctively shot over my shoulder and grabbed at Terry's head.

My fingernails scraped along his greasy scalp as I spun around a few times.

Finally I wrapped my hand around his head like a softball.

I ripped him away from my shoulder, suit fabric tearing as I did so, and threw him across the room like a... well, like a softball.

The need to hurt him was back, and I covered the floor of the diner almost as quickly as the flailing goblin.

My hands enveloped his narrow throat and I pulled him off the ground to eye level.

His eyes were bulging as he tried to gasp for breath. I could feel the start of something snapping under my grip.

The kicking of his legs slowed as I let out a snarling roar.

My face smashed into the dirty tiles of the diner and my arm bent behind me in a painful angle.

"You done, Bloodfist?" Denny asked.

I snarled what I thought was an approximation of yes and she let me up.

Terry had scrambled away from me and was gasping for breath underneath a booth against the wall.

Denny picked Ma's keys off the ground where I'd dropped them and tossed them on the counter.

"I'll drive," she said as she guided me to the door.

Ma met us at the door and opened it for us.

She cast a quick look into the diner, and seeing most eyes watching Terry, she turned back to us. "Karen. She will tell you what I can't."

I'm not ashamed to admit that I sulked a little as Denelle drove away from Jack's Place.

I sat in the passenger seat and stared out the window without really paying attention to the scenery. "You can just drop me off at home," I said.

She didn't say anything as she continued to guide the car along the curving road.

"Nothing to say?" I asked. My tone could have been friendlier. It wasn't her fault I was in a foul mood.

"What did you want to hear?" she countered. "Your family is awful? No. They're just scared of this guy. More scared of him than they are of me. What can you tell me about your homeland?"

I was a little surprised by the question. Our origins were mostly ignored. I know plenty in the city speculated, but for the most part Jackson's word was good enough. And that word had been to not ask too many questions. "They're here now. Get over it." That's paraphrasing, but you get the point.

"Not too much," I answered. "I was only six or so when we moved."

"You don't remember anything?"

"I remember playing with the wargs. A lot of shouting. I think everyone was pretty scared before Jackson showed up. Something my father did. I never really got the full story. I was always afraid to ask, honestly."

"Why were there only goblins at the diner?" she asked.

"The two families don't really get along," I said.

Now, just so it's clear, I say two families, but there are actually more than that. The orcs are all members of a single fist—the word we use for tribe or clan. The entire fist hadn't followed when we left.

Three households in the fist came: The Bloodfists, that's me. The Goretusks, such as the recently deceased Devin. And the Slayinghands. They had been the decision makers. Still are. My monthly check always had a Slayinghand signature.

The goblins, on the other hand, are much more numerous. I'd be lying if I said they were brave creatures. Smart, sneaky, ruthless. Those they are, but not brave. So when the option was put forth to migrate somewhere relatively safe, the whole horde agreed.

Ma and Gramps call the shots. Or at least they used to. I wasn't sure anymore. For the most part, goblins function with more of a primitive democracy than the orcs do. So I assumed there must have been a secret election recently.

The goblins usually pay me with a paper bag full of crumbled bills from the diner's till. And free food.

The two races had been brought together when my parents had married. It had been less than civil between them if what I'd been told was true, and I believe it.

But my father had been a smart a man and his schemes had made both sides wealthy in the old world.

While he'd been alive the two sides had been friendly enough. I still kind of miss the monthly barbecues. When he'd died, Ma just stopped caring and the goblins pulled away. I'd tried to keep things as they had been, but I'd given up after a while. And it wasn't that all my relatives hated each other. It was more that they just didn't give a damn what the others did.

Denny and I drove in silence for a while. Her face was its usual calm mask, but I could tell she was deciding what to do with me.

I made my decision. "I can help with this, Detective."

"I know," she said.

I considered our next move. Ma had said to talk to Karen.

"Have you talked to Karen yet?"

Denny grimaced. "Yeah."

"How'd she take the news?" I knew Karen well and had a decent guess.

"She said thank you, and asked after my day. We had a delightful conversation about her vegetable garden."

That was about what I'd expected. My father's sister had been the fist's weapon master. She had lost several husbands, some at her own hand if the rumors were true, and Devin was not the first of her children to die a violent death. It's not that she was cold. Just hard. Too used to tragedy.

"I'm assuming this was before we knew the guy's name."

She nodded.

"So, we going to see her then?"

Denny kept her attention on the road as she spoke. "If you make me regret this, I'll kill you myself."

She took the next turn and aimed the car toward Green Valley, the suburbs just outside of the city. The land of tiny, green lawns and perfect picket fences.

I called it Orc Town.

You'd be surprised to learn how many monsters live in the suburbs.

SIX

My aunt Karen lived with her son, my cousin Luke.

Their house is exactly what you picture when someone says, "suburbs." The lawn is green, immaculate, and the exact same size as every other yard in the cul-de-sac. The house is pretty, as these things go. A medium-sized, two-story, three-bed, two and a half bath with long a driveway and a two-car garage.

It's almost identical to every other house in the neighborhood.

The only real difference between buildings is the numbers on the mailboxes.

"Maybe I should have taken you home first," Denny said as we approached the front door.

"Why?" I asked.

She pointedly stared at me before nodding toward her shoulder.

I looked down to consider myself. The shoulder of my suit jacket was noticeably shredded where Terry had bitten me.

My shirt was stained brown. Maybe from dirt, possibly blood.

"Is that going to be a problem?" she asked, pointing at the shoulder.

I shrugged. "I doubt it. Might get infected, I guess. But he didn't bite that deep."

"If you say so." She turned from me and knocked on the door.

We waited for only a moment before Luke opened the door.

My cousin is a full-blooded orc. If you didn't know what you were looking for, you might think Luke was his dead brother's twin. But that would be racist, and I know you're not racist. Though the racial similarities are very apparent

Now, I'm a big guy, but my goblin blood took me from the towering seven-foot orc height down to a more inconspicuous six and a half. Luke stood at the full seven.

He, just like the rest of my full-blooded cousins, is also a lot broader than I am. Seriously, they all have shoulders that Schwarzenegger would have envied back in his Mr. Olympia days.

Luke's face split in a wide grin, the tips of tusks in need of a trim peeking from under his thick beard.

"Jack, Ma said you might be by. Hello, Detective Halldorson," he said, greeting Denny with a harm hug.

She hugged back. "Please, I've told you to call me Denelle," she said, amiably.

I narrowed my eyes slightly. What the hell, right? I had to call her Detective Halldorson. She could be a real dick sometimes.

"Of course, Denelle. I'm guessing you're here about Devin." He stepped aside and ushered us inside. He squeezed my shoulder fondly as I entered his home.

He didn't sound very upset about the recent death of his brother. I know I mentioned it before, but orcs aren't usually very sentimental. Especially when the deceased in question was never really a part of their lives.

"I'm sorry about your loss," Denny said, even managing to sound sincere.

Luke shrugged. "Can't say any of us are surprised. Did you need us to do anything about the body?" He looked at me when he asked. Part of my job was making those arrangements.

"We'll talk about that later," I said. "Den, um, Detective Halldorson and I need to talk to your ma. See if she knows anything about the guy that killed Devin."

"Alright. Let's get the formalities out of the way first." He pulled the knit cap he'd been wearing to hide his pointed ears and tossed it on the table by the door.

He turned into the house and bellowed, "Lise, Mik! Company."

Down the hall I could hear a TV click off and the rearranging of bodies on a couch.

"Come on." Luke led us down the hallway into the living room.

Lise, Luke's wife, is a small woman by orc standards, which makes her about average for a human, which she is. If she has her blond hair up in a bun she might come to my shoulders.

She rose from the couch when we came in, all smiles and hugs, just like always. She greeted both of us by name and gave us each the unavoidable hug.

Unlike her husband she did look a little sad. She's one of those genuinely good people you hear rumors about. Even though I'm pretty sure she'd never met Devin, she sincerely mourned his passing.

"Uncle Jack!" shouted Luke's six year old daughter, Mikaia, and for the second time that day a small creature leaped across a room and latched onto my back. I didn't mind this time.

"Miki!" I shouted back as I gently pulled her over my shoulder and dangled her upside down.

Her long, dirty blond hair fell down in knotty waves as she laughed uncontrollably.

Miki had been lucky in the genetic lottery. She looks more like her mother than her father, and as an unbiased observer, Lise is a looker. She did inherit the orc laugh, however. A loud, thrown-back-head, belly-shaker of a laugh.

And with her mouth open wide like that you could see the other gift her father had given her: Two small tusks sticking out of her bottom gums. They're small enough she should never have to worry about grinding them down like her father and I—and every other orc that tries to fit in—but they're there.

I held her by the ankle with one hand and tickled her mercilessly with the other, causing her laugh to grow louder.

Luke and Lise watched with that weird half smile only parents watching a childless bachelor can have. Even Denelle had the start of a smile on her face.

I ignored them until the girl begged me to stop. I put her down on the couch and she flopped on her side, still laughing loudly.

"Is Karen around?" Denny asked after Miki had quieted down enough for normal conversation to resume.

"She's out back by her shed." Luke indicated the sliding glass door that led to the back yard.

"May I?" the detective asked.

"Of course." Luke slid the door open and the detective exited.

I started to follow but Luke's hand fell on my shoulder. I stopped and considered him. Both he and Lise were eying me worriedly.

"What?" I asked.

"I didn't want to say anything in front of the detective, but are you okay?" he asked.

"You look a little worse for wear, Jack," Lise added.

"What do you mean?" I asked.

Luke gently poked my forehead, where a white bandage hid my stitches.

"Well, there's that," he said. "Then what looks like a bite marks in your jacket. And considering that's your work jacket..." He left the implications unsaid.

"Yeah," I said, embarrassed. "It is a little worse for wear."

"What happened?" Lise asked.

"Well..." I told them an abridged version of my run-in with Arthur Shield. I left out the goblin bite. No need to discuss family problems with them.

"Why do I feel like I know that name?" Luke asked.

"Right?" I said. "I told it to Ma and the rest of the goblin council and they freaked out. Refused to tell me anything though."

"And isn't Saban that Power Rangers guy?"

"That's what I said." Glad someone else had caught the reference.

A hand fell on my shoulder and I turned to find Denny standing just outside the door. She handed me a slip of notebook paper.

"My partner just called. He says your girlfriend's been

calling the station looking for you. She says you haven't been answering your phone."

As far as I knew, my phone hadn't survived the crash. I also didn't have a girlfriend. Not really. I would have liked that to be the case, but as it was, we had not progressed to that yet.

The number on the slip of paper was the one I had expected to see. Denny watched my face as I studied the number. I tried my best to keep my face impassive.

The corner of Denny's mouth threatened to turn up in a smirk as she turned away and walked back across the small yard.

Karen stood next to a well-cared-for vegetable garden, resting her forearms on the shaft of a shovel. Her shed stood behind her, open doors revealing a large collection of gardening supplies.

She raised a large, gloved hand in acknowledgment of my existence before returning to whatever conversation she and Denny had started when I wasn't looking.

"Girlfriend?" Lise asked, a knowing smile on her face.

"Ooo, Uncle Jack has a girlfriend," Miki said from the back of the couch in that tone that would make you want to punch an adult but is just adorable in kids.

Luke just smiled and raised an eyebrow.

"I don't—" I started, but gave up with a sigh. They would believe whatever they wanted.

I stared at the number a little longer. With today's technology, nobody needs to remember numbers. Some people don't even know their own phone number. We just need to find a name on a list and touch the screen. I make it a matter of pride to actually know phone numbers.

So, of course I recognized this number. And, no, as

much as I wished, she was not my girlfriend. I stuffed the paper in my pocket and started to walk outside.

"You're not going to call her?" Lise asked.

"More important things to deal with," I said.

"She's obviously worried about you. Just call her. Let her know you're okay. Miki, go get the phone for Uncle Jack." Lise waved the girl toward the kitchen.

"She's not my girlfriend, guys," I protested.

"Whatever you say, buddy," Luke said, settling himself into the couch, "Ma's not going anywhere. You'll be able to ask her whatever you need to after you let your worried lady friend know you're good."

Miki rushed back into the living room carrying a phone. They still have a land line, can you believe that?

"Thanks, Mik." I ruffled her hair as I accepted the phone.

I sighed deeply, just to let them know how much of a burden this was for me.

I dialed the number from memory and was suddenly very conscious of the room of people watching me intently.

I stepped outside and slid the door closed as the phone rang. I eyed the family inside suspiciously as Luke threw his head back and laughed. Miki sitting in his lap did the same.

After a few rings Mogayne Thornhill's melodic, almost Irish accent greeted me.

"This is Mogayne," she said.

She wouldn't recognize the number, of course.

"Hey, it's Jack. Uh, Bloodfist. You were trying to get a hold of me?" I didn't know if I was the only Jack she knew. Plus I'm not great at talking to women on the phone, okay? Don't judge me.

"Jack? Oh God, man, I heard you were in an accident. What happened?"

"Who told you that?" I asked. I really needed to know who was feeding her information about me.

"I have my sources," she said, I could hear the smile in her voice. "Now tell me you're okay. That should have been the first thing you said."

"I'm okay," I said obediently.

"Good. I was worried." She genuinely sounded like she was. "What happened? Did you lose your phone? I've been trying to reach you all morning."

"Kind of a long story," I said.

"I'm not that busy."

"I kind of am, though." I paused and then added an awkward, "Sorry."

"It's fine. Can you stop by the office later? You can tell me all about it over some donuts."

"Tempting," I said. I considered trying to get out of it. It's not that I didn't want to see her—that's something I always enjoyed—but it just was not the day for that.

"Perfect. See you this afternoon? That's enough time for you to take care of everything, right?"

"Well..." I started.

"Great, I'll see you then." She paused for just a breath. "You really are okay, though, right?"

My desire to get out of seeing her died. "Yeah. Just a few stitches. Some bruises. Nothing too serious." I added a silent "yet" in my mind.

"Good. Well, I'll do my best to help mend your wounds when I see you." I heard a second voice on the other end with her. She laughed at whatever had been said. "Kirk says hello."

"Oh, tell him I say hi."

"Will do. Looking forward to seeing you, Jack." She sounded sincere, though she usually did.

"Okay. See you this afternoon." I hung up the phone, feeling light and just a little giddy.

I slid the glass door open just wide enough to toss the phone to Luke. He caught it with one hand and grinned wider.

I ignored the Goretusks and their infuriating smiles and made my way to join Denny and Karen.

The two considered me silently as I approached. I stopped in front of them and waited for one of them to speak.

"I think I have what I need," Denny said finally. "Thank you, Karen."

The two women nodded at each other. They were too alike for there to be any hugging. I'm not really sure what happened to Luke to make him so lovable. You'd think it was his wife, but no. Can't even blame Lise. He was like that a long before he ever met her.

"Karen says she'll have Luke give you a ride home when she's done telling you about Shield," Denny said, an oddly friendly hand on my arm. "If you need anything, let me know."

"Thanks." I thought too late to ask after my car. But that would have been a stupid thing to worry about right then.

Karen and I considered each other silently for a moment, until Denny was back inside the house.

Then my aunt turned and indicated I follow. She returned her shovel to its place in her orderly shed and pulled two folding chairs out from the small structure. A large cooler followed.

We sat on the chairs and she passed me a beer from the cooler.

I don't usually drink—it had been almost five years since the last time—but I felt the occasion appropriate.

"To the dead," Karen said, pouring her can out on the grass.

I followed suit and she gave me another can, this one for actual drinking.

"My brother never told you what we did." It was not a question.

"No."

"Good. That was the decision we all made. That our children never had to know what we were before."

"You were thieves and killers," I said.

"True." she bobbed her head in agreement. "I think it would be better to say that we agreed you never know the full story." She drained her can and opened another.

I took a shallow sip of my own and waited for her to say more.

"Arthur Shield is dangerous," she finally continued. "His reasons make him very dangerous."

"Reasons?"

"For wanting us all dead. How he followed us is a mystery. Your mother and her whingeing clan are probably arguing about how coming here was a mistake, or wondering how to run away again."

"He followed us?" I asked. I had thought I'd recognized the man's accent, but the thought was still a hard one to accept.

"He must have. How else do you explain his being here?"

I shrugged. "I don't know. Who is he?"

"I will tell you the story, Garack Bloodfist. My brother would have wanted you to know. I know most of the fist don't appreciate what you do for us. But I do. My son and his family do."

She drained another can, and as she opened the next

one, she told me the story of how my family came to be here.

Some of it I knew. Some I even remembered from my early childhood.

But more of it was new.

SEVEN

Twenty years ago, on the continent of Anfang, there lives an orc named Garack Bloodfist.

And he is hungry.

Not for food. He has finally found ways to provide enough of that for his fist. Even enough for the goblins that follow his wife.

No, he is hungry for something else. For comfort, for wealth. For a bed that is not a pile of furs on a cave floor.

But he knows that he will never be able to sate that hunger.

He has done much in the last few years to improve the lives of those for whom he feels responsible. But he knows he has to stop soon.

He has earned himself a form of infamy that is reserved only for the greatest of criminals. His fame is the kind that comes with a large bounty. A bounty that, if he had the money himself, he would never have had to steal or kill.

His name is known across all of Anfang.

Merchants avoid the woods at night out of fear of his

raiding parties. Soldiers, on their way to war, march around the woods so they may save their blood for enemy swords.

In the capital city of Glanzend resides the Lawful Temple of the Order of Saban. The paladins of this temple have it in their heads that killing orcs would be in the best interest of Anfang.

This is a sentiment that Garack can actually understand, but being an orc, he cannot agree with.

The influence of the temple, as well as the impressive bounty, convinces others to seek the heads of Garack and his bandits.

For the past month the frequency of these attacks has grown. Almost every night a new group of bounty hunters has braved the woods in search of the orcs. Rangers, fighters, even the odd thief, stalk the trees hoping to kill an orc or goblin. Slice of the ears and return them for their reward. Ten silver coins for a pair of goblin ears, and ten gold for orc.

It is on one of these nights that Garack Bloodfist meets the wizard Jackson.

The wizard enters the camp at night. The goblin stoneslingers on watch are either too drunk or too stupid to see him enter and the rest of the camp is alive with celebration. The latest victory against those seeking their ears has earned them a night of drinking and song. None see the wizard as he slips inside the back of a tent.

Garack doesn't join in the merriment. Instead, he sits in the door of his tent, spear resting across his crossed legs, his wife nestled beside him as they watch their son roll in the mud with a warg pup.

"Don't make a sound, I just want to talk." A length of steel falls across the orcs throat; the voice is not dangerous, but conversational.

"Then talk." Garack keeps his face impassive. If this man wanted him dead, he would be dead.

"You are Garack Bloodfist? The bandit?"

Garack sneers at the title. "What of it?"

The sword is removed. "Good. Afraid I had the wrong tent for a minute there. How would you like to dethrone a god?"

Garack and his wife both turn to consider the young man, now sitting comfortably on a rusted iron chest.

"What? Who are you?" Garack demands.

"My name is Jackson. I'm a wizard." He says *wizard* as though it is the most ridiculous title anyone could hold. "And I need to remove Saban from his throne in the Lawful Temple."

"I..." Garack has no words. What is this madman talking about?

"Why Garack?" The slender goblin rises to her feet, a hand grasping at the dagger on her belt.

"Because Saban and his servants are the ones that placed that bounty." The wizard considers a speck of something brown on his sword, picking at it with a fingernail. "I thought you might like to stop that. There's also a vault stuffed full of valuable relics, as I understand it. Two birds and all that." He looks up and meets Pat's eye. She shrinks back at the intensity of those eyes.

Garack rises slowly, looking over his shoulder to make sure none are looking toward their tent. He closes the flap and indicates for his wife to sit. She does so, but her hand never leaves the hilt of her blade. Garack sits next to her, back straight, legs crossed. He indicates the hide covered ground in front of he and his wife.

Jackson slides off the chest and mimes Garack's posture.

"I've been considering a raid on the temple," Garack states.

Pat jerks in her seat and stares at her husband as though he were mad. And to even consider such a thing, he must be.

"That's what the numbers said." Jackson nods. "So here I am to make that happen."

"Numbers?" Garack asks, not sure if this is some obscure oracle.

"My advisor relies on mathematics to predict events. Based on your previously known habits he was able to determine that of everyone in this country, you were the most likely to be willing to attempt this. And also that with the warriors willing to follow you, you're also the most likely to succeed."

"I don't like this, Gar," Pat whispers to her husband. "How does he know so much?"

Jackson pretends not to hear her. "You're more than welcome to say no. I understand the risks. If we fail, it's very likely Saban will have every orc and goblin on the continent killed, not just those following you. And us? Well, death will be slow in coming and welcome when it does get here."

"And what does it get us if you succeed?" the goblin demands. "A few more coins? More angry paladins marching through our woods?"

"It gives you a fair fight," Jackson says. "Without their god, these knights have no power other than the strength of their arm. And while they have numbers and swords, so do you. You have berserkers and stoneslingers. They have old men in armor."

"Very well trained old men in armor," Garack clarifies. "Tell me why you want this."

"It's the job I've been given," Jackson says, shrugging. "I've found things are better when I do what I'm told."

"And you can offer us no protection? Your masters, whoever they are, cannot provide us with assurances?" Pat demands, almost rising from her seat again.

Jackson sighs. "I may be able to set something up. Give me a minute." He closes his eyes and begins an unheard conversation.

The orc and goblin eye each other, nervous at the close proximity of this strange magic.

"My advisor says there is something we can offer, but only for those that are willing to follow you."

"And what is this offer?" Pat asks, calming slightly at the touch of her husband's hand on her shoulder.

"If we fail, but are able to get out of the city fast enough, I can take you somewhere safe. Somewhere Saban and his paladins shouldn't be able to follow."

"Shouldn't?" She frowns at the weak assurance.

"Yes. Shouldn't. Best I can do."

"Tell me what you have planned." Garack leans forward, eyes fixed on the wizard. "If your plan is any better than one I can come up with on my own, I will see about convincing others to join us."

Jackson nods, unsurprised at the orc's willingness to listen. They talk into the night. They do not stop when the couple's son wanders into the tent and falls asleep in the corner. Outside the music dies and the feast ends.

The young man is gone by the time the sun comes up, and Garack is convinced of the plan.

Garack has a week to convince his fellows to join him and to make his way to Glanzend. If he does not arrive in time, Jackson will assume he could not muster the necessary number of raiders. In this case, he claims to be prepared with other solutions to his task.

The next morning, Garack meets with his sister, Shakill Goretusk, the fist weapon master. Where Garack leads the warriors in combat, Shakill ensures they are equipped and prepared.

"Absolutely not." Shakill stands, arms crossed and glowers at her elder brother.

"Why not? Do you fear death, Shakill?"

"You know I don't. I'm an orc, just like you. But, unlike you, I'm not stupid enough to throw my life away for nothing."

"Nothing? You think the chance to overthrow a god is nothing?"

She narrows her eyes. "How does our raiding a temple treasury result in a god being overthrown?"

Garack grins. He has her now. He explains the wizard's plan.

"You trust him?"

"Not at all. Why would I trust a human? But I think he's sincere. I truly believe he has a spell capable of exiling Saban. And if not," Garack shrugs, "it's a death I'm comfortable with, sister."

She studies him. "If it's a death you greet willingly, I might consider going with you. But who else has to die? And do they need to know why they're dying?"

"It depends. We'll need to take a goblin or two along. They won't accept death with any honor, but the promise of gold? That should be good enough."

Shakill snorts. "Why do we need goblins?"

"Well, for one, it was part of our agreement when they joined the fist. They must be included. They'll take it personally if they're not. And, you have to admit, they're a damned sight better than any of us with locks."

"Gods, fine. You do the talking. I'll stand behind you and look intimidating."

"That's why you're my favorite sibling, sister."

"I thought you liked Kaga more because he let your runt play with the wargs." She follows him as he heads to present the plan to the Slayinghands.

"Well, yes. But you still manage to overtake him two out of every five days."

"I'm honored."

The eldest Slayinghand listens calmly to Garack's plan. That is why the Slayinghands lead the fist. Despite all their thirst for blood and berserker rage, the orcs recognize that a level head is needed.

"Think of it," Garack insists. "If this works, if we dethrone Saban, we will be safe from the temple. We will be on even footing with the paladins. Their retaliation will be meaningless."

The old, half-blind orc nods. "I agree. And you think this wizard can really do as he promises?"

Garack does not know for sure, but he lies admirably. "Yes. I do."

"Good enough for me. I'm sending Hurck and Rit with you." The elder's children are capable warriors. Garack would have requested their help even if it had not been offered.

"Who else do you need?"

Garack and Shakill request two more orc warriors. Then they consult with the leader of the goblins, Garack's father-in-law.

The old goblin heeds the council of his daughter and agrees to the plan without the need of convincing.

"How many do you need?" he asks.

"Two will be enough. I know any of them will be silent, but we need someone who can handle locks. Most likely big, complicated locks."

"Terin!" the goblin shouts, his voice echoing down the cave the clan calls home.

There is more shouting as the clan carries the message farther into the cavern. Soon the sound of running feet can be heard and the goblin Terin rushes into the clan chief's chamber, his breath heavy.

"You called for me?" he asks.

"What are your thoughts on becoming obscenely wealthy?" the chief asks.

Terin's face contorts into a silent question. "Do you even have to ask?"

"Terin is one of our clan magicians. He is also the best lock pick we have," the chief explains to Garack.

"Magic and thievery. I like it. Ready for a trip to Glanzend?"

They are given another goblin and prepare for their journey.

Garack bids his son goodbye, and attempts to make another with his wife before leaving.

The trip is mostly uneventful. Shakill only has to save everyone from one troll, and is only a smug asshole about it for several days. Much better than everyone expected.

They arrive at the capitol city without any other major incident and manage to sneak through the gate without being noticed. Despite the bounty on orcs and goblins the city is so full of creatures of various races that none look twice at the six hulking frames, or the two miniature. With hoods up against uninterested eyes they make their way to the greeting place.

"This is the one," Garack says.

The sign hanging outside the tavern holds the face of a dog, cowl pulled up over pointed ears. *The Robber's Dog*.

"Subtle," Shakill says.

The tavern is full of the sort one might expect in an establishment named *The Robber's Dog*. Scarred and hooded faces consider the newcomers before returning to their own sinister planning.

A hand goes up in the back of the room. The eight of them force their way through close-packed tables and join the human that waits for them.

"Glad you could make it," Jackson says.

Garack sits across from the wizard and his followers fill the table, stealing chairs from around them and forcing themselves close.

"So," Jackson grins, "who's ready to rob a temple?"

It is surprisingly simple to infiltrate the temple. By the cover of night they climb the high walls of the fortress-like structure. Terin proves himself worthy of his chief's praise and picks every lock they come across as Jackson leads them deeper and deeper into the massive complex of Saban's temple.

"Alright," Jackson says after what seems hours. "We split up here. That way to the treasury, this way to the inner sanctuary."

"What?" Terin says. "Why are you going to the sanctuary?"

"Don't worry about that, Terin," Garack says. "Take the others and go clean out that room. Don't forget why we're here."

Jackson takes Garack and the two head for the sanctuary. The rest go to the treasure room.

"I feel like you may have been able to get in here yourself," Garack says, growing more and more concerned with the ease of their infiltration.

"The security is going to get much worse soon."

"But why are you only bringing me?"

"It doesn't really matter, honestly. You can go to the treasure room if you prefer."

His purpose there dawns on Garack. "The treasury is a distraction."

Jackson nods. "I'm sorry, Garack."

"You bastard!" Garack wraps a hand around the wizard's throat and smashes him against a wall. "Why?"

"You still have a chance to get out alive, Garack. I didn't send anyone in to die. But they will reach the treasure room before we reach the sanctuary. Saban's security will go there, leaving him exposed for me." He speaks as though he is not held against a stone wall by his throat.

There is the sound of a bell and Garack drops the wizard. "You bastard." He rushes down the hallway in the direction of the treasure room.

"Meet me outside the city, Garack. I'll keep my end of this. I promise." Jackson turns and rushes down his own hallway.

Garack finds the treasury's doorway surrounded by men in armor. He is relieved to see they are not paladins, just normal men in leather armor carrying pikes.

They are not looking at him as he charges, and their leather offers no protection from his ax.

The first falls silently with a hack that opens him from armpit to heart. The second dies with a gargled scream as the ax blade bites between shoulder and neck.

The rest turn to face the towering orc and Garack pulls himself up to his full height. The guards step back, intimidated by the massive creature stalking their dim hallways.

From within the treasury there is the sound of battle cries and Shakill and the other orcs hack a path through the weak humans.

In the end the guards are dead and the orcs study each other. Shakill and the others each carry a massive canvas bag on their backs. The clinking of coins and jewelry is obvious as they move.

"We have to go. Now," Garack says, and they begin to make their way back out.

"Where are the goblins?" Garack realizes they are two men short."

"Took off when the alarm started," Shakill snarls.

More guards round a corner and the orcs waste no time in relieving them of life.

One orc rushes into the darkness around the turn, sword arm swinging. There is a flash of blue fire and the orc dies soundlessly.

Garack steps around the corner to find Arthur Shield, the most feared of Saban's knights.

Garack does not consider his options. This is an acceptable death. He charges the paladin. He dodges under the swing of the longsword. He steps up close to the knight, and with a grunt of effort swings his ax with both hands.

Shield staggers back several steps, face turning grimmer. "What is your name, orc?"

"Garack Bloodfist. Did you know your god dies tonight, human?"

Garack manages to dodge another swing before his sister vaults over his shoulder, pointed ears scraping the stone ceiling.

Shakill's sword is stopped by the steel covering the knight's shoulder. His careless shrug throws her back a pace.

She swoops under another fire-shrouded sword swing, grabbing the bag that had once rested on the back of their friend. She shoves it into Garack's hand. "Run, brother."

Their three remaining comrades rush from behind and all five of them charge the lone knight.

There is the sound of steel on steel and the short, final sound of steel piercing flesh. Garack, Shakill, and the two Slayinghands leave Arthur Shield and the orc resting on his sword.

They are lucky enough to meet no other magic knights on their flight out of the temple, though the heavy footsteps of Arthur Shield are never far behind.

They break out into the night air, and almost trip over Terin the goblin as he cowers outside the main doors.

"Hurry, orcs!" he shouts.

As the fourth and final surviving orc passes the door, Terin slams it shut and murmurs the words of a prepared spell. The lock of the great doors click with a sound of finality.

"Hurry. Won't take them long to hack trough that." They follow the goblin as he leads them back to the rope over the wall.

"Where's the other one?" Shakill demands of Terin.

The goblin doesn't bother hiding his look of shame. "Saban killed him."

"You saw Saban?" Garack demands.

"Saw him kill. Please, we have to run."

The city is as alive as any metropolis would be at night. More so, as the sound of the temple's alarm brought excitement to the streets.

No one paid any heed to the five figures that ran through the streets, though some noticed the large bags and their suspiciously jingling contents.

Garack is more angry than relieved at the sight of Jackson waiting outside the city gates, though the eight horses he leads with him are a welcome sight.

"Only five?" The tone of his voice is almost enough for Garack to forgive him.

"Yes. Happy?" Garack forces any forgiveness from his thoughts.

"I'm sorry. No time. We have to ride. Fast."

Their flight from Glanzend to their home is long and hard. Every step of the way they are hounded by men in armor, but they make it to their woods before the pursuing knights.

"We have maybe a day before they get here," Jackson says as they stop just outside of the orc and goblin territory. "You have that much time to convince your people to leave. If they don't, chances are they will die."

Garack has already demanded to know what went wrong, but he asks again, out of principle.

"I told you. They knew. They saw us coming. A room full of paladins was waiting for me. I've apologized, now let me keep my promise."

Very few of the orcs like the plan. "Why should we leave?"

"We should meet them in battle. Die honorably or kill them. Those are the options of an orc."

The Slayinghands agree to Jackson's proposal. The elder is tired, done with battle. His children heed his council. Shakill also manages to convince her mother's family and the Goretusks agree to the journey.

There are less Bloodfists willing to join them than Garack would like, but his brother and several other families that carry his name agree.

Garack tells Jackson and the wizard shows his relief.

"Good. Now, I'm sorry about this, but to open the door I'm going to need a lot of power. I also need to make sure that they have no way of tracking us. The treasure. I'll need to use all of it as components in the spell."

"You just can't be happy taking our homes, can you? Have to take anything that might be considered a victory?"

"Do you want to live? I can leave if you don't."

"I'll talk to the others." Garack leaves the wizard to consult with his sister and the Slayinghand.

"Fuck him," Shakill says, "we earned this. I'm not giving it up."

"I think I want to live, sister." Garack realizes he doesn't want to die in battle. He wants to die comfortably on a pile of furs surrounded by children.

"Then we keep some of it. One piece each," Shakill insists, "just to prove that he can't control us."

The four agree and each pick their trophy, hiding it among the possessions the wizard instructs them to bring.

Garack picks something simple—a small stone bird, layers of blue and white. His sister takes a necklace made of the same stone.

The Slayinghands take larger trophies, a sword and a shield respectively.

Garack's wife has convinced the goblins that they should follow. Jackson has promised that this new home will be safer. They will no longer need to hide in caves, but can live among all the races as equals.

"Land of the free. That's what they call it." Jackson says. "Everyone's legally obligated to treat you as equals. That's the theory, anyway."

The goblins like the sound of that and agree with almost no argument. Only Terin seems hesitant, but he goes along with his clan.

Jackson gathers everyone in the center of their camp, a pile of gold and jewels sparkling in the firelight.

The orcs that refuse to leave gather their own possessions and march away, disgust at their cowardly kinsmen plain.

In the distance the sound of charging horses can be heard.

Jackson speaks the words of a spell, a language none recognize but one they will soon learn.

There is a flash of fire, and the ground shakes. The pile of riches glows and is gone as the air above rends and tears.

The charging horses are intercepted by the orcs that refuse to flee and the air fills with the sound of dying men and monsters.

"Hurry!" Jackson shouts as he waves the orcs through the doorway between worlds.

Garack is the last of his people to walk through the hole in the sky. His sleeping son drools on his shoulder, unaware of the changes awaiting him when he wakes.

Garack spares one final glance for the world that birthed him. He bids a silent farewell to the trees and caves, and then, with a single step, he steps over the unimaginable distance and enters their new home.

Jackson jumps through the doorway, as close behind him a mounted knight charges.

The massive horse screams with its rider as the man strains forward, sword outstretched.

Arthur Shield lets out a cry of triumph as the point of his sword reaches for the wizard's face. Then the weight of universes collapses together around the length of steel.

All that remains of the paladin is a point of steel, glowing orange from the heat of the closed door. Jackson kicks the broken sword with a leather boot before turning to consider the orcs and goblins.

They stand, studying the woods that surround them, the noon sun blinding after the darkness of their world's night.

"Alright, everybody," Jackson says, "this is your home now. We're going to make sure you're comfortable, safe. But you need to make sure you respect the laws of this world. You're done being bandits. If I hear that you've fallen back into old habits, I'll fix the problem." His smile informs them of just how he'll fix the problem. "I've risked a lot bringing you here. Don't rock the boat."

Jackson helps them find homes, jobs. They become part of their new city.

Garack is still hungry. But as he listens to his small son playing in the street, his warcrier lungs filling the air with youthful joy, he doesn't care about the hunger.

He thinks he has made the right choice.

EIGHT

Karen finished her story with another 12-ounce sip of beer.

I sat silently and considered. Arthur Shield had found a way to cross over.

It honestly made sense. His accent, why everything he had said to me seemed to strike some chord in my mind.

And, really, it was only logical to accept that he had found a way over. If one wizard could open the door, couldn't another do the same? Though, I'm not claiming to be an expert in magic, so my opinion on this is really worthless. I'm passable when it comes to imaginary magic systems, but not the real thing.

The end of the story struck me as important.

"The treasure you divided up, where did it all end up?"

I knew my dad had kept the stone bird for himself.

"That garbage?" she asked, cracking open another can. "Nothing really valuable. Ceremonial crap. I took the necklace, your father kept the little stone bird."

The bird Shield had convinced Keelee to steal from me.

"What did the necklace look like?" I asked, remembering something from my meeting with the paladin.

She shrugged, dropping another empty can in the cooler. "Haven't seen it in a few years. Gave it to Snaga when he left home. It matched that bird your father kept. Blue and white stone, I think." She had a faraway look on her face, can halfway to her mouth. She shook her head and took another drink. "I'll have to ask Denelle if he had it on him."

"He didn't. Shield has it."

She studied me silently, slowly lowering her beer. "And the bird?"

"Took that too."

She scowled. "Must really have wanted that junk back."

"What about the sword and shield?" I asked. I had the beginning of an idea. If nothing else, maybe a way for us to find the bastard.

"Slayinghand took the shield, and her brother took the sword. They weren't anything special. Old and rusted pieces of iron. Only good as trophies."

"Maybe. But that necklace and bird are just chunks of stone, and he seemed to want them badly enough."

She grunted her agreement through yet another can.

"Hurck and her brother Rit..." I trailed off. I remembered those names. I'd arranged their funerals a few years before.

"Both dead," Karen said, voicing my thoughts. "Have kids though. I don't know their names."

It was a start. I knew the orcs in question fairly well. It was the Slayinghands that signed my checks, after all.

"Thank you, ma'am." I finished my drink as I rose. "I'll get out of your hair."

She grunted noncommittally and remained seated. She stared off into space, as though lost in thought. Maybe reliving more memories from her past.

I made my way back to the house and found Luke had dressed in his usual plaid shirt, blue jeans, and massive boots.

He dangled his car keys and inclined his head toward the door to the garage. "Where to, cousin?"

"I know it's your day off, but do you mind taking me to the office?" I asked.

The first few minutes of the drive were awkward. Luke fiddled with the radio, changing from country to rock stations every few seconds.

"Luke," I started, still not really sure how to say it. We're not very affectionate in my family. "I really am sorry about your brother.

He shrugged. "I know. Denny'll find the bastard, though. If we can help that happen faster, all the better."

"We will," I promised.

"So what's at the office? Letting the boss-man know what's happening?" He asked.

"Hopefully he already does. I asked Ma to give him a call. If not, then yeah, I'll tell him. The main reason, though, is that your ma told me the Slayinghands might have something the bastard is after. Looks like he's rounding up stuff our parents stole from him before the big move."

Luke nodded in understanding. He was silent for a little while.

When he spoke again I could still hear some hurt in his voice, but it was masked well with his usual good humor. "So, what's the story with your reporter friend?

"What?" I asked, thrown off by the resurgence of the discussion.

"You know. The pretty one. Redhead?" He watched the road, a playful grin on his face, as he waited for my response.

"What do you mean, her story?" I must have sounded angrier than intended because Luke just shook his head and changed the radio station again.

"I just meant..." He sighed. "Never mind, just be glad Lise isn't here. She'd interrogate you, and you'd answer."

I nodded. "Yeah, I probably would." I considered telling him. Explaining that I liked her, but I wasn't sure if it would actually go anywhere. But I seriously hate those conversations, so I was grateful when he spoke again.

"Did you need a ride to her office later? You said you'd stop by, right?"

I glared at him. "Couldn't resist listening in on that, huh?"

"It was Mik's idea." He had the good grace to look guilty.

"How much did you hear?" I asked.

He gave me a sickly grin. "All of it?"

"You son of a bitch." I wasn't really angry. Luke was my best friend. It hadn't been the first time he'd listened in on one of my private phone calls. Hell, I'd done it to him before. Of course, we'd been kids. It's a little different when a grown-ass man eavesdrops.

"Sorry. We just worry about you." He changed the station one last time, stopping on one that was somewhere between country and pop.

We made the rest of the trip in relative silence.

On the other end of town, inside a dusty, well-lit shop, the goblin Terry—once Terin—examines a wall of antique weapons.

He searches for one particular piece. One he does not see here.

"Looking for something?" the short man behind the counter asks, setting a large book down to examine his customer.

"Yes. A shield." Terry does not look at the dwarf. It is nothing like the bearded berserkers he remembers from his home.

"Well, looks like you found them." The dwarf eyes the wall. "Any catching your eye?"

"I'm looking for this shield." Terry walks to the counter. Reaching up he slaps the drawing on the wooden surface.

So long ago he had held that in his hands, and he had traded it for a bag of gold and jewels. He had thought they would be worth more. Now he knew better.

"Blue and white?" the dwarf asks, voice dropping in volume.

"You have it?" Terry exclaims, just stopping himself from jumping on the counter.

"Orc brought it in years ago. That one's gonna cost a lot."

Terry glances around the empty store and pulls out the small leather pouch. The dwarf's eyes open wide at the glittering golds and reds that spill across the pocked wood.

The goblin stops, bag still holding most of its contents. "Is that going to be enough?"

The man rubs the stubble on his chin. "Maybe." He eyes the bag. "A few more coins ought to do it."

He holds a questioning hand over the pile and Terry nods.

The dwarf pulls out a jeweler's loupe and inspects a small ruby.

Terry picks through his bag and drops an emerald down. "Now?"

The dwarf deftly sweeps the pile into a drawer. A key clicks as he locks away his new treasures.

"Follow me." He locks the store's door and leads Terry into a back room.

Boxes of wood and cardboard are piled in neat and orderly piles. The smell of dust irritates Terry's nose.

The goblin's innate gift in the arcane warns him as he enters the room. There are objects of power in here.

"I had no idea you were a collector of this sort of thing," Terry muses.

The dwarf raises an eyebrow. "Can sense it, huh? I didn't know there were any of the magical inclination in your horde."

"Just me." Terry stops behind the dwarf as he digs through a large footlocker.

"Here it is." He pulls out the shield.

It has been cleaned since Terry saw it so long ago. The rust is gone. It seems to pull in all the light of the dim back room and reflect it back at him.

He reaches out, his hand aching to touch it. This will please them, please that god that so long ago spared him.

"Need anything else?" the dwarf asks.

"Maybe later." Terry's eyes see only the shield.

"Need a bag for it?"

"I think that would be a good idea." Terry pauses. What are the chances he will be discovered? It shouldn't be long before all is done, but he has always been careful.

He pulls out three coins and spreads them in his fingers, like gilded cards. "If anyone asks, a large man with a big gray beard bought this."

The dwarf narrows his eyes. "Okay," he says slowly. "Is someone going to ask?"

"At most, one orc. Maybe an elf."

"Drow?" he asks, voice low.

"Possibly."

"Gonna need a few more coins for me to lie to the detective."

Terry gives him the three coins and a rough-cut diamond.

Much easier to kill the dwarf, but his new master has instructed that only orcs are to die this day. Justice can only be meted to the guilty.

Terry's obedience has earned amnesty for his horde, so the dwarf lives.

At least, until Terry comes back to collect a few more pieces for his own private collection. But that will have to wait.

Slaying Construction made its home in a large warehouse with a small, two-story office building attached to the front.

The same vinyl banner has been hanging over the front door for the last ten years: A crudely drawn orc holding a bloody spear over the tag line, "We slay the competition." Not the most original, I know.

Hurck Slayinghand, the matriarch of the Slayinghand family, had inherited the company from the previous owner. She and several other orcs had turned the company into a profitable enterprise. And now, most of the orcs that chose to live responsible lives were employed by the company. My own paycheck had the company logo in the corner.

"Want me to come with you?" Luke asked as he parked on the street in front of the building.

"Nah, I know the way." I opened the door and stepped out. "Shouldn't be too long.

The front entrance was about as clean as you'd expect from a small construction company. Buckets of paint and boxes of caulking tubes were piled up in front of the receptionist's desk. A few couches, caked with sawdust and plaster, rested against the wall.

Several orcs and a couple dozen migrant workers all stood around the door to the main office, loudly asking after their next paycheck or which job site they were expected to visit next.

I offered a friendly head nod to Marge, the short Hispanic woman that answered the phones and manned the front desk. She smiled and waved, not bothering to ask if I had an appointment or not as I headed up the narrow stairs. I wasn't a regular at the office, but I'd make enough appearances over the last few years that even the non-orcs knew who I was.

I knocked on the door of the CEO's office. Charles, formerly Gravak Slayinghand, was Hurck's youngest son. He was only a few years older than me and had taken over the company after his mother's death. Natural causes, if you were wondering. That was becoming more and more common for us, this past morning being the exception.

"Jack." Charles looked up from his desk. His tone wasn't unfriendly, but it wasn't that of an old friend, either. "What can I do for you?" He indicated the cheap, plastic chair in front of his cheap particle-board desk. He leaned back in his leather office chair and waited for me to sit down.

Unlike myself, Charles was clean-shaven, and his under

bite fairly apparent, but it doesn't matter that much when your suit costs as much as I'm sure his did.

"Did my mother call you earlier?" I asked as I sat down.

He shook his head, unconcerned by the question.

I cursed as I eyed him. How much did he know? He was the current head of the Slayinghands, and they were the unofficial community leaders as far as the orcs were concerned. Better to assume he knew as much as I did then. "Ever hear the name Arthur Shield?" I asked.

He shook his head. I took a deep breath and gave him the abridged version of Karen's story. Then I told him about Devin.

"Well, shit." He sat silently for a while. "What does Detective Halldorson need from us?"

I frowned slightly at not being included in that question, but I had to admit, it was probably better to just let her handle it. But God damn it, this was my job.

"Well, I think this guy is after the trophies our parents kept. He has two already. Karen Goretusk says that your mother and uncle each kept two of the four. A sword and a shield. I think this Shield guy is trying to get them back. I figure if we know where they are before he does, maybe we can stop him." I may have put too much emphasis on the word "we" but he didn't seem to notice.

"My mother had a shield. Gave it to me a few years before she died," he said.

"Still have it?" I asked, hope rising.

He shook his head. "Pawned it pretty quickly. Needed the beer money."

"The usual place?" I asked with a sigh.

He nodded. "Paid top dollar, too. Who knows if it's there?"

"Can you tell me anything about the sword?"

"Sorry, no. Uncle Rit could have left it to any of his kids. You know how many of them there are."

"Yeah." Rit had been known for his, well... let's just say he got around. "Do you have any contact info for any of them? Anything could help," I said.

"Sure. A lot of them work for us. Give me a second."

He began to type on his computer, clicking his mouse and staring at the screen intently for a few minutes.

The old printer in the corner of the small office began to whine in complaint and a sheet of paper was dragged out.

"Names and phone numbers." Charles passed the sheet across the desk. "Not everyone, but maybe some of them will know something."

"Thanks, that's all I needed." I pushed myself out of the chair and turned to leave the office.

"Let the detective know she has our full cooperation," Charles said as I closed the door.

I nodded at him through the streaky window before leaving the building.

When I got outside I found Luke on his phone, his expression frantic. "When did it happen?" he demanded. He waited impatiently for the answer to come. "Okay, we're heading back now."

"What is it?" I asked.

Luke turned to face me, his face a mask of rage and hurt. "He killed her."

NINE

Shakill sits in her uncomfortable lawn chair as the boy leaves. She drinks another weak drink as she considers the talk of Arthur Shield.

She had known the paladin once. Feared him in the way one feared any worthy foe. But the man had been old even back then. Twenty years could not be kind to such as them. She herself has felt the effects of hard living and time's unforgiving advances. Shield would be worse off. She no longer fears him.

Her son had been weak. How else could she explain his death at the hands of an old man? And her nephew had goblin blood in his veins. If he were full orc, like his father, he would have had no trouble facing the vengeful zealot.

She sighs to herself as she considers the weakness of that generation. This land makes them soft.

Even she is soft now. She knows this to be true. Where once she had been hard and strong, carved as though from an old oak, she is now soft. Old and plump. She hates it.

She does not know how long she sits and considers her failings as a mother and as a warrior. But it feels long.

Her son's wife, Lise, and her granddaughter, Miki, come and say goodbye as they prepare to leave to buy the family's groceries for the week.

"Can you find me something stronger than this water?" Shakill asks the woman, holding up another empty can.

"I'll see what I can find," Lise promises, though Shakill recognizes the distaste in the woman's eyes.

They leave Shakill alone again, her thoughts growing more troubled as the minutes pass by.

There is movement in the house. She knows no one should be home. She approaches her tool shed and draws the crossbow she keeps in there for emergencies, or for crows. Damn birds always eating from her garden.

Before she reaches the house the back door slides open and a large man steps outside to greet her.

Shakill's chest tightens in fear at the sight of the man.

He is older, true, but he is as large and dangerous as she remembers. His gray beard lifts slightly as he smiles a dangerous smile.

"Shakill Goretusk," he says in the common tongue of their shared homeland.

She finds herself again, recovers from the unexpected fear.

Her arms whip up with a practiced ease and there is the sound of the weapon cracking the air, the bolt flying true.

Arthur Shield leans back, almost casually, and allows the bolt to speed past. Something ceramic and fragile shatters inside the house.

The gray man is on her now. Hands, glowing with unnatural blue fire, grasp for her throat.

Instinct, earned by years of killing, saves her. She swings the spent crossbow up in a deadly arc.

Shield is faster than his old joints should allow and his hand is in the path of the weapon.

The strength of the swing and the opposing force of the block cause the wood to splinter.

Shakill steps back quickly, one hand up as though wearing a shield, the other holding the cracked bow like a club. She swings it again.

Arthur raises his arm, catching the blow on his forearm. He lets out a grunt of pain as the wood hits.

Shakill winds up again and strikes a second time, then a third, each blow falling faster than the last.

The man's hand darts out and catches the length of wood. His fingers dig into the cracking wood, smoke curling up into the air.

He lets out a triumphant cry as his free hand flashes out, blue fire trailing it in the air.

But she still has some speed left over from her youth. Still has some of the hardness required of an old warrior. She releases her weapon, drops beneath his strike, and tackles him. The two fly through the air together. The glass of the sliding door shatters as they hit it.

Arthur Shield hits the ground first, Shakill on top. She straddles him, her fists striking wherever she can find a target.

His hands lose their fire, and now he covers his face as her blows grow in ferocity. She lets out a war cry that would still freeze the blood of lesser enemies. Shield screams his defiance back from behind his protecting hands.

With a grunt of effort he rolls to his side, all his strength focused on pushing her considerable weight away. She is knocked of balance and falls to the side. She scrambles to her feet before he can overpower her.

He rises slowly, blood running from his left temple. He

wipes the stream of blood with his hand and admires it before closing his fist around the red of it.

"Still good, Goretusk. I'm glad."

"For an old woman. And you still have strength in your bones," she concedes in Orcish.

"Yes. A gift from Saban. After twenty years he has finally found me here. He has provided a way for me to find you." His hands begin to burn once more. "I have waited a long time for today, Shakill," he says, eyes slowly growing brighter. "Too long. Justice for your defilement of the temple. That will earn me my place in Saban's holy hall."

She snorts at this. "You can rot in hell for all I care. Now stop talking. I'm tired and my family will be home soon. I don't want them to see me like this." She knows she will die.

He nods his understanding. "Once I have killed you, I will kill your son. Then his family. I will try my best to make it quick, painless."

"No!" she bellows. "You leave them alone. They are innocent. You owe them no vengeance."

"Your son has your blood. He is Bloodfist as much as he is Goretusk. Both families are at fault. The child has the same blood in her veins."

"She's a child!" Shakill screams as she charges Arthur.

The attack surprises him and she wraps her powerful hands around his throat.

She coughs, unable to breathe. A flaming fist is slowly pulled from her chest, where it has punched through the ribcage and crushed her lungs with a painful, cold fire.

"Yes. A child. A child with your blood. Innocent, I know. But the sins of the parents corrupt. It will be quick. And I know, now you think: what of the wife? Why does she deserve to die?" He leans in close as he gently lowers her to the ground. "Because she gave your son a child. No other reason. She stained this world with one more of your blood. If not for that I would have been content to leave her a widow, but for that sin she must die."

The last thing her mind registers before all is oblivion is the sound of thunder. Or is it gunfire?

Shakill Goretusk dies, alone and fearing.

TEN

Luke and Lise's living room was in ruins. Bullet holes pocked the walls and the carpet glittered with the glass of broken picture frames and the shattered back door.

A few uniformed officers casually stepped around the shattered glass and pool of blood in the middle of the floor where Karen had died.

I stood on the grass of the backyard with Denny's partner, Matt Fitzpatrick, both of us looking in. Denny was in the middle of a whispered conversation with Luke and Lise. Thankfully, Miki had been dropped off at Lise's parent's place after Denny had called with the news.

The neighbors had heard shouting, and, most of them being orcs had ignored it. Then when they'd heard the gunfire they'd decided to call the police. Or I should say, their human spouses or in-laws called the police.

By the time the first officer had arrived it was already over.

Karen had been found dead on the carpet with no one else in the house.

From the little I'd been able to get from Matt, Karen

had not been killed by the gunfire. Which was surprising considering just how many bullet holes there were.

"It actually looked like whoever did it was being gentle," Matt said.

The man is, using one word to describe him, boring. Not that he's a bad guy or anything, it's just that compared to Denny, any human detective is just kind of dull.

"Gentle?" I asked, turning from the activity inside to consider him.

The man nodded, boring brown eyes still focused on the evidence collection. "Yeah. I mean, not in the killing. Looked like someone rammed a flamethrower through her chest and cooked her lungs. But the way her body was laid down. Seemed almost gentle."

"I think we have very different definitions of that word, Matt."

The longer you spend with Matt the more he talks. This has proven useful before, but right then I had all the information I needed. Shield. Not that I had actually suspected anyone else, but the presence of a small, concentrated fire just confirmed it.

Luke caught my attention and I slapped Matt on the shoulder in lieu of a goodbye as I started toward my cousin.

"We're heading to the station. Need to ID Ma." He was starting to show some of the hurt that we orcs are so good at denying. "Don't think I'm going to be able to chauffeur you around today."

I nodded. "I'll make all the arrangements." It had been a while since I'd arranged a funeral. Now two in one day. Three if we couldn't find anyone from Keelee's family to take care of her.

"Maybe you should head home too, Bloodfist," Denny said, her voice uncharacteristically soft.

I chose to ignore the statement. "Where are you guys staying tonight?" I asked, trying to keep the topic practical and away from myself.

"My parents have a guest bedroom ready for us," Lise said.

She was looking much worse than Luke. Both her nose and eyes were red and running, though her voice was still strong. If I'd had to pick which of the two of them was stronger right then, I think I would have said Lise.

I'd been ready to offer them the extra trailer, but it was probably for the best. I'd actually managed to forget about the other murder that morning. The trailer was most likely still surrounded by a perimeter of yellow tape.

"Here." Luke pressed the keys to his truck into my hand. "Get yourself home. Take care of whatever you need to."

I couldn't think of anything else to say, so I just watched as he and his wife were led away by an officer.

"You really should head home," Denny said to me, her voice insistent.

I turned to consider her. Why was she trying to send me home? I knew I could contribute to the investigation. She had conceded as much earlier. Besides, it was my damn job to help take care of this problem.

I thought of Charles Slayinghand encouraging me to let the police handle it. Of Luke telling me to go home, just moments before, and now Denny, again. I found myself angry at them all.

"Oh." Denny reached into her jacket pocket and handed me my phone. "We found that in your car. Still works. Looks like you have a bunch of messages."

I nodded dumbly, accepting the phone without a word.

"Need me to give you a ride home?" she asked.

I was about to say something I might have regretted when I actually looked at her and noticed her face. She had been crying. As impossible as it was for me to accept, cold, distant Denelle had been crying. Her eyes had the telltale red rings. That was it, but it was enough that I could tell.

I suddenly felt like a total ass. Karen was one of Denny's best friends. Possibly her only friend. This couldn't have been easy for her.

"No, I'll be fine." I dangled Luke's keys. "How are you holding up?"

She seemed surprised at my concern but recovered quickly. "Three murders. Not the best day of my life."

"I'm sure," I said, feeling awkward in these uncharted waters.

"Listen, Jack, go home. Seriously. This psycho is targeting orcs." She looked around to make sure no one was close enough to hear her, then she still whispered the word. "I don't want you making yourself a target."

"Wouldn't my sitting on my couch make me a pretty big target?" I asked. "I mean, he knows where I live. Remember murder number two?"

Denny considered that.

A thought occurred to me. "And how do you think he found Karen? He was running off into the woods last we saw him, and somehow he got here almost right after we did."

She scowled at me. "I'm already working on that, Blood-fist. Let me do my job. You do yours."

I was ready to protest, but stopped myself. "Wait. Really?"

She sighed. "Yes. It's pretty obvious this guy's targeting orcs. That does mean you have a right to help. But the second you get in the way, I have the right to send you home."

"Do you think he's going to try and kill all of us?" I asked.

She shook her head. "I don't know. According to Karen she was the last of the orcs he should have had an issue with. Everyone else died years ago. Still goblins. We may want to warn them again. If they'll listen. I'll have Matt work on finding somewhere safe for all of you. Call Luke and anyone else you can think of to get the word out. Let's get everyone to the station for now." She paused for a moment, considering. "Yeah, call the goblins as well."

"Of course. I'll call Ma while I drive." I turned to leave.

"Where are you going?" she asked. She didn't sound reproachful, just legitimately curious.

"Gotta go see a dwarf about a shield," I said over my shoulder.

"Bloodfist," she shouted. I stopped and waited for her to finish. "Don't do anything stupid."

Danyl Ironbeard is a dwarf. I don't mean little person. He stands over five foot. Like, one inch over five, but still, too tall to be considered a little person.

No, I'm talking axes, beards, mines. That kind of dwarf.

Ironically though, he doesn't have a beard. Weird, I know.

He owns a pawnshop in town, just off Main Street. *DI Pawn and Loan*.

The exterior of the shop is less than impressive. Peeling paint over crumbling brick. The O on the Open sign doesn't light up, and hasn't for as long as I can remember. So I usually just call it the Pen.

Inside doesn't look too impressive either, unless you actually know what you're looking for.

Danyl is the preferred pawn broker for the city's non-human crowd, as well as the humans that actually do know what they're looking for.

The cheap bell on the door bounced uselessly on the glass as I pushed it open. The musty smell of some of the older merchandise replaced the smell of sunbaked asphalt as I went inside.

"Jack, good to see you." Danyl waved from his seat behind the counter, a thick fantasy novel balanced on his ample stomach.

"Dan. How's business?" I asked, approaching the counter.

"Can't complain," he said with a smile that said it was doing better than was probably legal. I couldn't blame him for that. "You looking to buy or sell? Just bought a box of minis from some lady cleaning her attic. Her son's gonna be pissed when he finds out. Even had a few dragons in there."

He leaned over in his chair and pulled a small plastic figure out of a box.

He flicked it up at me like a coin and I snatched it out of the air.

"Is that an orc bard?" I asked, studying the thing.

"I dunno. Is it? I think the kid made his own custom pieces."

I turned the little orc in my hand, looking closer. Yup, it was a bard. It held an ax in one hand and a lute in the other, mouth open in what I imagined was some moving ballad.

"Hm," I said, finally turning my attention back to

Danyl, "Might have to look at that box later. I was actually hoping to ask you a question."

"Okay." He eyed me suspiciously as he closed his book and placed it on the counter.

"It's about something you bought from Charles Slayinghand a while ago."

His eyes narrowed at the name. "How long ago? I don't think I've seen him in here since before his old lady went belly up."

"It was actually a few years before she died."

"Might be hard then. He used to bring in a lot. His bar tabs were impressive back in the day. Or so I hear." Danyl's ex-wife owned one of the bars in town. I imagined he had probably seen one of Charles's legendary tabs himself.

"They were. I think you'll remember this though. Not something you'd see every day." I stopped and looked around the packed showroom, my gaze lingering on a wall of swords. "Well, you may actually."

"I can try. No guarantee, though."

"Thanks. It was a shield. I'm not entirely sure what kind, but I'm pretty sure it would have been blue and white."

He nodded, recognition in his eyes. "Yeah. Shit, man, I hope Charles doesn't want it back." He actually looked concerned.

"No," I reassured him. "I'm guessing that you sold it." I wasn't really surprised, it had been a while. "Do you remember who bought it?"

"I actually just sold it this morning. Man, not even an hour ago. I don't think Charles knew this, but that shield was just packed with arcane energy. I'm talking Arthurian-sword levels."

He said it as though it were nothing more than a signed

vinyl he'd found at a yard sale. I guessed he found a lot of magic stuff with his clientele. Half of us probably had no idea what we had when we brought in a family heirloom for a little beer money.

"Who bought it?" I asked. The timing could not be a coincidence.

He seemed to sense the urgency of my tone and spoke quickly in response, his voice nervous. "I didn't get a name. He paid with cash. Came in, showed me a drawing of the thing."

I rested my hands on the counter and leaned in closer. "What did he look like?"

He stepped back, his face scrunched up trying to remember. "Uh. Human. Old. Gray beard."

"Kind of look like the Dude?" I pressed.

Something clicked for him and he nodded. "Yeah, that's a perfect description of him. You know, minus the robe."

"Shit." I pushed off the counter and paced back and forth. "You said he came in just an hour ago?" I asked.

"Yeah. That's what I said." He nodded again, his face anxious.

I ran a hand over my dome and considered. Had he been in before or after he killed Karen? It would have to have been before. I didn't think she'd been dead that long before she'd been found.

But maybe I had the time-line wrong.

Another thought hit me. "You wouldn't happen to have sold him a matching sword? Would have been another Slayinghand that brought it in."

"No." his eyes opened wide. "But shit, having a matching set like that would have been amazing. That sale alone could keep me in luxury for life."

"Okay." I paced some more, Danyl shifting nervously

behind the counter. This wasn't good. I'd had no idea the shield was magic. I doubted Karen or the Slayinghands had known either.

"Alright, I have to go," I said finally after deciding I wouldn't figure anything out pacing around a pawn shop. "Thanks, Dan." I turned to go, stopping at the door. "And save that box for me. I'll try to swing by tomorrow."

He smiled and tossed the orc bard at me again. "Whole mess of you ugly bastards in the box."

"Thank you, sir." I pocketed the plastic orc and made my exit.

I tried to keep my mind on the matter at hand as I climbed into the truck. Magic was in play. Orcs are not the most magically inclined of the races, which meant the normal pool of people that might be able to help me would most likely be useless.

I'd known Shield had powers, but for some reason learning that the trophies Karen had told me about had magic properties as well scared me. Well, not so much scared me as made me nervous. I was not scared.

I did have one option, though. Of course, he might not even be in town. Or even in the same dimension for that matter. He should have been my first call when I had learned who Arthur Shield was. But it had been a stressful morning. I'd almost died, lost my phone, other people died. I only felt slightly stupid for not thinking of him sooner.

Jackson had given my father his number years before and I had put it in my phone, just in case. It also made me feel really cool having a wizard's phone number. It's okay, you can be jealous.

After a few rings it went to voice mail. *"This is Jackson, I'm probably in the middle of something. Just leave a message, and I'll return all calls in the order received."*

I looked out the truck window at the Pen and sighed as I waited for the beep. Danyl was watching me through the bars of the front window.

I ignored him as I left my message. "Mr. Smith. This is Jack Bloodfist. We've met before, but it's been a few years. Um. I have an issue that I think you can help with. It actually has something to do with you, and what you did for us. Uh, it looks like someone followed us over somehow. I was hoping you could help out with that? He's kinda killing folks. Thanks."

I left my number and hung up. I stared at the phone in disgust. What the hell was that?

I tossed my phone in a cup holder and started the truck. I had another stop I'd promised to make.

I hoped Mogayne would be willing to help me find the sword. I had a list of Slayinghands to call, and I knew from experience she was good with that sort of thing. Plus, it would be nice to see her.

I hummed that song from The Wizard of Oz as I pulled onto the road.

ELEVEN

Phases is the best-selling newspaper in the area. Considering that print is supposedly dead, it's doubly impressive that this particular publication is still selling.

Why? Well, its primary market is lycanthropes. You know, werewolves and other were...things?

The first issue of every month includes a full page detailing the phases of the moon for the next thirty days, as well as any other condition that may or may not trigger transformations. That was the original intent anyway. Now it reports news for the entire community.

The classifieds alone are worth the price of admission. A lot of people, humans, buy it to laugh at the ads.

"Wanted: goblins for position in Chinese eatery. Must be able to skin rats without training."

No one takes it seriously, unless they know it's serious.

And, if you're wondering, no, I have not gone back to that particular Chinese restaurant.

Most people just assume it's a tabloid, albeit one with really good photo editing, but the truth is, it's one of the most honest and reputable news sources in the state. They even have a website now. Mogayne runs that.

Part of me was pretty sure that's why she kept calling. There was a story involving the city's orcs and I was the best source for that information.

I was always willing to comment on any potential story for Mogayne. For one, the paper actually paid a decent fee for sources, and, of course, I like talking to Mogayne. Didn't matter what the topic was. I really do have a thing for that little redhead. I like to think it's a mutual attraction, but it's hard to say.

The paper's office is a storefront in a strip mall. Dollar stores and fast food joints flank it on either side. Standing in front of the doors you'll catch the distinct whiff of all you-can-eat pizza from two units down. The silhouette of a howling wolf that they use for their logo actually fits in pretty well with the picture of the smiling cow serving burgers next door.

Directly through the glass door was the receptionist's desk.

The young man behind the desk looked up and waved as I entered, "Mr. Bloodfist. Good to see you again."

I nodded my greeting to the pretty young man.

Seriously, he's pretty. I'm comfortable enough in my sexuality to say that. I also know that the only reason he was hired was because the owner has a thing for pretty men. And despite his being straight, he still has the job because he's actually a good receptionist.

"Hey, Nat. Mogayne should be expecting me," I said.

He scanned a sheet of paper. "Yup. You're actually earlier than she expected. Just head on back."

I walked around the free-standing wall and into the open room behind.

The rows of desks were exactly as I remembered them, either piled high with papers and full in trays or organized by OCD zealots.

It wasn't the crazy bullpen of papers that you always expect thanks to television, but it was fairly busy. There were about twenty desks, most of them empty, but still a few with someone hard at work.

One old guy may have been playing solitaire, but I wasn't going to rat him out. A few of the people in the room eyed me as I walked past.

"Hey, Mo." I waved at the woman as I approached her desk.

She looked up from her laptop, half a donut sticking out of her mouth.

She quickly pulled the pastry out of her mouth and stuck it on a napkin that rested on top of a pile of papers. She smiled at me as she rose, dusting donut crumbs off her shirt. The effect was distracting.

"You're early," she said, walking around the desk, her eyes lingered on my bandaged forehead, but she didn't say anything as she wrapped me in a fond hug.

I'm always impressed with the gentle firmness whenever she does that. I made sure to hug back.

The hug seemed to last longer than usual. Her question explained why. "Are you okay?" she asked. "I heard about your aunt. Detective Halldorson told me when I called her."

I swallowed the sudden lump in my throat. I'd been holding up pretty well, and I didn't want to lose it in front of her. As an orc, I didn't want to lose it in front of anybody. It would be shameful.

I was actually a little surprised at the sudden rush of emotion, but I felt like I played it off pretty well.

"I'm alright. Listen, I was hoping you could help me with something."

She looked up at me as she released the hug, which was a shame. "What's that?"

I pulled the folded list of names out of my back pocket and handed it to her. "The guy that's been killing my family? He's after some old heirlooms. The last one is probably with someone on this list. Or, at least, was at one point."

"So it's a murder-robbery thing?" she asked, carrying the list back around her desk and sitting down.

"He has a little bit of a grudge against the fist." Mogayne is one of the few humans that know about orcs and all the other races, and as a reporter that frequently writes about the goings on in the community, she knows all the terminology.

"How big a grudge?" she asked.

I could tell by the way her eyes were focused that she was mentally recording everything I said.

"Very," I said simply.

"And this list?" She held it up.

"If the pattern sticks, his next victim is on there. I'd really like to stop that."

She indicated a chair at an empty desk and I pulled it closer.

She placed the list on the desk between us and drew a line at the halfway point, "I'll take these, you take those. Sound good?"

"Sounds good."

"What are we looking for again?" she asked.

I explained the situation and she nodded her understanding.

"Old sword from pops, got it."

"Oh, and while you have them on the line, tell them it's been recommended that all orcs make their way to the local police station. Tell them to ask for either Detective Halldorson or Fitzpatrick. Just in case."

For some reason that earned me a smile.

For the next thirty minutes or so the two of us dialed numbers and questioned the orcs on the other end. Mogayne was her ever-friendly self, joking with some, consoling others on the recent losses in the community. We ended every call by encouraging each of them to contact the detectives.

I had two names left on my list and dialed the first one.

I was more than a little surprised when Denny's voice answered.

"Hello, Bloodfist," she said.

"No," I said, with a groan.

"Afraid so," she answered. "Two this time. One orc and a goblin. A few others injured."

"Where?" I demanded.

"The Bearded Lady." Danyl's ex's bar.

"I'll be right there," I said.

"Sure you shouldn't be at the station with your cousin?" she asked, tone sharper than I expected.

I ignored the question. "Den, this is John's phone, right?" I asked, checking the name on the list.

"It was in the dead guy's pocket, yeah."

"You need to get people to his house." I read the address off the list.

"Why?"

"John most likely had something Shield wants."

"Any chance that something is a sword?"

I froze, my stomach a knot. "How did you know?"

"Witnesses say the two were discussing terms. Goblin wanted to buy the sword. Had a decent amount of cash."

"And?" I pressed.

Denny sighed. "According to my witnesses, big guy stormed in, said he'd waited long enough and killed both of them."

I cursed. That was it. Shield had everything. I had no idea what that meant, but I had a feeling it didn't mean he was going to leave town and not try to kill anymore orcs and goblins.

"Head to the station, Jack," Denny said. "We'll figure it out there."

"Yeah," I said, numb.

"And, Bloodfist, thanks for letting the others know. We've been getting calls for the last little bit. We're setting up protective details for everyone that requests one."

"Thanks, Detective. I'll head there now."

I hung up and found Mogayne studying me quizzically.

I told her what Denny had just told me.

"Alright then. You drive and I'll keep you company." She rose from her chair, throwing her laptop into her messenger bag.

Despite myself I smiled. "Yes, ma'am."

"Ma'am? No, that's Miss Thornhill to you, young man."

A door opened at the back of the room. "Where you headed, Mo?" Kirk Brown asked.

"Chasing a story, boss." She waved at the man who nodded approvingly.

Kirk Brown is a werewolf. A very well dressed, very gay werewolf.

At this moment he was human, because there was no full moon out, obviously.

He's also one of the richer members of the community.

Besides being the owner of Phases he also founded a very exclusive club. For a monthly fee he offers secure housing for some of the more violent members of the were-community. They pay him and he sticks them in a bunker somewhere for however many days their transformation lasts. Because of that, we actually have a higher number of lycanthropes than anywhere else in the country. At first everyone freaked out, but most of us are monsters to someone, so we got over it. Well, most of us did.

It helped that the club draws in the werewolves that don't want to hurt people and are willing to pay to make sure they don't.

"Hey, Jack." He winked at me. "How you holding up?" His voice transformed form its normal exuberance into a tone I'd heard far too often that day.

"Just fine, Kirk. You?"

"Selling papers." The three of us stood in awkward silence, with a roomful of people pretending not to hear us, before Kirk spoke up again. "Well, I'll let you two darlings go. Be careful out there. Crazy motherfucker killing folks." He waved over his shoulder and closed the door.

Mogayne grabbed my hand and led the way outside. So it wasn't the worst day of my life.

Jackson Smith stands in the mud, his naked body covered in blood. None of it his.

His breath is as heavy as his sword feels as he watches the remainder of the army marching to meet him.

Their cries are filled with bestial hate. Sharp teeth and sharper blades are waved at the storm-darkened sky as they slowly close the distance.

Jackson uses a bloody hand and wipes a strand of his long hair away from his face, leaving a trail of acrid black blood over the already dry layer of gore.

The blood is beginning to burn his skin, the itching adding to his discomfort.

The army of manlike creatures are at the base of his hill now. In their hundreds they begin the steep climb. The air fills with the thump of ten dozen bows loosing into the air.

Jackson throws back his head and laughs in defiance as the black shafts rain down around him.

The days of fighting in the rain and the mud and the blood have had their effect. He is all carnal violence.

He is death. Let them try and kill him.

A sound, louder than the bows and Jackson's laughter is heard. Like a peal of thunder Jackson looses a small portion of the energy he holds within himself.

The arrows halt in their paths and scatter in splinters and failure.

The beastmen do not halt their charge. They fear their masters more than they fear Jackson and his magic.

He will teach them the error in this.

The talons and hoofs pound over fallen comrades as they close the distance.

Their numbers give them false courage, and they are too stupid to consider that in the past days this man has already killed twice their number.

But these are the last. Their hooded masters crack their whips from the rear, harder and with more urgency than they have before. So they march, charge, to death at the laughing man's hand.

Jackson lowers his gaze to meet the eyes of the lead creatures.

They falter when that gaze meets them and they are passed by the more eager and more blind.

Jackson peels his lips back, white teeth standing out against his blood-stained skin, and jumps forward, feet first, down the hill.

His legs still hold some strength and he meets his first foe while still in the air, sandaled feet crushing the muzzle below the human eyes.

His sword arm swings as his feet hit the ground and two more fall, black blood washing the living in death.

He has killed five more before those around him realize he is there, in the midst of their ranks.

Their cries of anger threaten to deafen him, their press of bodies promise to overwhelm.

He laughs again in the face of these odds as his sword pierces a throat, his empty hand crushing a skull.

He pulls a spear from the hands of a fallen abomination and stabs and slashes. Soon, there is a circle around him and he has room to throw the spear.

It pierces three of the monsters before its momentum is spent.

They roar in fear and anger once more and the press of hundreds pushes in around him again.

Many slip and fall down the hill in the rush to smother the man.

There is another crash of his inner thunder and several rows of the creatures fly into their comrades, red fire peeling their skin, and more stumble and roll down the incline, clawed hands grasping for holds in the mud.

Jackson dances around the blows and strikes as he charges into the mass of monsters. His sword and fists, feet and knees, create a path of blood and corpses.

He pushes through the army at the base of the large hill and runs far enough to give himself some space.

They cry with their beast mouths and human tongues and the mass turns to face him again.

Jackson does the calculations in his mind and decides it is time to end things.

He stabs his large sword into the ground and it vanishes in a shower of glittering, blue light, returned to its home for now.

He holds both hands above his head, the back of his right hand resting in the palm of the left.

As the beasts charge closer, misshapen feet slapping on the blood soaked ground, Jackson closes his hand into a fist. The faint outline of a narrow blade forms out of nothing in his hand.

Eyes closed in concentration, he whispers the first word of the first spell he ever taught himself, "Zen," then with a cry that shatters the sky he swings his empty hand. "So!"

The trees on top of the hill collapse to the ground, their trunks neatly cut with one stroke of Jackson's magic.

Below, struck with the same magic, the beastmen all lie in the mud; blood and organs spill from the perfect slashes that leave every one of them in two pieces. Cut swords and spears are still held in angry hands.

Jackson collapses to one knee, breath ragged.

There is the squelch of a booted foot in the mud behind him. The gentle rasp of sword brushing leather.

He forces himself to his feet and turns from the dead to face those still living.

The robed man holds a whip in one hand, half-drawn sword in the other.

This is the same whip used to drive the beastmen to

their deaths. The sword that was intended for Jackson's back.

The figure steps back, fear showing even with face unseen.

Jackson raises his right hand, first and second fingers held out like a gun.

There is no sound as the back of the robed figure's hood explodes outward, littering the ground behind.

A voice whispers in Jackson's mind. "Sir?" it says.

"Yes, Sigmund," Jackson thinks in response.

"You received a call a short while ago."

"And?" Jackson asks, impatient and tired.

"It is from one of the orcs you saved from PF-27."

Jackson thinks for a moment, his mind still foggy from the battle, "Oh." He remembers now. "What did they need?"

"I will play the message." There is a click and the message plays in Jackson's mind.

He smiles. Someone followed. Just as he'd hoped they would.

TWELVE

I tried to call Ma as we made our way to the station.

There was no answer at Jack's Place, or her apartment.

I'm not so stupid that I hadn't been able to figure out the goblins were up to something. They'd somehow known what Shield was after before I had.

Dad had probably told Ma something about the trophies. The two hadn't had many secrets.

What I couldn't figure out was what they'd thought they'd could do with the sword. Whatever it had been had obviously not worked. It seemed like the only thing they'd managed was to let the good Sir Arthur know they were involved, if he hadn't already.

I tried the number for one of my cousins who worked at Jack's Place, hoping he could tell me something about Ma.

After a few rings someone answered, "Ello?"

"Ricky, it's cousin Jack," I started.

"Oh, shit." The phone clicked off.

"What the hell?" I slammed the phone into a cup holder and glared at the road. "Little shit hung up on me."

"Why don't they want to talk to you?" Mo asked.

"No idea. They refused Denny's help, too. It's probably that bastard Terry. He's been up to something. Trying to make himself the new glorious leader." I shook my head in distaste. My shoulder still hurt from his bite.

My phone rang, and I snatched it up expecting the number from Jack's Place. Instead a picture of Sir Ian as Gandalf stared back at me. It was Jackson.

"Holy shit," I said. I wiped my hand on my pants before I swiped to answer.

"Who is it?" Mogayne asked.

I excitedly mouthed the word, "Jackson," as I held the phone to my ear. "Hello." I tried my best to keep my voice in a normal octave.

"Is this the young master Bloodfist?" a friendly voice asked.

"It is," I answered. I felt like some fangirl talking to Ryan Gosling. My heart was beating fast and I knew I had a goofy grin on my face that I couldn't do anything about. Don't judge me.

"This is Jackson Smith. You left a message earlier today."

"Yeah, I know. I mean I know it's you, not the message. I, I know I left a message, just, um. Never mind. Yeah. I was hoping to talk to you. Hopefully figure out what happened."

"I'd be happy to talk. Your fist is my responsibility after all. Do you remember where I live? I think you came by with your dad once?"

"Yeah, about ten years ago. Could I get the address again? Just in case." I looked to Mogayne and she nodded, her eyes focused, ready to remember what I said. Never need paper with her around.

Jackson gave me the address and I repeated it back, Mogayne nodding to let me know she had it.

"Should be there in about thirty minutes. That okay?" I asked hopefully.

"Should be fine. I just got back into town, so if I don't answer just wait, I might still be in the shower. See you when you get here."

The line disconnected and I held my phone at arm's length, studying it with awe.

"Who was that?" Mo asked again, an amused smile in her voice.

"That was Jackson Smith," I said, with, I'm sure, a smug grin on my face.

"Who's that?"

"The wizard?" I grinned at her, a little surprised she hadn't heard the name.

"I don't think I've met him," she said, returning my grin. "But he must be impressive to get you so excited. I doubt I could get you to smile like that in my most risqué undies."

I coughed in surprise. "What?"

"Nothing. So are we going to see the wizard?" She sang the question.

"Hell yes we are."

You going to let the detective know?"

"Uh." I gave her a sidelong glance as I considered. "Yeah, I probably should."

Denny answered on the second ring.

"Hey, Denny, I just got off the phone with Jackson. He's asked me to meet him. See if he can help."

"He's back in town?" she asked, tone not nearly as excited as I'd expected.

"Yeah. Said he just got back. How'd you know he was out of town?"

"He's always out of town. I think in the past twenty years he's been in that apartment twice. I also called him this morning after speaking with Karen. Thought he might be able to help. This is his mess, he should clean it. Nice to know he returns your call." She sounded a little bitter. Well, a little more than usual.

"It comes with the card, Detective," I said, not really meaning to be smug, but I'm sure she just heard me talking out my ass.

"Whatever," she said with an exasperated sigh. "Ask him if he can do a tracking spell. He can probably use some of your blood to find the guy."

"Huh?" I asked, confused at the sudden mention of spells.

"Just trust me, Bloodfist. I'm an elf, I know a little bit about magic."

"Then why couldn't *you* do that?"

"Shut up, orc. I know magic. Not the same as being able to do magic. Not that kind, anyway."

"Ah, you're stuck with elf magic. Like making bread that fills you up after one bite, or magic rope, or—"

"If you list one more thing I will reach through this phone and show you just what kind of magic I know."

"Understood, ma'am."

"Let me know what you learn."

I promised I would and she hung up with no further ceremony.

"Detective Halldorson totally loves you," Mo said, doing a good job of keeping her face straight.

"Oh yeah. That's why she always tells me not to do something stupid, or actually just calls me stupid? Term of endearment with elves?"

"It might be," she said, lips pursed as she considered. "At least for her. I'm serious. I think she considers you a friend."

My mouth hung open as I tried to think of a response. I finally settled on, "Think so?"

"Oh yeah." I could see the smile now and I scowled.

"That's mean. Doesn't matter, though. I like Den, whether she accepts my love or not."

"Aw, it's love now?" Mo teased.

"And what if it is? Maybe I have a thing for older women."

"Well we all know you have a thing for elves." She rolled her eyes in mock disgust. She ruined the effect when she glanced at me to gauge my reaction.

"Can't help it. It's the ears." I flicked the point of my right ear in emphasis.

"Yeah, pointy ears are kinda sexy." I jumped a little as she pinched my ear gently.

We rode in comfortable silence for a little while before she spoke again. "So, this the new ride?"

I laughed. "I could never afford this on my pay. Nah, this is my cousin Luke's truck."

"I see. So what presets does he have in here?" She flicked the radio on. It was still the pop country station Luke had left it on and vocal talents of the latest country diva greeted us.

"Hm, interesting," Mo said. After a few notes she began to gently sing along. I guessed she was very familiar with the song.

If I'm being honest, Mo's voice is much prettier than anything I hear on the radio. Something about her accent just adds something to any song that I find very appealing.

Despite all the events of the day, my spirits were at an all-time high, so I joined in.

Not loudly—I tend to drown people out when I'm loud,

and I wanted to be able to hear Mo—so I just provided a little harmony.

Or tried to. It had the opposite of my intended effect and Mo stopped singing.

"You have a great singing voice." She sounded legitimately surprised.

"Nah," I said with false modesty. I know I have a good voice.

"I didn't know orcs sang."

"Some of us do. Dad used to a lot. He always said I would have been a warcrier back home."

"What's a warcrier?" she asked, sincere interest in her voice.

"Well, Dad and Ma never really talked about the old country too much. But I think warcriers were warriors that led others into battle. I think Dad said once that they gave orders through song. Used their voice to bolster morale and to scare enemy troops."

"Really?" She turned in her seat to consider me. She cocked her head to the side, eyes narrowed as she focused on my face.

"What?" I asked, surprised by her sudden inspection.

"Just trying to picture you leading an army of orcs into battle. I'm picturing a loincloth and warpaint. I hope that's not racist." She bit her bottom lip as she ran her sea green eyes up and down my body.

I felt like a piece of meat. I also kind of liked it.

"Loincloth, huh?"

"Oh yeah. That part is very important," she said, dropping her voice.

I laughed. "I don't know what the traditional garb was, but sure, we'll go with loincloth."

"Good, because you have no choice in the matter.

Whenever you lead an army into battle, you have to wear a loincloth."

"Yes, ma'am."

"But seriously, singing?"

"Yeah," I shrugged. "I guess the different notes meant different things. Dad said that some of the best warcriers could even steal their enemies' strength with their songs."

"That would be something." She studied me for a moment longer before turning back to face the front of the truck.

"What about you?" I asked.

"What about me?"

"No fancy Irish stories to explain your beautiful singing voice?"

"Oh, it's beautiful now, is it?"

"Well, it's about the best word to describe you." I was surprised by my own forwardness, and she didn't seem displeased with the statement.

She smiled. "No, just lucky. Most of my family sound like seals on a beach when they sing."

We drove in silence for a few minutes. I couldn't decide if I should follow up my statement by asking her to dinner— it had been a while—but she spoke up first.

"Thanks, by the way."

"For?"

"Saying I'm beautiful. I don't hear that nearly enough." Her tone was teasing again, but I just grinned back at her.

"Anytime."

"I think I need to make you dinner when this is all over," she said thoughtfully.

"I wouldn't say no to that."

"Good, but I wasn't going to give you a choice." She ran a gently hand through the mess of my beard.

The rest of the drive was incredibly pleasant, as I'm sure you can imagine.

———————

Jackson's apartment building is in the small town of Camden, a little over thirty miles from Summervale. It's a small building. Two stories tall, with five units on each floor. The doors all face the playground of an elementary school, with only a small strip of pitted asphalt separating the two lots.

I knew which door was Jackson's without even looking at the lopsided unit number.

Nine of the ten apartments had faded red, almost pink paint on the doors and surrounding frames. Jackson's was a very distinct blue.

"Huh," I said as I stared up at his door.

Mo raised a questioning eyebrow.

"Nothing. Let's go."

She followed me up the warped wooden stairs to the second story. We stopped in front of the door and I gave it three solid raps. My hands didn't shake at all, I swear.

There was the sound of a chain lock and then the door swung inward.

Jackson stood in the doorway, just as I remembered him.

He looks like he's in his early to mid-thirties. It's just how he looked the day he led us through the door in the sky.

His light brown hair was cut short, still wet from a shower, and his face was freshly shaved. The skin around his hazel eyes wrinkled as he smiled at us.

"Jack, please come in." He stepped out of the way and indicated we go inside.

"Hi, I'm Jackson." He extended a hand to Mo as she followed me inside.

"Oh, I know." She smiled at me as she accepted the offered hand, "I'm Mogayne, call me Mo."

"Pleasure to meet you, Mo."

He turned his attention to me. "How much does she know?" His expression was serious, and it aged him considerably.

"Uh, not much, actually." I hadn't considered this. Our origins were supposed to be a secret.

"Do you trust her?" he asked.

"I do." I answered. I always will.

"Good enough for me." He smiled, making him look young again as he closed the door. "Please have a seat, and we'll get down to business."

We sat down and Jackson handed each of us a cold can of Coke without asking if we were thirsty.

He opened his own can as he sat down. "So, someone followed us? Got a name?"

"Arthur Shield," I answered, opening my drink. The caffeine tasted amazing.

He nodded, as though he had already suspected. "Makes sense. I wouldn't be surprised if he was trapped somewhere between for a while. Worked his way through over the course of years." He was talking to himself, so I didn't interrupt. "That does things to a person, though. Never leaves them the same."

"Is that the killer's name?" Mo whispered to me.

I nodded.

"What do you mean, he followed you?"

Jackson looked up from his private conversation and studied her face, eyes intent. "From the orc homeland," he answered for me. "He's a member of an order of holy knights. Jack's old man and I pissed them off pretty badly about twenty years ago. I brought the fist here to give them a chance of escaping."

"You said stuck between. What does that mean?" I knew she was storing all of this for later.

Jackson looked to me for approval and I shrugged. "I'm okay telling her if you are."

His eyes went from me to her and back again, smiling.

He turned to Mo and, in the most matter-of-fact voice possible said, "Between Jack's world and this one."

To Mo's credit her only reaction was a surprised blink. Her lack of any follow-up questions was the only other sign of her shock at the news.

"So you think you know how he got here?" I asked. "Any way we can get him back, or, you know, kill him?" I really wanted the second option.

"You can kill him the same way you kill any man," Jackson said. "I'm guessing the real issue is finding him."

"That, and do you have any idea how he's tracking us down?"

"What do you mean?" Jackson asked.

"So far he's killed three orcs, a half-elf, and a goblin. But I don't know how he found them. My only theory right now is magic, but..." I shrugged, not really sure how to finish the thought.

"Any connection with those he killed? I feel like there must be something significant with that elf to have made Shield's list. He's a paladin. He doesn't kill unless he feels the dead man deserved it."

I sighed. Karen had said Jackson had been unaware of the trophies. I figured all the guilty parties were dead, so that would hopefully not make him angry. I've heard scary things about angry wizards.

I told him about the trophies and about how Shield seemed to have been collecting them.

"How long ago did he get the last piece?"

"About an hour ago," I said.

"Hm. So a necklace, a holy symbol, a sword and a shield. That's a full set of ceremonial gear. Good thing Saban has no way of endowing the man."

"What do you mean?" I asked.

"His god. There's no way he could have found him here. With those relics, Shield could technically open up a doorway, but he'd need some power first."

"Yeah, about that." I grimaced. "Would glowing blue eyes be an indicator of anything?"

Jackson let out a short laugh. "Awesome. That means his god found him."

"Okay, but what does that mean?"

"Like I said, Arthur Shield is a paladin. Unlike a wizard," he pointed to himself, "they rely on the borrowed power of their chosen deity. It's actually an interesting system..." he trailed off.

"So?"

"Well, if Saban was able to track him down, which should have been impossible, he would be able to give him enough power to open that doorway I just mentioned."

"If it should have been impossible, how did he find him?" I asked.

Jackson stared at me like I was an idiot.

"The trophies," Mo said.

Jackson nodded slowly. "The trophies. I told them to leave everything." His voice was low, dangerous.

I met his gaze, forcing myself to not look away.

"We should probably find him before he does anything, right?" Mo asked.

"Yeah." I remembered my conversation with Denny. "I was told I should ask you to try a tracking spell."

Jackson blinked. "Well, that would work, if I had something to link to Shield. Or if I had the frequency of Saban's power."

"My blood," I said. "We're from the same world. I was told that should work."

Jackson frowned, a look of concentration on his face. "How many orcs and goblins are left that crossed over?"

"Oh." I dropped my head, disappointed that I hadn't thought of that.

"No, I'm asking. How many? It should be a simple calculation to eliminate them from the spell. In fact," he jumped up from his chair and rushed into his kitchen, "I can use your blood,—half and half, right?—To remove anyone of orc or goblin descent. Should just find Shield, then."

He came back carrying a large plastic bowl full of water and placed it on his coffee table. He held up a small knife. "Cup o' blood for a good neighbor?"

I held out my hand to Jackson. He pulled me closer and cut a small gash in my forearm. He pushed a wadded paper towel onto the cut after only a few drops fell into the water.

He pushed my arm away and turned his full attention to the bowl.

I glanced over at Mo, who had her recording eyes on. This was going to make one hell of a story. The kind that sold a lot of papers.

Jackson lowered his face to the bowl and whispered something I couldn't hear. The surface of the red-tinted water rippled and then a blurry image appeared just beneath the surface of the water.

"This could be bad," Jackson said.

"What? Why?" I asked as I tried to make sense of the upside down and obscured image.

I turned my head and squinted at the bowl until I could see it. It was Arthur Shield, in all his bastardly glory.

He was kneeling in a clearing, surrounded by trees. On the ground in front of him was the sword and shield. He pulled the necklace from around his neck, and the stone bird from a pocket, and placed both of them between the other two trophies.

That was when I understood Jackson's concern. The water filled with a blue light as the air in front of the paladin tore open.

THIRTEEN

Arthur Shield rises from his prayer, heart full of thanks to Saban. On the other side of the canyon between worlds his brothers wait.

For the briefest of moments he considers stepping into the rift, returning to the home he has missed for the past two decades.

But he allows the fancy to pass quickly. His purpose now is not to return home, but to lead his brothers in their quest for justice. It is to rid this world of the plague he had allowed to escape so long ago.

The tear in the sky emits a soft, orange glow, the rift wavering in his vision like the surface of a gentle lake disturbed by pebbles.

So far away he can see his brothers. He strains his eyes and catches the glint of sun on plate mail. Hands raise in greeting, swords wave in victory.

He stands straight, feeling ill-dressed for the occasion. But despite the long wait, he has succeeded.

His brothers cross that infinite chasm now. With a single stride of plate-clad feet the first warrior steps into this world. Then the second, and the third. In the end he surrounded by a sea of metal and gentle, blue fire.

The last few to cross the expanse between worlds carry his armor. His sword. Tears rise, unbidden and unstoppable, at the sight of what he had thought lost.

The men all stand straight, arms crossed over chests in salute for their long missing commander.

A grizzled veteran that Arthur remembers as his squire indicates the armor, now piled neatly at Shield's feet. "Sir Arthur, it has been a long time. May I have the honor of preparing you for battle one last time?"

Arthur nods, emotion preventing the words from coming. The man smiles, the scars of his face twisted and noble.

He pulls a short, sharp blade and cuts away Arthur's sweater and jeans as the old paladin steps out of the cheap leather boots he had been forced to steal.

Padded pants and robe are placed on him. Chain mail that once felt like a second skin on top of that. Finally the plate. He places his helm on his head himself and turns to consider the watching mass of knights.

His old squire offers him the hilt of his sword, something he thought lost in the void. The tip is severed, removed by the weight of worlds, but the edge is keen. Sharp enough to remove any orc head.

"Are you ready, Sir Arthur?" a voice asks.

Shield spins at the sound. One had passed through the door without his notice.

He drops to his knees and the rest follow his lead.

Saban considers his faithful warriors, a grim smile spreading. "Let us bring justice to this world."

"Do you have any weapons?" Jackson asked as the three of us watched the steady stream of armored orc-haters file through the hole in the sky.

"No," I answered. Denny had not returned my gun.

"Are your people taken care of?"

"Most of the orcs should have contacted the local police. Ma and the rest of the goblins aren't answering my calls, so I don't know about them."

"The cops won't be any help. Not against these numbers. We need to get them somewhere safe. Preferably somewhere with less collateral damage."

"Like where?" I asked, still staring into the bowl as a blurry figure started cutting away Shield's clothes.

"I think I have an idea," Mo said. She hadn't looked away from the water.

"Where?" I asked.

"Will five feet of reinforced concrete slow them down?" she asked Jackson.

"Better than nothing." He'd moved away from the coffee table and was unlocking a closet in the hallway.

"What are you talking about?" I asked.

She ignored me and pulled out her phone.

"Boss?" she asked. "Hey, I need you to do me a huge favor. You up for saving some lives today?"

She waited for a response. "Okay, I need you to call Detective Halldorson. Tell her she needs to get all the orcs and any goblins she rounds up to your clubhouse. Then have her call Jack. He'll explain the rest. Thanks, boss. You're the best." She made a kissing sound into the phone and hung up.

"Clubhouse?" I asked.

"No questionable lunar phases tonight, so all the rooms are free."

I smiled in sudden understanding. Kirk's clubhouse was built to keep big, scary things in, so it would probably do just as well keeping men in armor out.

"I'll just need to keep Saban away from them," Jackson said.

"What? He's here?" I asked, checking the bowl again. Shield was currently being fitted with armor to match his friends, but I didn't see anyone that I might consider godly.

"Yeah." Jackson pulled the closet door open and looked at me. "Come pick something out. You're going to be helping me, and I like to make sure my allies are equipped for what's coming."

I rose and approached the closet. The room inside extended far beyond what should have been possible in that small apartment. It was twice the size of the whole unit.

"Bigger on the inside?" I asked.

"Just magic, Jack," he said with a knowing grin. "Don't get too excited."

The walls were lined with weapons, swords, guns, spears. You name it, he had it.

My eyes were drawn to a vicious ax that hung on the back wall. Crescent ax head on one side, stiletto blade on the other, with a short spike on the top. The logical part of my brain told me to pull a rifle down, or to at least take the ax and a gun. But when my hand wrapped around the rough wood of the handle I knew it was all I needed.

"Hm," Jackson said, "interesting."

I looked up at him, quizzical.

"Its name is Ukufa."

The ax seemed to vibrate in my hand at the sound of its name.

"Mo, if you don't mind, I'll pick for you." Jackson pulled a pistol of the wall and passed it to the woman.

"Why don't I get to pick?" she asked.

She didn't sound upset as she stuck the pistol and extra magazines in her bag, next to her laptop.

"Because I know which one you'd take." He glanced inside the closet again. I think he was eying a silver net, but it may have been the trident hanging next to it.

There was a loud knock at the door and Jackson jerked to attention. He hurried me out of the armory and locked the closet behind us.

"Who is it?" Jackson asked, cautiously approaching the front door.

"We know he's in there," an angry woman's voice shouted. "Open up!"

"Who's in here?" Jackson asked, glancing at me.

"Oh, for God's sake." There was a loud boom and the splinters of the door flew inward.

A woman stood in the doorway, her brown trench coat fluttering dramatically in the settling dust.

Jackson hadn't moved at all; pieces of blue wood stuck out of his body, dripping blood.

"Take them alive," the woman ordered.

That's when I noticed the others around her, all with rifles aimed inside.

"May I help you?" Jackson asked, right before he threw his fist out and caught the woman in the stomach.

She doubled over and flew backward off the second-story walkway. The instant her feet left the ground guns began to fire.

I grabbed Mo and threw her behind the couch. I jumped over as well, landing on top of her. My chest gave me a painful reminder of my morning's excitement as I landed.

Mogayne had her hands over her ears and her eyes shut tight.

I covered my own ears as I made sure I was between her and the bullets that were filling the apartment. I'm a nice guy like that.

"I said *alive!*" The woman shouted again.

The gunfire died down and I peeked up over the couch to see the woman in the trench coat as she gracefully landed on the wood of the walkway outside, coat flaring like a cape.

Jackson had his back against the wall between his kitchen and the entrance, his expression somewhere between annoyance and boredom.

The woman and her subordinates, another woman and three men, marched into the apartment.

The guns were shouldered and they all pulled out extending batons. The sticks snapping open menacingly.

Jackson and I locked eyes for a second and he nodded his head toward the intruders, as if asking me, "You want to do this?"

I nodded, hand tightening around my new weapon.

Jackson moved first, spinning out from his cover in a blur. His fist caught one of the men, a squat barrel of a guy, on the chin.

The man fell like the ugliest bag of bricks in the world and Jackson moved to the next.

His knee connected with the plump woman's stomach. She collapsed as quickly as the first.

I decided I didn't want Jackson to take all the glory so I charged in next. Ax over my head and a battle cry ripping from my throat. I swung at the first guy I came to.

He was the most stereotypical Russian I had ever seen. If you've seen Rocky IV, just picture Ivan Drago and add a couple dozen pounds of muscle. He stared down at me as he nimbly dodged my swing, and countered with his own.

The baton smacked me on the shoulder and I snarled in pain and growing anger.

Drago blinked, apparently surprised that I hadn't gone down, and swung again.

I charged him, getting close enough that he hit me with his arm instead of the baton. It still hurt, but far less than the last hit.

I wrapped my arms around him, ax flat against his back, and lifted him off his feet. I carried him a few steps before dropping us both to the ground.

I sat up, leaving the ax under him, ready to start pounding him in the face. This was my go-to strategy. My aunt Karen had taught Luke and me how to fight as kids and she recommended this move for bigger opponents.

I'd expected the guy to cover his face, which is what usually happens, but instead he sat up, pushing me back. Both his arms shot up with an impressive speed and wrapped around my chest.

He stood up, still holding me, and lifted me up off the ground. His face twisted with the effort as he squeezed.

I groaned as my already injured chest began to scream.

I stared down at him, my lips peeling back, ready to roar if only I had the breath.

His eyes opened wider, probably surprised at the sight of my trimmed tusks.

I brought my head down on his face, smashing my forehead into his nose.

He let out a soft grunt of pain and I brought my head down again.

After the third one he let go, staggering back and holding up a hand to slow the rush of blood.

The sound of a gunshot distracted me and the man collapsed backward into the apartment wall.

He slid down until he was sitting, his face contorted in pain.

I glanced over my shoulder to see Mo, eyes wide, holding her new pistol.

I grinned, and she tried to grin back.

I turned to help Jackson but was surprised to find he was on his last opponent.

He casually dodged around the woman's blurring fists and impressive kicks.

Her whole body glowed with a deep red. As her fists tore through the air they left trails of orange fire that turned into embers, then disappeared.

Jackson sighed loudly as he dodged another blow. He seemed bored as he caught her flaming fist in his open palm and twisted her arm around. She let out a pained cry and the fire blinked out.

"Why don't you tell me who you're looking for before we resort to violence?"

Her eyes darted around the apartment, settling on me. Her mouth opened in an angry snarl.

"Him." She jabbed her head toward me, "We need him to find Shield."

"You're looking for Shield?" Jackson asked, releasing her.

She stood up straight, angrily rubbing her arm. "Yes."

"And you need Jack why?"

"They're from the same world."

"Tracking spell died on you, huh?"

"How'd you know?"

"Wizard."

She nodded as though that made sense. "You're strong."

It seemed hard for her to say. "Now give us the ugly one, and we'll go."

"Tell you what. He'll forgive you for calling him ugly if you just shut up and listen."

"Yeah, bitch," I said, picking up Ukufa. "We've already found Shield. You could have just asked."

"Where?" she asked urgently.

"With friends," Jackson said.

Her face paled. "How many?"

"A lot of paladins. Didn't get a count." He nodded to the bowl on the coffee table. A bullet had passed clean through, draining the water onto the table and carpet.

She looked around at her fallen comrades, some of whom were stirring. The big Russian rubbed his chest and gave Mo a respectful nod.

The leader seemed to be doing math in her head.

"You're going to need a lot more men. They also have a god with them," Jackson said.

She studied Jackson's face as though looking for any hint of a joke. When she saw none she sighed. "Well, fuck." Her blue eyes betrayed only a hint of fear.

Everyone conscious stood or sat up straighter at the sound of sirens in the distance.

FOURTEEN

"You should go," Jackson said, peering out his front window.

"You have a GPS?" He turned to the woman and she nodded. "Good. Meet me at these coordinates." He listed some numbers so fast that I couldn't catch them.

"Got that?" he asked.

Everyone shook their head. Except Mo.

"Yeah. I got it."

"Good. Give it to them. Let's go."

Jackson had me help his guests down the stairs to their car.

The sirens were coming closer, so we moved fast. Gunfire near schools usually warrants a quick response time.

As I loaded an unconscious woman into the back of what looked like a modified prison transport vehicle, Mo gave Jackson's coordinates to a silent, dark-skinned Indian man, who punched them into a fancy handheld GPS unit.

The big, blond Russian casually tossed the remaining member of his squad in the back of the truck. Then he climbed in the back himself. He gave me a respectful nod, his eyes and nose still red, and closed the door, effectively locking himself and the other two in the back.

Jackson and the woman hurried over to the rest of us. "Alright," he said, "you two follow Leonora. Go. Now!"

Mo and I rushed to Luke's truck and climbed inside, as the woman, Leonora, and the Indian man climbed inside their own ride.

"So we're working with them now?" Mo asked as we pulled onto the road behind them.

"Apparently." I checked the rear view mirror and caught sight of the flashing lights, just blocks away. They'd probably rounded up every cop they had from every town in the county. The only city with enough manpower to respond to something like this call was Summervale, but that was a thirty-minute drive. No way any of them had made that drive.

I followed Leonora around a corner just as the cruisers sped into the small parking lot and blocked the street around the building. People in the gas station across the street peeked out from windows and around cars, trying to see what was happening.

Once the flashing lights were out of sight and we couldn't hear the sound of sirens in pursuit both Mo and I let out a breath. I couldn't see anyone in the car in front of us, but they weren't driving like they were concerned.

"Why do you think they're after this Shield guy?" Mo asked.

"I don't know. That could be one point in their favor. Really wish they hadn't shot at us, though."

"What do you think Jackson's going to tell the police?" she asked.

I could tell she was still a little frazzled. I don't think she really cared about the answers to any of her questions. Just needed to hear someone talking.

"Hell if I know. He's a wizard, maybe he'll just teleport somewhere before they show up."

"I can't believe I'm having a conversation where teleportation is a perfectly reasonable topic."

I'd intended my answer as a joke, but it had the opposite of my desired effect—if anything her tone grew more panicked.

I didn't like it. Partly because I didn't like to see her scared like that, but mostly because it made me realize that I was actually scared shitless.

"Do you really think he expects us to fight?"

Of course, I was showing no fear. I was the perfect orc warrior. My hands were not shaking, and there was absolutely no way you could hear the pleather of the steering wheel creak from my too-tight grip.

"I doubt it," I said. "I mean, you saw him back there. He doesn't need our help." I really hoped he didn't.

I could feel the ax, Ukufa, nestled next to me on the seat. Why had he had us pick weapons, then? I glanced sideways at Mo, and the sight of her terrified face broke my heart.

I reached out and wrapped my ham of a fist around her slender fingers and started to hum. I figured if it could calm me down, maybe it would work for her too.

Battle Hymn of the Republic. Always works. After a few notes she squeezed my hand and slid across the seat of the truck until she was right next to me. We sat like that for the rest of the drive.

The coordinates Jackson had given us led almost all the way back to Summervale. About ten miles out we turned down a small dirt road, conveniently marked with a hand-painted street sign.

"Possum Ridge," Mogayne said, laughing a little. "God, I can never decide if I love this place or not."

"Trust me, it's better than the old country," I said as I followed Leonora's van down the road.

"Oh, I doubt that. No orcs in loincloths here."

I was relieved to see her in high spirits again. It really improved my own mood.

The van in front of us stopped a short while after the road ended, in a field of tall grass at the edge of the woods. I parked behind them and the two of us climbed out.

Leonora and the Indian man climbed out of their ride and she walked around to the back and flung the back doors open.

"Let's go," she said to the three in the back.

There was a gruff sigh of resignation as one of the men stepped out first. It was the short man Jackson had knocked out first.

This might be rude of me to say, but he may have been the ugliest person I had seen in my life.

I say this as a guy who has to grind his teeth down to fit in.

He had a bulbous nose that had definitely been broken at least a dozen times and never set properly. Close-set eyes the color of dog shit. And his potato-shaped head was shaved just enough that the grease reflected the early afternoon sun a little too well.

He cleared the distance between us with bow legs and held out a friendly hand that also looked like it had been broken a lot.

"Name's Burt. God, you're kinda ugly." Despite myself, I liked him immediately.

The goblin Terry stands at the edge of the ring of trees. His knees shake, unwilling to listen to his demand that they stop.

It has been twenty years since he has seen so much sword steel.

When the first of the armored men had stepped through the tear in the sky he had instinctively cowered behind a tree, hands held over his ears protectively.

Now he stands in the open, the hate-filled eyes of the men studying him.

Arthur Shield, the man he had been forced to obey for the better part of the week, approaches him, a broken sword grasped in a tight grip.

Terry swallows his fear—if he dies now it was all for nothing. But Saban is supposedly a god of justice. He must keep the promise made so long ago. Right?

Terry fears the answer.

Shield looks as imposing as his brothers in his armor. The boots add inches to his height, causing him to tower even higher above the goblin.

"You have fulfilled your promise, goblin." Shield refuses to acknowledge the magician's name.

"Yes, and you have done it well." The sea of plate parts and another armored man steps in front of the goblin.

While all the others wear the simple gray plate without adornment other than the stamp of their temple over their hearts, this man wears a long, red cape. He looks to be no older than his fortieth year, but all know he is much older.

Terry's eyes open wide at the sight of the god. He had not known Saban would come himself.

He drops to one knee, wise enough to show the reverence he had promised. Even if it had only been out of self-preservation at the time, he has come to almost believe the lie.

"Rise, magician," Saban says. "You have done well. I knew when I first saw you that you would be a useful servant. Is your price for obedience the same?"

"Yes, my lord." Terry rises, keeping his eyes trained on the god's chest, afraid to raise them any higher. "I wish for my horde to be safe."

"Do you wish to return home?" Terry feels the eyes of the paladins studying him.

He looks up and meets the eyes of Arthur Shield. The gray-bearded man smiles a cruel smile.

"He wishes to stay here, my lord. They have grown far too soft for the homeland."

"Have you?" Saban turns to his commander. "Twenty years without combat is a long time, soldier."

Shield shakes his head. "I have not, lord." His eyes are troubled, but Terry senses the truth in the statement.

"Very well, goblin." Saban returns his gaze to the diminutive creature. "Your horde shall be spared. And after we bring the justice needed down on the orcs, we shall leave you."

There are grumbled complaints from the ranks of paladins, but a slow glance from Saban silences the noise.

"The orcs have grown soft, lord Saban," Shield says. "I have killed three of them in the past day."

"And one goblin," Terry says, eyes growing wide when he realizes it was spoken aloud.

"Yes. And one goblin." Shield takes the long stride necessary to loom directly over Terry. He leans over, eyes narrow and full of vile promise. "Pray to Saban that it remains one."

"It shall remain one." Saban places a hand on Arthur's shoulder and pulls the man back.

"Thank you." Terry allows himself to stand straight again. "I have one last gift, lord." He holds out a strip of rough, gray cotton.

"What is this?" Saban takes the offered fabric.

"It is from an orc. It is a piece of clothing that he is wearing today."

"And how is this a suitable gift for our lord?" an angry paladin demands.

Saban looks at the goblin, curious for the answer.

"I have enchanted it, lord." With a shaky hand he pulls out a leather cord with a plastic clip on the end. "Clip it to this and it shall lead you to him."

"Which orc?" Shield asks, eyes narrow.

"Jack Bloodfist. Garack's son."

Shield cocks his head, recognition in his eyes. "I fought him today, one of this world's law enforcement intervened. Why does he matter, other than his name?"

Terry grimaces. Why does the pup matter? He is a worthless fool, posturing and miming his father. A nothing. But he matters.

"He holds the orcs together. Whether or not any of them would believe it. Mostly they ignore him. But when he tells them something needs to be done, they do it. He is their tie to this world. He will convince the police to protect all of them, if he hasn't already. And despite any ideas they have about their leadership, he is the head of that fist. Kill him and it crumbles."

Saban holds the fabric in one hand and pops it inside the clip held in his other. There is a faint glow of yellow-green light around the leather and cotton.

The god holds the strange amulet by the leather strap and the cotton strains away from him.

"So the young Bloodfist is that way?" Saban points a finger into the trees, a grin on his face.

"Yes, lord." Terry bows low, he hides his surprise to see that the pup is not in the direction of Summervale.

"Good. We'll deal with him first then."

The paladins march away. Several spit at the ground in front of Terry, others throw slurs and curses at him.

But he is alive, and happy. With them going the other way, maybe he has time to organize the horde. Prepare them for what is coming.

Most have accepted his plan, are grateful for his sacrifice to save them. But there are still those that object. The Bloodfist woman and her father will need to be dealt with.

He hurries back through the trees to his parked car. By turns he feels giddy and terrified. What has he done? He has saved his people. But why then does he feel like he has consigned them to death?

We got to know Burt and the others as we trekked the rest of the way to Jackson's coordinates.

The Indian man, Umanand, guided us silently using his GPS. I think he chose the most miserable path possible. The terrain was hilly. And if we weren't going up a slope, we were going down. Down was actually worse. Especially when the hillside got extra steep. Every time I slid on a patch of damp grass I was sure I was going to fall and cut my balls off with the ax sticking out of my belt.

Then there were the puddles of stagnant rain water,

every one accompanied by a cloud of gnats and mosquitoes that our silent guide led us straight through.

It didn't take long before I was missing the comfort of my shitty couch and the roof of my shittier trailer.

The whole hike was made worse by the fact that I was still dressed for work. Even with the tattered jacket draped over my shoulder and the tie loosened, my shirt didn't allow that much air in. My pants were too tight. And the shoes? Do not go hiking in dress shoes.

Almost immediately I had dark spots under my arms and could feel the damp down my back, as well as the starts of what I knew would be blisters from hell on my feet.

Burt walked next to me as I struggled down the nonexistent trail, prattling on in that easy way some guys do when they have the ability to make friends with everyone they meet.

Our guide stood on my other side. He hadn't said anything other than his name when I'd asked for it. He didn't say anything, but he watched. I could tell by the way his eyes studied the trees that he would see anything well before it made the decision to do violence.

Behind us was Leonora. When I'd first seen her I'd thought she was closer to my age, maybe in her thirties, but I realized now that she was actually closer to her fifties.

Flanking her on either side was the short, chubby girl, Bryanna and my good friend Drago—his real name is Vladik.

All five of them carried guns. Sleek, black, and fancy. The kind of guns the well-funded bad guys always have when the hero only has a shotgun and two shells left.

After all the introductions had been made I decided I needed to ask the important question. "So, who are you guys?"

Burt looked up at me. "What do you mean? I'm Burt, That's Umanand."

I stopped him before he rattled of everyone's name. "You know what I mean, smart-ass."

"You don't need to know that," Leonora answered. She gave her group a meaningful look.

Burt shrugged. "Sorry, she's the boss."

"Why are you after Arthur Shield?" Mogayne asked. Probably more important than who they were.

Even Vladik looked nervous at the mention of the paladin's name.

"Why are you?" Leonora countered.

"Because Jack is, and I'm just that good a friend," Mo said.

"He's killing my family," I answered, hoping if I was honest they might be as well. "A few cousins, my aunt. He has a history with my family."

Leonora nodded. "I'd imagine. Your tie with him is close," She grimaced. "I suppose I should apologize. Given your obvious connection with him, you would have been the easiest way to find him." She shrugged.

"Are you a wizard?" I asked, interrupting whatever she might have said next.

"I am." She didn't even bother hiding the pride in her voice.

"I thought women were witches?" Mogayne added.

Vladik snickered, and Leonora snorted as she eyed the big Russian. "No. They spend their time over potions, waiting for the moon and stars to be just right. We are much more direct."

"I'd say. Blew up Jackson's door pretty good," I said.

"Well," Mogayne corrected me before turning her attention back to Leonora and raising her hand, like she were in a press conference. "One more question, not that I'm complaining, but why did you knock first?"

"Told you we shouldn't have knocked," Bryanna said.

"Shut up, girl," Leonora snapped. "It was a feeling I had," she answered Mo, uncertain. "I try to trust those."

"What are you going to do when you find him?" I asked.

"Our instructions were to bring him in alive," the wizard said.

"Alive?" My heart sank a little at that revelation.

"Those were our initial instructions. I phoned the situation in to our command. Lethal force has been approved."

That was reassuring. "Was it you that shot up that house earlier today?" I asked.

"We tracked Shield to a home. He had just killed a woman. Burt ignored orders and opened fire." She gave the short man a disapproving glance.

"Sorry," he said, trying to ignore the glare.

"Wish you'd killed the bastard," I muttered.

For the first time during our hike, Umanand said more than two words. "We're here."

Okay, so it was only two and a half words, but I was impressed.

We rounded a grove of pine trees and saw the little cabin.

The front door stood open and Jackson sat on a camping chair, feet up on a cooler.

"What took you so long?" He waved a glass bottle over his head.

I swear, I could see the condensation on that bottle from across the clearing.

Jackson rose from his seat and kicked the cooler at his feet open. He indicated the ice-filled chest and went inside the small building.

The seven of us piled around the treasure chest and each grabbed a drink. I pulled out a glorious red and white jewel of my own and drained the caffeine in one swallow.

I wasn't surprised at all when Leonora pulled out a bottle of water instead of any of the other options. She slapped a bottle of beer out of Burt's hand before it made its way to his lips.

"Really?" Not even today?" He grumbled to himself as he found something non-alcoholic and followed the angry woman into the cabin.

None of the others even tried for the beers nestled in the ice. I was more than a little impressed.

Mogayne was the only one to pop open one of the brown bottles, draining half in one swig.

She held the sweating bottle to the back of her neck as the two of us started to follow everyone else inside.

My phone rang and I jumped at the sound. "How the hell do I have a signal out here?" I asked quietly.

Mo shrugged. "Magic?"

The caller ID told me it was Denny.

"Detective." I put on my most official tone.

"Bloodfist. Just had an interesting call from Kirk Brown. Know anything about that?"

"Ah, yes. Let me hand you over to my assistant, she'll explain." I handed the phone to Mogayne, who rolled her eyes.

I leaned up against the wall and listened to her explain her plan to Denny. Smart woman, that Mogayne Thornhill.

FIFTEEN

To call the inside of Jackson's cabin cozy would be generous. It was the most spartan room I had ever seen, and I've
spent a night or two behind bars. It was one small, square
room that somehow earned a front and back door. There
was no stove inside, as I'd expected, but a small fire pit
outside. No bed, just a bedroll tossed in the corner, spider-
webs connecting the fabric to the wall.

The only furniture in the shed—that's a better word
than cabin—was a table and a few folding chairs stacked on
the wall next to it.

It was a nice table. I've never been the craftsman others
in my family are, but even I recognized it had been well
made. I was certain even Luke would have been impressed.

The surface, a dark, stained wood, was smooth and
polished to a mirror sheen.

Jackson indicated we all take a spot around the table.

Burt opened up a chair and sat down with a world-
weary sigh. I considered grabbing one myself, but instead
decided to be chivalrous and offered one of the remaining
two chairs to Mo.

She looked at it and shook her head. Bryanna sat in the chair before I could offer with a cheerful, "Thank you."

"Alright. First order of business." Jackson looked around the room, studying each of us carefully. He let out a thoughtful, "hm," before turning his full attention to Leonora. "Why are you after Shield?"

"As I told your subordinates—"

"Whoa," I interrupted, "I am no one's subordinate."

Jackson gave me a patient look before indicating Leonora continue.

"We were under orders to bring him in," she finished.

"Orders from?" Jackson pressed.

"None of your concern." She folded her arms over her chest and raised a challenging eyebrow.

"You're powerful, Leonora, I can see that." He leaned forward, resting his hands on the smooth surface of the table. "But you're not strong enough."

"Excuse me?" she bristled.

"Shall I break it down for you?" He pointed a finger at Bryanna. "She is the weakest in the room."

"What?" Bryanna sat up straight in her chair, mouth open.

"True." Leonora agreed.

Bryanna's mouth moved soundlessly.

Jackson pointed to me next. "Then the orc."

"The fuck?" I stood up straighter, instinctively trying to intimidate the room with my size.

The big Russian smirked at me.

"Orc?" Leonora turned to me, curiosity plain.

Jackson continued before she could ask any questions.

"Then Miss Thornhill." All eyes turned to consider Mo, who shrunk into herself, blushing slightly.

She met my eye, and blinked in surprise at what must have been a less-than-friendly glare.

"Then the silent twins." he pointed to Vladik and Umanand. "They're close enough to the same level. Then your bruiser."

Leonora looked confused at that. "He is stronger than Vladik?"

"He hides it well, but yes. Then we have you. Your magic is strong. You've obviously been trained well, I can see that, but," he pointed to himself, "I am Jackson Smith." His name was said as though it were all the explanation needed.

I'll be honest, I'd really stopped caring right around the time he's said Mo was more powerful than me. I didn't know if he was just talking in terms of magical ability, which came as a surprise, because I thought Mo was just a regular human. It was fickle of me, I know, but for some reason I couldn't help but feel a little jealous of the slight woman.

Jackson's little show must have convinced Leonora, because she sighed and nodded her head. "You do seem to have power. Any wizard that can travel as fast you did must have considerable reserves of power."

"Oh, I cheated for that," he grinned, "but we'll talk about that later. Now answer my question. Who sent you?"

She unfolded her arms and reached down the collar of her shirt. She pulled out a thin, silver chain with a dog tag hanging on the end. There was a strange symbol engraved on the thin piece of metal. It looked like an eye with a dagger stabbed through the center.

"Should I recognize that symbol?" Jackson asked.

"No, I guess not. The chances you might were good though. Our employers—" Burt snorted at the word, but

Leonora ignored him and continued, "Our employers like to recruit any powerful magic users they find. I thought you may have been approached."

"They want you to recruit Shield?" Jackson ventured.

Leonora laughed. "Not exactly. Shield has been in the service of the company for the better part of twenty years."

I snapped out of my silent sulk and focused on the woman. "What?" I demanded.

"The company is... let's just say unique. These three," she indicated Burt, Vladik and Bryanna, "are a few of the most dangerous killers and thieves on the planet."

The smile on Burt's face didn't waver, and I decided I liked him a little less.

"Clients hire us and, using their skills, we fulfill each contract."

"And you two?" Jackson asked.

"Umanand and I are their handlers. If they disobey an order from either of us"—her dog tag began to glow and she grinned the most humorless grin I had ever seen—"they die. If I die, they die."

"Must pay well," Jackson said.

"Very. Shield was one of them." She jerked her head over her shoulder toward Burt. "But he did something to break the spell the company had placed on him. Then he got out of his cell. Killed a lot of guards doing it."

"And he's been in Task Force X for twenty years?" I asked.

"What?" Leonora looked at me like I was an idiot.

Some people just don't appreciate good literature.

"How long has he been one of your little puppet slave thingies?" I said, trying to speak slowly so she'd understand.

She narrowed her eyes, but answered, "About twenty years. He's been with the company longer than I have. That was why they wanted him alive. Reward for faithful service, I guess."

I locked eyes with Jackson, hoping he understood my unspoken question. How had he been here as long as we had?

"Why now?" Mo asked. "Why did he escape now?"

Leonora shook her head. "We don't know. The powers he started using when he escaped were new too."

"Of course they were." Jackson sighed and slapped a hand on the table. It lit up with a blue light that slowly faded in intensity until the table looked like a TV screen.

"Hand on the table please, Mr. Bloodfist." Jackson nodded his head toward the table.

I obeyed the command without thinking about it. It still felt like wood, but it looked like a glass screen, one that was now flickering gently as an image began to appear.

On the wooden screen, marching quickly through the forest, was Arthur Shield and his paladin buddies.

Leonora stepped back in surprise and the rest of her followers, except for Vladik, all let out some sort of surprised sound. Even Umanand let out a sort of surprised grunt.

"Want to know why he escaped now? How he got his powers back?"

"Back?" Leonora asked, confused.

Jackson nodded and tapped a finger on the screen.

The man looked unremarkable. Short, graying hair, a well-trimmed beard, and eyes a boring brown. The red cape bolted to his armor was the most impressive thing about him.

"Saban." I hadn't seen him before, but I knew it was him.

"Yup. The god of Shield's order. All of Shield's power

comes from here." He tapped Saban again. "With him here, everything you thought you knew about Shield is wrong. He's stronger, faster, far more dangerous than he ever would have been before."

"If we need it, we can have backup here within the hour," Leonora said.

Jackson shook his head. "That's a lot of paladins, even before factoring in their god. It would take a literal army." he paused, "How many wizards does your company employ?"

Leonora considered. "There is at least one for every squad. So twenty or so."

"All as powerful as you?"

I could tell she wanted to be proud of herself; the smug smile said she was the strongest they had.

"Well, twenty wizards of your level, each with a squad of skilled fighters beneath them, might be able to take at least that many of them."

"How many?" Leonora asked.

"Twenty."

She blinked at the answer.

"Only twenty?"

"The wizard would be able to counter the paladins' magic, running defense, constantly keeping them in check, then the others might be able to get close enough for a successful attack." He paused as he watched the table. "I don't even know if I'd be able to take more than five of them at a time. You should definitely call for that backup."

She looked over her shoulder at Umanand who nodded and pulled a satellite phone out of his pocket. He made a hushed call in the corner of the cabin while the meeting continued.

"So, what's your plan, Jackson Smith?" Leonora asked.

"We have a few options. Best thing would be if we had an orc."

All eyes turned to me.

"Oh, so now you need the second weakest person in the room?"

Jackson shook his head. "I'm afraid you might just get in the way. Do you know if any of your cousins are warsingers?"

"Warcriers?" I corrected.

"Whatever. Do you know of any?"

"I don't know. My dad always said I—"

Jackson spoke over me, "That's fine then, we'll figure it out without one. Mogayne, can you point to this bunker you found for the orcs?"

He tapped a couple of fingers on the table and a map of the county popped up over the image of the marching paladins.

Mo squeezed my arm as she walked past. It calmed me down a little.

"Right here." She pointed to the map and Jackson nodded.

"Alright, I'm sending the two of you there now. It'll probably be for the best if you're there to greet your family as they start showing up. We'll stay here and finish up our preparations. Get Leonora's people up to speed."

"Sure," I grunted. It made sense, I should be there when they showed up. "How far are we?"

"Won't take you any time at all, I promise. Just keep your weapons handy," he gave both of us a comforting smile, "but if everything goes according to plan, you won't need them. I'll get them back from you when this is all over."

"This looks familiar." We all jerked around at the sound

of Umanand's voice as he studied the armored men on the screen.

"What do you mean?" Leonora asked.

"He's right." Burt stood up and pointed. "I pissed on that rock on the way in. I remember 'cause it kind of looks like a pair of—"

"Breasts. Yeah, I remember. You wouldn't shut up about it." Leonora looked to Jackson. "They're coming here."

"Must be using a tracking spell. Looks like you're next on their list, Jack." He looked at me and grinned. "Well, let's get you kids somewhere safe."

He reached into his jean's front pocket and pulled out a small square of fabric that looked like burlap. Rushing to the back door he slapped the square onto the wood of the door.

From where I stood I couldn't tell, but it looked like letters spread across the length of the material. He poked at the words, as though he were navigating a menu on a tablet, then he grabbed the doorknob and swung the door open.

"Mr. Bloodfist, Miss Thornhill, if you wouldn't mind."

I only moved when Mo grabbed my hand and pulled me toward the opening. The doorway just framed trees. I had expected something similar to his magic closet, and was a little disappointed to see the summer sunlight filtering through leaves.

"Come on, guys, don't really have time." Jackson waved us toward the door urgently.

Mo stepped through the door and I followed, ready to bolt when Shield and his friends arrived.

Jackson closed the door as soon as we were clear. I turned around to find the cabin gone. We stood in the middle of a thick grove of trees, the sound of buzzing bugs and chirping birds the only thing other than trees.

"Where are we?" I asked.

"I think we're at Kirk's clubhouse," Mo said, sounding impressed. "Come on." She still held my hand, and I squeezed back as she began to lead me through the trees.

Jackson closes the door behind the orc and the girl, silently wishing them victory in the battles they will have to face soon.

Leonora and her team prepare weapons, taking positions by the doors and windows. They believe they are ready for this.

"How far out is your backup?" Jackson asks.

Leonora looks to Umanand who holds up a single finger.

"One hour," she tells him.

Jackson nods as he approaches the door. He does not know how many of his new acquaintances will leave this clearing alive.

He will. Somehow, he always does. And in the years of his service to the Machine he has grown used to losing friends and allies. And he does not really know these people. Their deaths will mean very little to him, compared to others he has had to endure.

He places a steady hand on the door-knob. "Leave Saban to me. And the first chance you get, run."

Leonora nods. Like him, she has seen enough death that it no longer bothers her. The thought of Jackson dying means almost nothing to her. Maybe a day of guilt, then nothing. Just a forgotten face and a name that might haunt her in dreams.

Jackson sees all this as he studies her. She is strong. Not just of will, but of body.

Sigmund fills his mind with the numbers. He can see them around the others. Their power, their potential. If Leonora does not die now, she will one day be very powerful.

"You should find Jack again, track him again if you can. Do your best to help him against Shield."

He opens the door and steps into the light of the noon day. He has already slaughtered one army today. But now another waits. And with this force marches a god.

He has never defeated a god before. And until the order had been given, years before, he had never thought he would have to fight one of his own.

The paladins already stand in the clearing. One holds a strip of leather, an oddly glowing amulet on the end. His face is contorted in confusion as his fellows complain in a language Jackson has not heard in years.

"He's gone," Jackson shouts across the clearing as he casually walks toward the armored men.

The normally whispered sound of steel on leather is loud as a hundred swords are drawn and leveled toward the lone man.

"I know why you fear them, Saban." Jackson stops, just out of sword range of the knights. "You're right to fear them. They could have destroyed you in the temple. I should have let them. But you don't need to worry about the orcs right now." Jackson brings his hand up, his fingers dancing in a rhythm that has long been familiar to him. The air above his hand shimmers and his sword appears in a flash of electric blue. "Right now, you only need to worry about me."

The paladins stand still, murmurs of surprise at this show of magic.

A gunshot destroys the tense silence that dominates the

forest air. A plate helm cracks and a paladin collapses to the ground, life leaving through the break in his skull.

"And them." Jackson rushes forward as Leonora and her warriors stream from the cabin, guns firing.

Blue lights erupt around the paladins, brightening the clearing even more. Bullets bounce off their shimmering shields, splintering trees and digging furrows in the ground.

Jackson slides under the swing of a sword, a halo of blue covering its length. His own sword darts out, his considerable strength allowing the steel to bite through armor and flesh, grazing bone.

As the man's concentration wavers at the pain his shield blinks out and he is riddled with rifle fire.

Sliding past the now-dead knight has left Jackson surrounded by men eager to kill him. His arms blur in the blue glow of holy fire as he blocks the swings of large swords.

With a grunt of effort he throws a blocked strike back up. The wielder of the parried weapon staggers back and Jackson kicks him in the chest. The paladin flies back through the air, cracking a tree with the force of his impact.

Jackson dodges and counters attacks from the pressing throng of armored knights. Swords and gauntleted fists come close to hitting him, but never seem to find their mark.

As Jackson battles through the sea of plate and chain, trying to get close to Saban, Leonora and her team charge forward. They hope to catch another by surprise. Umanand has the honor of the first kill, and all of them took part in the second, but there are so many left.

Leonora has trained for years. Her body is stone and steel, carved by masters of arts both mystical and martial.

She has faced strong foes before, but these men scare

her. She can feel the power radiating from them. Can sense their intent to kill.

A small group of paladins have left their comrades to battle Jackson and charge to meet Leonora and the others. Arthur Shield himself is leading them.

Leonora has worked with Shield before, back before his escape, before his powers made themselves known. He is a good warrior. Leonora is almost disappointed that he has to die.

The escaped knight brings a hand up and a glint of silver steel flashes through the air.

Leonora sidesteps just in time to dodge the thrown dagger.

There is a pained gasp accompanied by the sound of blade meeting flesh.

Leonora ignores it. Bryanna is dead, or dying, it doesn't matter. The girl was weak. Weak and cruel. Her death in this forest clearing is better than she deserves for the things she had done before being taken by the company.

The small portion of Leonora's power that rested within Bryanna so she could be controlled, or killed if needed, returns to the wizard. She sends the spark, along with a larger surge of power into her arm as she throws it up to catch a flaming sword.

The blue flame of the sword meets the magically enhanced stone of her skin. She brings her other hand around in a powerful strike. The hand, glowing with her own inner fire, shatters the helm the man wears.

He does not fall, just staggers back one step, then returns, his attack more vicious than before.

She blocks his second strike but screams out in pain when another blade pierces her side. The blue fire burns her like ice.

Vladik is there at her side, picking her up and throwing her over his shoulder as though she were no more than a bag of grain.

As the large man runs, she looks back and watches as Burt, sweet, murderous Burt, covers their retreat. He is fighting three of the armored men. He laughs as a sword pierces his chest, clean through, the red tip sticking out his back. Burt punches the man holding the sword, sending him flying through the air to land in a heap of twisted metal.

The short, ugly man pulls the sword out of his chest and cuts the legs out from under another paladin. The man collapses to his knees, scream cut short when the same sword slides through the narrow eye slit of his helm.

Arthur Shield steps up to Burt, who pauses at the sight of the familiar face.

His pause is his death as Shield swings his broken sword and removes Burt's head.

Shield spares no second glance for the dead man, but instead watches as Leonara, bouncing on Vladik's shoulder vanishes through the trees.

There are only three of them left, Leonora realizes. Umanand has joined Vladik in the flight through the woods. They run from death, but Leonora knows they only run toward more of the same.

Still in the clearing, Jackson can sense the three in their retreat. He is actually glad the woman is not dead. It was not that often he met warriors with her potential. This world needed someone like her.

Of course, there was still the chance she may die later in the day.

He is growing tired now. He uses a burst of speed and leaves the paladins spinning as they try to keep up. He stops just outside their circle, doing his best to hide his fatigue.

He holds his sword in a fighting stance he learned decades before—an easy, quick fighting style he has relied on countless times.

But he knows he cannot fight all these men. He has barely managed to kill four of them. Too many more still live. He has his first spell. His final spell. But he has used so much power this day. And Saban is there. He doesn't even know if it will work.

The god stands, just behind a row of gleaming steel, arms crossed, studying Jackson. His face holds no fear, only a mild curiosity.

The impassive face worries Jackson, but he has an ace up his sleeve. A trap he had prepared twenty years before, in hopes of just this day.

"May I ask one question before I die?" He asks, feigning fear.

"No," Arthur Shield snarls, approaching from behind him.

"Stop," a voice says. The wall of armor parts and the red cloaked god steps out to face Jackson. "Ask wizard."

"Why did you betray us?" Jackson asks, all fear gone from his voice, just stern reproach.

Saban's eyes flash with what might be his own fear. "Who are you?" he demands.

Jackson pulls himself to his full height, his eyes beginning to glow with a pale red light as he allows what little he has left within himself to shine.

"I am Jackson Smith, Saban. I am the Deus of War," he says as he aims his sword through the protective rank of armored men, "and I am your end."

"No. That door has never opened." Saban rushes forward, pushing men out of his way, trying to see Jackson.

"It opened for me," Jackson says, his voice heavy with a

meaning only he and Saban can understand. "And now I must close yours."

Jackson is gone. Only empty ground and a gentle breeze where he stood an eye blink before.

The paladins know fear now. They glance from one to another, unsure of what to do. Their god trembles. Can a god tremble?

But it is not fear, it is rage. His unarmored face shows the rage well as he screams.

"This world must be purged! All must die!"

"But, lord," Arthur Shield bows low, "there are innocents on this world."

"That man's presence here makes them all guilty." He points to the empty space where the man had stood.

"What of justice?" Arthur asks, not wishing to anger his god further, but needing to know. "What of those that would, in another life, have served thee? Would it not be against thine own laws to kill those that protect?"

"Do they protect those that desecrated my temple?" Shield's silence is his answer. "Then they are more guilty than the rest."

None argue. It is not their place to question his will. Their place is at his side, as his swords.

SIXTEEN

"Where the hell did you two come from?" Detective Hall-dorson demanded as Mogayne and I broke out of the trees into the landscaped area around Kirk Brown's clubhouse.

As I answered, Denny signaled some of her men to cover the foliage behind us. "Long story, Denny. Has anyone else showed up?"

She narrowed her eyes at my familiarity, but nodded. "Yeah. Mr. Brown is inside showing them to their rooms."

"I'll go see if he needs any help." Mo squeezed my hand warmly before rushing up the long drive to the large building.

I was quick enough to catch the hint of a smile on Denny's face before I barreled forward with my questions. "Who's here?"

"We've got about twenty of your cousins inside. About the same still at the station waiting for the vans to get back and pick them up." She waved me toward the building and we followed after Mo.

Before that day I'd never seen Kirk's clubhouse. I knew he'd built it to keep werewolves from running around killing things, so I'd expected a big slab of concrete, no windows, and thick steel doors. Inside I was sure there would be rows of cells with thick iron bars and deep claw marks in the walls.

But it was nothing like I'd expected. It was a big log cabin. It looked like what I'd imagine to see on a fancy ski resort. The entire east wall was one giant window looking out on a small lake. I'm pretty sure the lake was man-made, put in just because Kirk wanted something other than the trees and hills to look at.

Even from our spot all the way down the drive I could see the soft armchairs through the window. They looked incredibly comfortable.

My initial thought was that the building looked nice, but I was seriously doubting if it was siege-ready.

Before I could ask my next question Denny spoke up, her eye on Mo as the redhead went up the wooden steps to the entrance two at a time. "You two seem awfully close."

"Yeah, I guess." I kept the smile off my face.

It was easier to do when I looked down to be met by a serious scowl on Denny's face. "So Luke's truck was seen fleeing a crime scene in Camden. Please tell me you don't know anything about that."

"Um, I don't know anything about that?" I tried to put on a charmingly roguish grin, but I don't think it worked. I don't really have the face for it.

"Son of a bitch, Bloodfist," she sighed, "at least tell me your visit with the wizard was worth it."

"Yeah. He's fighting Shield and his men right now."

"Okay, good. Maybe we'll get lucky and he'll finish everything—" She froze. "Wait, did you say men? There are more of them now?"

"Yeah, a lot of them. And they brought their god with them, apparently."

"Okay. How are they armed?"

"Swords, spears."

She started walking again, "Okay, so we at least have superior firepower, if not numbers. Twenty officers with guns, that going to be enough?"

I grimaced. Jackson didn't think so, but he also apparently thought I was really weak. My pride really didn't want to believe anything the man said.

I decided to be honest. "Jackson is of the opinion we need a lot of magic to fight them."

"Well, that's just too damn bad. We'll make do. Are you sure they'll come here?"

I nodded. "I'm told they're tracking me."

"Of course they are." She let out a snort as we reached the stairs.

"So who's here?" I asked, remembering my original line of questioning.

"Charles Slayinghand and his family. A few Goretusks. The three Jacks." She said the last as though it were a curse.

I suppose to a cop it might be. Of all my cousins, the three Jacks are the most well known in the local police department.

They spend enough time in the drunk tank they might as well pay rent. I've spent more than a little time bailing those three out. Not out of jail. Let them rot for all I care, but I've had to pull some weight to convince the former Mrs. Ironbeard to not press charges after some of their more legendary nights in the Bearded Lady.

I've just been lucky so far that they usually only pick their drunk fights with other orcs, or that one time with Denny. That didn't happen again.

"What about Luke and Lise?" I asked. The more I looked at the clubhouse the more I hoped they hadn't made it yet.

"Still at the station. Vans should be getting back soon, then they'll be on their way."

"Are we sure bringing everyone here is a good idea?" I asked.

"Don't trust your little girlfriend?" she asked.

"I trust her, it's just, I'm starting to doubt that bringing them to the place the angry glowing knights and their god are coming is the best idea."

Denny let out a humorless laugh. "They're tracking you, right? What says they can't track everyone else later? Trust me, trust Miss Thornhill. This is the best option."

"Okay. Just hope they get here before Shield does."

"How long do you think we have?" she asked.

"No idea."

She gave me a trademark Denny look of exasperation. "You said they were tracking you."

"Yeah, but magic."

"What?"

I gave her an abridged version of everything that happened after we made it to Jackson's apartment.

"Alright, give me an estimate then. How much time do you think we have?"

"I wouldn't take any chances," I said, looking over my shoulder.

Her officers all had guns drawn and were patrolling the area. It made me really nervous.

Denny led me inside the high-scale lodge and I wasn't surprised at all when it was as nice on the inside as the outside had led me to believe.

Expensive looking paintings hung on the walls, and two

huge fireplaces flanked either side of the large main room. Wide stairs led up to a second floor and I could see a hallway lined with thick wooden doors from the front entrance.

Jack Goretusk, one of my three infamous cousins that shared my name, waved down at us from where he leaned against the knotted wood of the railing, a fancy glass in hand. It was filled with, I was sure, an amber liquid worth more than a month's worth of his pay.

Charles Slayinghand was in the main room, his hand resting on the back of a thick leather armchair as he studied a painting that hung over one of the fireplaces. His wife, a human, sat in the chair, trying to calm a squealing mass of fat that I could only assume was a child.

More orcs lounged in chairs or poked at expensive-looking fixtures of the lodge. Some paced the thick, definitely expensive carpet, while others, out of sight, shouted at each other about something they'd found deeper in the building.

I offered the room in general a quick wave of my hand. Some returned the gesture halfheartedly. Charles offered me a patient smile and a head nod.

Denny led me around a corner into an enormous, very well stocked kitchen. The two remaining Jacks and a few younger orcs stood around a large granite island, the surface covered with a massive tray of sandwiches.

Jack Slayinghand, the one on the left, looked up, hand still forcing a fistful of bread and turkey into his mouth.

"Hey, Jack," he said, spraying crumbs over the island.

"Jack, Jack." I nodded to each of them in turn and grabbed a sandwich of my own off the table as I passed.

I made sure to give everyone in the kitchen a friendly nod or wave as I followed Denny out of the room.

Just past the kitchen was a small hallway that led to an inconspicuous door that I would have guessed was a pantry. She pushed the door open to reveal another very nice room. Even if it was a little small.

Big leather desk chairs faced a wall of monitors, and a fancy coffee machine percolated in the corner.

Mo waved from her seat in one of the comfortable-looking chairs. I went and stood behind her as I studied the monitors.

Only half of them were on, and showed footage of the grounds around the lodge. Occasionally an armed officer walked past a camera.

Kirk hovered over the shoulder of a uniformed officer, an overly friendly hand rested on the muscular cop's shoulder.

"Then this switch turns on the electrical fence. And this," he leaned over the man in a way that made the cop appear very uncomfortable, "will bring up the storm windows."

"Got it, Mr. Brown." His tone was terse.

"Oh, come on, Mike. Call me Kirk."

"Officer Jensen," Mike corrected. Apparently working closely with Denny had its side effects.

"Whatever you say, Mike." Kirk's hand lingered on the officer's shoulder as he turned to face Denny and me.

"I think Mike's got it, Detective," he said to Denny. "Any idea how many more guests we'll have today?"

"Not sure. And I'm told we may not have enough time to get everyone here before trouble shows up."

"What should we do about everyone that doesn't make it?" I asked.

"Station will have to do for now." Denny was watching the monitors as she answered me.

On one of the screens, two officers could be seen leaning against a cruiser, passing a flask back and forth.

"Excuse me a moment." Denny stalked out of the room.

"This covers the whole area?" I asked, pointing to the screens.

"You got it, dear." Kirk patted me on the back. "We'll see anyone coming from any direction."

"What about the other screens?" I asked.

Kirk leaned over Mike again and flipped a switch and the other screens all turned on.

Each of them showed an identical room. Gray, cement walls and floors. The only thing that distinguished them were the scratches.

Each wall had a different pattern, but all had obviously held something big and well equipped with claws, and, I can only assume, teeth.

"These are the rooms for paying guests," Kirk said.

"How much do you charge?" I asked, the sight making me slightly queasy.

"Depends. Anyone that asks for a room gets one. I just ask that everyone pitch in somehow to keep the club running."

"Must cost a lot to keep it going."

"A lot of our members have useful skills. Between the money of our wealthier members and the hands of our skilled ones, we keep the place going."

Officer Mike looked uncomfortable with the conversation, and Kirk smiled when he noticed.

"So how's the food, Jackie?" Kirk turned to me, catching me with the last bite of my sandwich halfway to my mouth.

"Uh..." I paused, not sure if I wanted to answer or finish eating.

Kirk winked at me. "Why don't you and Mo take some

for the boys and girls outside before your family finishes them all? I try to make sure all my guests are taken care of."

The orcs in the kitchen booed as Mo and I loaded a small plate from the heaping pile, but we ignored them as we left the kitchen to make the rounds.

We stopped at every group of armed officers and offered them food. Kirk had also encouraged us to take a few thermoses of coffee, so we made sure each of them also got a paper cup of nourishing caffeine.

After seeing to the officers we left the empty plate and containers on the porch and walked the grounds of the clubhouse. I say grounds because it sounds fancy. Like the grounds of a mansion. I felt very out of my element.

We ended up in front of Kirk's lake after a while. Resting along the paved walkway that wrapped around the lake was a bench, and for what felt like the first time in days, I got to sit down.

We were both on edge, not sure when Shield and the other Power Rangers were going to show up, but Kirk had assured us that we'd have time to get inside when the cameras spotted them.

"It's beautiful out here," I said, staring out across the smooth surface of the water.

"You sure do throw that word around a lot, don't you?" Mo said.

I looked at her, expecting a playful grin, but she wasn't looking at me. She was staring at the lake, a strange, sad look on her face.

I don't know how to explain it, how I knew what that look was. But it was the look of homesickness. I guess I had seen it enough on my parents as I grew up.

"Only when it's deserved." I turned from her to study the lake.

She slid the distance between us and wrapped herself around my arm.

I was suddenly very unsure of myself. I felt as though an injured bird had just landed on my hand and any unexpected movement might startle it away. Might cause it more hurt.

"Tell me why they're after you." It was not her normal reporter tone. It was the voice of a scared woman that wanted to know why she was scared.

I told her the story. All of it. Just as Karen had told it to me.

She didn't move as I spoke, only once to rest her head against my arm.

She asked no questions, just listened. When I was finished she took a deep breath. "Okay." I could hear the hesitation in her voice, the words that were unspoken. She wanted to say something, but couldn't decide on the words.

My phone rang.

"Better answer that," she said, pulling away from me.

"How do I still have service?" I mumbled as I dug my phone out of my pocket.

It was Ma.

I hurriedly swiped the screen. "Ma?" I said, standing up.

"Jackie boy? Oh thank any gods. Gramps and I have been so worried. Where are you?"

"Somewhere safe, Ma. Where are you? No one's talking to me."

"You're not at the police station are you?" she asked, tone urgent.

"No, but you should be. Detective Halldorson has people ready to protect you from Shield."

"No, Jack. If anyone is at the station, you need to call

them. Tell them to get out of there. Get them somewhere safer."

"What are you talking about, Ma?"

"Your uncle Terry. He has done something very stupid."

I could feel the fist of fear that had been slowly tightening in my stomach all day clench closed.

It was a few moments before I could even find the strength to curse. I turned and began to run toward the clubhouse.

"Denny!" I shouted as loud as I could. "Call the station! They're going to the station!"

"Jack!" I stopped and spun at the sound of Mogayne's shout.

She stood facing down the lake's path. Two paladins strode forward, swords in hand, dripping twin trails of blood behind them.

———

Luke Goretusk sits in the police station. He is a little disappointed by the turnout. Only twenty orcs loiter around the bullpen.

It seems that not many in the fist have taken the threat seriously. Everyone now knows about Arthur Shield. Know that he has come to town to kill them all. But too few of them even know who the man is, or what he represents.

Luke only knows because his mother talks—used to talk —when she was drunk.

Those stories had not always made sense, but today he was able to piece them together.

Knowing what he does, Luke is glad he has listened to Denelle Halldorson. He considers what Shield may do to his wife and daughter and a rage builds in his chest.

The two women left in his life sit behind a desk and laugh with a female officer. The woman is teaching Miki a magic trick with a quarter.

The girl throws her head back and roars with laughter every time the officer pulls the coin out of a nose or ear.

Next to Luke is old man Hull Bloodfist. He is one of the last true Bloodfists. Perhaps the last full blooded orc to carry that name. The old orc's head shakes as he speaks to Luke. Age and hardship has left him a shell of the warrior he once was.

"I killed a few of them, you know," Hull says, his weak voice quaking, but even the quake cannot mask the pride. "One of those paladins. Crushed his throat with my boot." He holds up his arm to show Luke one of countless white scars on his green skin. "He stabbed me right through the bicep before he died. Kept the sword for a few years. Sold it for grog eventually."

Luke smiles what he hopes is a fierce smile as he half listens to the old man.

"Really, all this fuss is too much over one knight. You could probably kill the man." Hull tries to smack Luke on the shoulder, but it is more of a tap.

"He killed my mother," Luke points out.

Hull blinks in surprise. "Shakill? No, that can't be right." Luke has told him this three times already. He decides he won't tell him a fourth.

A radio somewhere in the room crackles to life. Numbers that mean nothing to Luke are repeated over and over again. The officers look at each other, confused and more than a little afraid.

"*Eleven ninety nine,*" the voice says again. "*We're—*" The radio cuts out.

It comes to life again and Luke recognizes the voice of

Detective Halldorson. *"Get ready!"* she yells through the radio. *"They're coming for you. Get the fucking orcs out of there!"* There is gunfire in the background. Lots of gunfire.

Luke stands as the door to the large room is forced open.

Armored men stream inside from the hallway. The hallway, which through cracks in armor is seen to be full of blood and bodies.

The desk sergeant sits in a pool of fast spreading blood, his head staring up from his lap.

Luke is at his wife's side in an instant, his daughter in his arms, her eyes covered by Lise's hand.

He wants to ask the female officer about a back way out, but her gun is drawn and she begins to fire. Every cop in the room begins to fire.

Miki screams and covers her ears.

Orcs and humans are scrambling for cover. They hide behind desks and cubicle walls. Some run out a door in the back of the room.

There is screaming, but Luke cannot hear it. The gunfire has left him with only the sound of explosions and a ringing.

The armored men enter the room, pacing casually as bullets deflect off armor and the blue light that protects them.

Swords flash through the air, and those not fast enough die where they stand, or where they huddle in fear.

Spears stab from the second row of knights, catching some that were able to dodge the swing of swords.

Luke gets Lise's attention and shepherds her toward the door out of the room.

He places a hand on the officer's shoulder and urges her after his wife and daughter.

She does as he bids. His face is grim, and for an instant she fears him more than the killers in the room.

A broken blade is leveled at Luke. The knight pulls off his helm and eyes glowing blue consider the orc.

"I am Arthur Shield, Goretusk. I promised your mother I would kill you." Even through the ringing in his ears Luke can hear the man.

He takes a deep breath. The smell of blood is strong and he lets the scent coat his nose, his lungs.

He is his mother's son. If he is to die, he will die on his feet.

Shield's eyes open wide in surprise as Luke charges forward.

The orc releases his held breath in an earth shaking roar. Shield's eyes narrow in recognition of this sound. It is the roar of a berserker. An orc warrior that fears no death.

Luke grabs a chair from behind a desk as he runs. Others follow him, his roar stirring something in their blood.

More cries rip from orc throats, drowning out the dwindling sound of gunfire.

Arthur cuts the chair in half as Luke swings it down toward him. Then three hundred pounds of orc muscle carry the paladin back into the row of knights behind him.

Shield and several of his brothers are knocked to the ground by the surprise tackle.

A spear carrier spins, aiming his weapon at Luke's back as the orc raises a foot to stomp on Shield's breastplate.

Old Hull Bloodfist wraps a hand around the shaft of the spear. His hands no longer shake. There is the crack of splintered wood as Hull breaks the spear in two, leaving the paladin holding a worthless splinter.

The old orc spins the tip back toward its owner and

jams it between helm and breastplate. A wash of dark red falls over polished steel as the servant of Saban dies.

Luke's booted foot smashes into Arthur Shield's breastplate again and again. By the time the paladin has recovered himself enough to roll to the side there is the beginning of a dent in the gleaming plate.

Another paladin tackles Luke, carrying him to the ground. The man straddles Luke and raises his sword, ready to plunge it through the orc's chest.

Luke, his mind no longer his own, laughs as he brings up a hand and wraps it around the blue flames of the sword.

He pushes the weapon to the side and pulls it down. The blade sinks into the floor next to his head, a trickle of blood escaping from his cheek.

The knight is close enough now that Luke's hands can reach him. Luke flips the visor of the helm open and digs his bleeding hand into the paladin's face. The man screams, releasing his sword, and stumbles back off Luke.

Luke rises quickly, a fresh roar already leaving his lungs as he pulls the sword from the tile of the ground and slashes at the paladin.

He swipes gauntleted fists away from the face and stabs the point where the man's eye had once been.

Lukil spins to find another victim. All around him is death. Dead and dying humans and orcs.

The paladins are winning. This thought pushes through the red cloud of his rage. The blood of orcs and officers fuel the holy fire of the paladin swords and spears.

Old Hull has jumped onto Arthur Shield's back, one hand wrapped around the man's throat, the other striking at the unprotected head.

Before more than two blows can be struck, Shield flicks his broken blade over his shoulder with a careless motion.

Hull slides off the paladin's back, his blood mingling with that on the ground.

The orcs that haven't fled, those still stuck in the thrall of their berserk rage, attack the paladins. But they do not attack as one.

The paladins group together, swords and spears flashing in unison. Blood sprays the walls as blades swing and swoop through the air. They remove hands, limbs, heads.

Luke does not wait to count the dead. He makes it to the door in the back before any notice he flees.

He rushes down a hallway and through one final door into the afternoon sun. A large van is parked in the station's lot.

"Just a little longer," Lise is shouting at the driver.

The officer Luke had asked to protect his wife raises a gun as Luke exits the building.

She closes her eyes and lets out a relieved breath. "Anyone else coming?" she demands.

Luke shakes his head as he forces his way into the vehicle. "Drive. Drive fast." The harried-looking man behind the wheel nods and with the squeal of tires they leave the station.

Luke does not fear death. He has learned this about himself today. But he does fear leaving a widow, a fatherless child. So he runs. He lives.

SEVENTEEN

I forgot about everything else when I saw those two men approaching Mogayne.

I was charging back toward them before I even knew what I was doing. I didn't even register the gunshots until it was all over.

I raised my ax over my head, a wordless snarl growing in my chest.

The man closest to me turned, sword up and ready to intercept me.

I threw Ukufa at him and his sword flashed up to block the flying ax. While his sword was out of the way I tackled him. The two of us flew off the path and slid a short distance along the gravel beach of the lake.

My shoulder hurt like hell where I'd connected with his armor, but I managed to ignore it as I struggled to stay on top of the writhing mass of steel and muscle.

I grabbed his wrist as he tried to get his sword between us and ripped the length of steel away from him, tossing it into the water.

His punch hurt more than I could have imagined. I

don't know if you've ever been hit by a gauntleted fist, but it hurts.

I fell back off him and he rose over me, a long dagger seeming to appear out of nowhere.

At this point, on my back, unarmed, and dazed, I was pretty much out of options. So I did what anyone in that situation does. I kicked him in the balls.

He was wearing armor, so I doubt it did much damage, but he staggered back from the force of the blow.

Right at the water's edge his feet slid on the uneven gravel and the ground gave way behind him.

I couldn't even enjoy the sound of his thrashing in the water as I rose.

I was just lucky the second paladin was in a bludgeoning mood and not a slicing one.

I staggered forward, almost falling into the lake myself, as the man smashed the back of my head with the hilt of his sword.

I was able to swing around fast enough to bring my arm up to block the second hit.

The hilt struck me on the forearm and I swore loudly at the crack. I was sure he'd broken something.

And then Mogayne was there.

She leaped from behind the man with a thin gray and black spotted piece of fabric in her hands. Her face was a mask of the purest animal rage, with her thick red hair wild in the wind. I think it was the most beautiful thing I had ever seen.

She wrapped the length of fabric around the man's neck, and with the momentum of her jump pulled him into the lake behind her.

There's no gradual decline in Kirk's lake. It's the gravel of the shore, then a straight drop to the bottom.

Which is lucky when you're trying to drown men in armor.

I rushed to the edge and looked down, ready to pull Mo up as the knights sank to the bottom.

That's not what I saw.

Through the murky water one of the knights was struggling to kick himself to the surface. I couldn't see the other.

The man had already managed to remove his helmet and gloves and was working on undoing whatever held his breastplate in place.

A graceful shape darted from the murk of the water toward him.

A stream of bubbles burst to the surface as the paladin let out a silent scream of pain. He held one of his hands tightly as the water around him began to cloud red.

The gray shape darted away and back again, and again, and again. Each time there was more red in the water and the armored figure sank lower and lower in the murky water until I couldn't see him anymore.

It didn't take long before the air stopped bubbling to the surface.

There was a splash a short way down the shore and someone let out a pained gasp for air.

I spun, hoping to see Mo, though I knew it wouldn't be her.

This paladin had managed to remove most of his armor and had made it to the surface.

His shortness of breath seemed to be affecting his ability to climb out of the water. His hands grasped at the gravel uselessly and he kept sliding back in the water every time he gained an inch or two.

I scanned the shore quickly and grabbed the first thing I thought might be useful.

The man Mo had dragged into the water had dropped his sword.

I took my time as I approached the man.

This may come as a surprise, but up to this point in my life, I had never actually killed anyone. I knew I had to. Part of me relished the idea. My orc blood sang at the prospect. But most of me was nervous.

The man looked up at the sound of my footsteps, or maybe it was my humming. Mine eyes have seen the glory, I thought, recalling the hymn again.

His eyes opened wider as I stood over him. My shadow fell across his terrified face and I watched my silhouette raise the sword.

I kicked his hands off the shore when it was done, and he sank to the bottom, taking his friend's sword with him.

I considered vomiting then. I didn't feel sick, but it felt like the right thing to do.

There was another splash behind me and I spun, angry with myself for giving up a perfectly good weapon.

"Mo," I shouted as I rushed to the woman.

She was trying to pull herself up, just as the paladin had been.

Without thinking I reached into the water and grabbed her under the shoulders.

I pulled her up easily and placed her gently on the shore.

That was when I realized she was naked.

The gray fabric she had wrapped around the man's throat was the only thing keeping all of her from the world.

The gray and black speckled fabric was smooth against my hand. I've never slept on silk sheets, but I imagine that would have been the correct way to describe the large square of fur that Mo held tightly over her chest.

"My clothes haven't washed up anywhere have they?"

I think I said something eloquent, like "Uh."

She stared at me, one eyebrow raised, an attractive blush on her cheeks, but she didn't look away. I suddenly realized I was being a jackass.

"Sorry." I spun away, removing my jacket and passing it back to her.

"Anything with more coverage?" she asked.

I unbuttoned my shirt and passed that back as well.

"So, what just happened?" I asked. I'm not the quickest on the uptake sometimes, but once the gears start turning I can usually figure things out.

"What do you mean?" she asked, voice guarded.

"Are you a, uh, a were or something?"

"Or something." Her voice was quiet and I could tell she didn't want to talk about it.

"Okay. Cool." I risked a quick glance over my shoulder and was rewarded with an eyeful of smooth, pale skin before a spiteful button blocked my view.

I looked away quickly, hoping she hadn't noticed.

"Okay," she said, after what felt like forever.

My shirt was big enough that it draped down past her knees. She'd tied the still-wet square of gray and black around her waist. It was not a bad look for her.

"What's happening at the clubhouse?" she asked, with an urgency I had almost forgotten was necessary.

I really wanted to ask what she was, but I figured it would be rude, and inappropriate considering the situation.

We both turned to look up the incline that hid all but the top of the large building from sight. The large window had been replaced with a wall of gray steel—the storm windows Kirk had mentioned.

I finally caught up with my mind and realized that I

couldn't hear gunshots, and I knew that just a short time ago I had heard gunshots.

Denelle Halldorson has always been a good shot. She knows this, and it frustrates her to no end that none of her shots have been able to find a mark.

She can feel the magic radiating from the armored men as they march up the long driveway of the lodge.

Mike Jensen has activated the storm doors from the relative safety of the security room. The large steel wall replaces the fragile glass, hiding the orcs inside from view.

Denelle's sharp ears catch the sound of Kirk Brown hurrying the orcs down the hidden stairs, down into the labyrinth of steel and cement created to hold the man's inner beast captive.

Some of the orcs argue. They are a bloodthirsty race. They want to partake of this battle. But many have families. The humans convince them.

Some of the older orcs, those who claim to have faced these foes before, tell them the stories, and soon Halldorson can hear no more arguments. The only sound is that of gunfire and the steady approach of steel-clad feet.

The knights have made it to the line of cruisers. There are several officers crouched behind the cars, guns ready.

One of the cops snaps up, spinning around and aiming her rifle at the nearest target. The rifle bursts twice before a thrown spear takes the officer through her neck.

With seemingly no effort, one of the paladins hops up onto the hood of the car in front of him, his weight crumbling the thin metal.

He casually paces across the vehicle as his companions do the same along the barricade.

Several more officers die to sword and spear. Two stand and try to flee, but thrown daggers take both in the back.

One man, too afraid to move, huddles in place as a paladin drops to the ground in front of him, his attention firmly locked on the line of men and women closer to the building.

Denelle and the others had stopped firing when their comrades were in the line of fire, but now, all but the one are dead and they level guns once more and open fire.

The air in front of the paladins ripples with the blue light as slugs ricochet into the asphalt and surrounding trees.

The cowering man, without rising, aims his shotgun at the back of the knight towering over him.

His training allows him to empty the seven shells in a matter of seconds.

There is a moment of silence after the burst of gunfire as the paladin falls forward, a jagged hole pounded into the back of his plate.

The closest knight rushes to his fallen comrade, face twisted in rage. He raises a sword to drive it through the cop as he tries to reload with shaking hands.

The angered paladin falls to a shot from Denelle.

Her .45 automatic cries from far down the length of paved ground, driving a round through a space in the knight's armor.

The knight rests on one knee, a gauntleted hand pulling away from his side covered in a layer of deep red. He looks at the man huddled before him before falling, helmed face first, to the ground.

Her next shot meets a blue shield as her target kills the uniformed man without even looking at him.

"Distract them," the detective says to her remaining force.

She has lost almost half of her men, and there are still eighteen of the twenty attackers left.

"Distract them or get in close. But be fast."

"How are we supposed to do that?" one demands.

Still far down the path, a knight hefts a spear and throws it. The heavy shaft of wood sails through the air and buries itself between Denelle and the questioner.

"Inside, now!" she shouts, and they all rush backward, firing weapons as they do.

She slams the door closed, sure that the thick wood will not hold the men for long.

"Get behind cover, be ready for close quarters. Their shields don't seem effective at close range. Use that to your advantage."

"What the hell is going on, Detective? What the hell are those things?"

"Men. That's all. Now move!"

They start to scatter, but Denelle freezes at the sound of running feet up the stairs. That was fast.

She barely has time to roll out of the way as the door smashes inward in a shower of kindling.

The officer closest to the door panics and opens fire, his rifle's cry ringing off the walls.

The knight that had charged through the door takes the rapid fire in the chest, unable to pull a shield up in time. He is pushed unceremoniously to the side as more men enter the building.

The gunmen scatter, ducking around corners and jumping behind couches.

From her position behind a wall Denelle waits patiently.

A knight steps past her and she darts in using all the graceful speed her kind were blessed with. She ducks under the swing of the surprised sword and, running in a crouch, she aims her gun up, firing into the unarmored section between arm and chest.

The chain mail and linen offers almost no resistance as her bullet finds its mark.

She does not watch as the man falls to the ground. She knows he will bleed out. It's usually a matter of seconds with that artery, but she expects his armor will hold the wound closed. He will still die.

She stands up and charges the next closest knight. This one does not see her coming; he is too busy striding toward the weak cover her men have chosen for themselves.

He freezes when he feels the warm barrel of her gun slide up under his helmet. He has no time to react before she pulls the trigger.

She gasps in shock as a steel plated fist strikes her in the ribs, sending her flying.

She lands gracefully enough a few feet away, rolling to face her new opponent.

There is a cry from above and the paladin looks up in time to see the large orc falling toward him. He is too slow to pull up his sword, however, as the mass of green muscle carries him to the ground.

One of the three Jacks, the Goretusk, is laughing as he flips the knights visor open and aims a pistol Denelle is sure is not legal at the man's face.

Another of the knights tries to save his comrade, but one of the Slayinghand Jacks appears from around a corner and tackles him.

The third Jack is helping Denelle's men by darting in and distracting other knights, allowing the officers to get in close enough to get past the shields.

But there are too many of them. The screams of wounded men fill Denelle's ears as the knights begin to gain ground.

She doesn't have the time to help though. One of the paladins has somehow circled behind her and she only just dodges the swing of his broadsword.

She rolls in toward him, hoping to kill another with a shot to the exposed armpit, but the man moves fast enough that the slug hits the plate on the upper arm.

The slide of her gun locks open and she rolls away, hand scrambling to find a fresh magazine. The blade catches her jacket, slicing it cleanly. She can almost feel the sword as it touches the fabric of her shirt.

Jack Goretusk comes to her rescue, his size belying a surprising speed as he sidesteps the same sword and gives her the space she needs to reload her weapon.

The orc is not fast enough. The knight swings a fist, catching the loudly laughing criminal with a vicious blow across the jaw.

Goretusk's feet leave the ground from the force of the blow and he travels, head first, into the bricks of the room's fireplace.

Denelle charges the paladin, her sudden burst of speed surprising him. She finds an opening in the armor and fires two rounds.

The man drops to his knees with a grunt of pain.

She holds her gun to his side, in the same weak spot in the armor she has used already, barrel resting on the chain mail under the plate.

A hand wraps around her throat and whips her away

from the wounded man. The paladin smashes her against the wall with enough force that a human may have died.

She grimaces as she brings her legs up and wraps them around the man's chest.

With a grunt of effort she brings her gun up and fires at the man's face.

The bullet bounces off the plate of his visor.

Denelle gasps in pain as the knight's other hand rams a foot of glowing blue steel into her gut. He removes the blade and there is a shower of glowing silver blood.

The detective lets out a scream of pain and rage as she forces herself closer to the man. Breaking his grip around her throat, she wraps a hand around his neck in return.

Her chest pressed against his, he stumbles backward, surprised by the strength she is still able to summon.

With a snarl she places her gun right against the slit in his visor.

Sparks fly as the rounds scrape through the narrow opening to find their target.

The dead man collapses in front of a plush leather chair.

The dying elf pulls herself into the seat and surveys the battlefield.

The two conscious Jacks have picked up their cousin and are dragging him down a stairway hidden in the wall.

Only three knights are left alive, she realizes.

A proud smile spreads as she slips away. Three. She can handle three.

But she can't. Darkness clouds her vision, and instead of fighting, she sleeps.

EIGHTEEN

I found Ukufa at the base of a tree as Mo and I made our way up the hill toward the lodge. I wasn't sure how the ax had been knocked this far but I am not one to question providence.

Mo had retrieved the gun Jackson had given her from her bag and held it in a surprisingly calm grip.

We crested the short hill and the building came fully into view. Down the driveway the cruisers had been parked in a line across the path.

Two armored men lay on our side of the barricade. And far too many dead policemen surrounded them. I really expected the worst when I saw the door to the lodge smashed in, one large chunk of wood still dangling from a hinge.

Inside was far worse than out. It looked like a storm had passed through. Or at least a group of very large men with magic swords.

Every wall had at least one big slash and several dozen bullet holes.

I felt a fierce pride in our local PD as we stepped over

the legs of the paladin gasping for breath against the wall. His chest plate was peppered with holes leaking red. He didn't look up as we passed.

From what I could see our side had been outnumbered, but there were more dead knights than cops.

One of the comfortable-looking armchairs had been chopped in half; the foam of the seat lay on the ground mingled with the gore of the dismembered man that had apparently been hiding behind it.

The scene was somehow made worse by the fact that it was inside. Not an hour before this room had seemed so peaceful, civilized, even if full of orcs.

I realized I didn't see any orcs and panicked.

"Where is everybody?" I asked.

Mo's face was paler than usual as she tried not to look too closely at the room. "Probably downstairs. Safest place."

"Which way?" I asked.

We both spun around at the sound of a cough, weapons ready. The back of the chair was facing us, so I stood up straight and strained, trying to see over.

All I could see were a pair of jeans and a pair of small, heeled boots. Boots I recognized.

"Denny?" I rushed over to the chair.

As I rounded it Denny's hand shot up, gun held tight.

She pulled the trigger a few times but the slide was already locked open.

At the foot of the chair was a paladin. His helmet pocked with bullet holes, most right around the eye slit.

Denny slowly lowered her empty gun and considered me with a pained expression. Her empty hand was held over her stomach, a glowing, silver fluid oozed from between her fingers.

"What took you so long?" she asked. She looked pissed.

"Are there any others?" I asked her as I pressed my own hand over her wound.

She nodded. "Three more got inside. Chasing after your three idiot cousins. What's it look like outside? Any more coming?"

I shook my head. "I don't think so. There are definitely more of them, but not here."

"Good." She closed her eyes in a pained grimace.

"Were you able to get word to the station?" I asked.

"Yeah. You're a loud bastard, you know that?" She pushed my hand away from her stomach.

I jerked back, not realizing I had been pushing so hard. I looked around, trying to find something to wrap around the wound.

"Don't worry about me, jackass. Head downstairs. Everyone else is down there." She tried to sit up but collapsed with a snarl of pain.

"I'll look after her." Mo came up behind me carrying a first aid kit. "Basement's that way." She nodded toward one of the fireplaces.

A door disguised as a wall panel stood open. I swallowed, tightening my grip on Ukufa.

"Be careful." Denny gave me a stern look. "Don't die."

"Yes, ma'am." I slowly crept toward the door and started down the stairs.

I spared one glance over my shoulder and watched as Mo lifted Denny's shirt away from her wound. The silver blood began to pump faster and Mo quickly placed a wad of bandaging over the hole.

I was halfway down the stark, white stairway when I realized I was doing something very stupid. I was pretty sure if Denny hadn't been almost dead she would have forbidden me from coming down here.

Three paladins. And me. Though Mo had said all my cousins should be down there as well. Maybe they'd already taken care of the knights.

I knew that was wishful thinking. I'd seen video of the cells. No orcs would be getting out to help me.

At least that also meant no paladins would be getting in to kill them. I hoped, anyway.

At the bottom of the stairs was a hallway, the same blinding white as the stairs. It ran straight for a fair distance, but the light from the stairs only extended a short way so I couldn't tell how long the hallway was.

I crept forward, deeper into the suffocating darkness of the basement. Once I left the light behind me I had made it ten feet with my hand following the left wall when I almost fell over. The wall had vanished and was replaced with a hallway. Another, identical hall stretched into the opposite wall as well.

Squinting in the darkness I could see that both of these branched again a short way down. And just before the new turns there were thick steel doors set into the wall.

I was willing to bet money that behind those doors were orcs.

I turned down the hallway to the left and followed it all the way to the end. I passed six cells before that, three on each side. After each cell had been another hallway leading deeper into the basement.

I had a general picture of the complex after that short hike. It was a grid system, each cell standing alone with a path around it. And even though I thought it might be easy to navigate knowing that, I still half expected a minotaur to pop out and gore me.

I inched my way through the darkness, always keeping one hand on the whitewashed cement walls when possible.

I stopped at every intersection and stared down, hoping, or dreading, to catch a glimpse of movement.

I don't really know how human eyes would work in darkness like that, but I wasn't totally blind. I'm not saying orcs have low light vision, but I was able to make out the general outline of things.

I'd lost count of intersections before I saw the light. It was ten cells away from me, a faint, blue light.

It moved slowly across the hallway, the outline of a man visible in the light. He looked tired; a gauntleted hand held his other arm up against his chest.

He passed the opening in the hallway and I lost sight of him, the after-image of his fire all I could see.

I took a deep breath, steeling myself for what I had to do, and took off after the man.

I cut through the intersection, stopping one lane short of the one he was in, and started to run as quietly as possible in the direction he had been going.

I continued to stop at every intersection and check to make sure he wasn't waiting for me.

I thought I was getting close to the stairs again when I caught sight of the blue fire. I jerked back out of sight quickly. He had just turned down the hall toward me.

His footfalls were heavy, and I guessed one of his legs was injured based on the "stomp, scrape," sound he was making.

The faint, blue glow stretched out past the wall I had pressed myself against as he came closer.

I gripped the handle of my ax tighter and tried to keep myself from breathing too loudly. Which seemed impossible. You always seem to breathe too loudly when you're trying to hide. Then your chest starts to hurt because you feel like you're not getting enough air. At least, that's how it is for me.

So I stood there, in almost total darkness as the magic blue crept slowly across the floor. The steady click, scrape, growing louder.

The closer he got, the more nervous I grew.

By the time he was next to me I had started humming. I didn't realize it until it would have been too late. Too late if he hadn't already been injured and walking very loudly.

I almost didn't do it. The thought of bringing my ax down into his skull seemed too barbaric. Bile was rising in my throat at just the thought of it. I think the problem was I'd spent too much time in the dark with my thoughts.

Even with that man in the lake with the sword through his face on my conscience, this one felt like too much.

I got over it.

He was wearing his helmet, obviously, so my first hit didn't do too much other than make a satisfying ring/thud.

The force of my attempted killing blow knocked him to the side and he staggered into the wall.

He spun, trying to bring his sword up, but now I could see the extent of his injuries.

Blood was dripping from his vambrace, coating an unarmored hand with a layer of dark red—though it looked black in the relative darkness—and his other arm hung uselessly at his side.

His uninjured arm didn't move fast enough and I was able to hook the back of his right leg with the crescent blade of my ax. I jerked the weapon back with a grunt of effort and the knight went down.

His helmeted head hit the wall with another satisfying fleshy bell sound and he slid the rest of the way to the ground.

His blue fire started to sputter and I narrowed my eyes against the faltering light. My hum demanded to be more as I stepped over the man, and I began to sing quietly.

"*He is trampling out the vintage where the grapes of wrath are stored.*"

His light blinked out entirely and I found myself nearly blind again.

He started to flail about weakly and I chopped my ax at any faint outline I saw move in the darkness.

I felt Ukufa bite into something and an instant later his sword clattered to the ground.

I kicked at the sound and was rewarded with the clattering of steel sliding across the floor.

He made a weak noise under his helmet, but I couldn't make out if he was talking or crying out in pain.

I followed the sound, though, and ripped the helmet off. He let out a sharp cry of pain as the leather straps snapped.

I used the sound of his pain to aim my ax.

I kept singing as I felt the blade crushing bone on the first swing.

I swung again and again, each swing capped with a growl or a roar that interrupted my song for just one note.

"*I have seen him in the watch-fires of a hundred circling camps.*"

The warmth of his lifeblood covered my hands, arms, chest. I stopped singing when blood splashed in my mouth.

I reeled back, spitting left and right as I went, stopping only when I hit the wall. I couldn't breathe, and my eyes burned.

I somehow managed to stay upright on legs that felt like jello before you stick it in the fridge. I stumbled away from the dead man I couldn't see and tried to remember which way I was supposed to go.

It was only after the sword cut a shallow line down my back that he turned on his glow.

"Orc filth!" the new paladin bellowed as I turned to face him.

His helmet was off and his face was covered in scratches, one eye nothing more than a gaping hole.

At this point I felt I'd expended my supply of adrenaline for the day and just managed to fall backward out of the way of the next swing.

And that was when the prayer I would have prayed if I were religious was answered. Kirk Brown stabbed the man through the throat.

"Hi, Jackie," the werewolf said.

I couldn't see him since the light had died with the paladin, but I thought I couldn't hear his normal smile.

The sword I'd kicked away earlier clattered to the ground as Kirk dropped it.

"You're alive," I said, too tired to sound happy.

"Yup. Perks of being a werewolf." He let out a bark of bitter laughter. "Silver bullets, Jackie. You should invest." He sounded tired and in pain.

There was the sound of footsteps behind me and I spun, almost falling over as I did so, ax ready for the third knight.

"Cousin Jack?" A voice called from the dark. I recognized it as one of the Jack Slayinghands.

"Yeah."

"Was that you singing earlier?" the other Jack Slayinghand asked, "Creepy as fuck, cousin."

When they were close enough that I could make them out I saw that each one of them was supporting a second body.

"Who's that?" I asked.

"Jack took a hit to the head," Jack One said.

"This is Officer Mike, took a sword to the heart. Tough bastard," Jack Two added.

"That's Officer Jensen to you, shit stain," Mike said, voice pained.

"Whatever. Don't worry about being grateful. We didn't just kill a man to save you or anything," my cousin said.

"You okay, Mike?" I asked.

"Officer Jensen," he corrected with only slightly less venom in his voice, "and yeah, I'll be fine."

The Jacks carried their loads past Kirk and me toward the stairs.

"He really going to be okay?" I asked Kirk as we followed them.

Kirk sighed. "One of these days, that boy's going to have to come out of the closet."

"Mike's gay?" I was having a hard time keeping up.

"I wish." There was another sigh.

"He wishes!" came a pained cry from down the hall.

Jackson Smith fears he is dying.

He has been pulled away from a world into the nexus without the use of a door. He has used no spell to prepare a path. No machine has been turned on to devise a safe course.

He has sacrificed of his own power, his own life force, to escape from Saban.

This is power he cannot spare. He will need all of it to face that foe.

He staggers through the halls of his home, clutching his chest in pain.

He passes a window; outside is the darkness of space.

There are no stars in that view. No stars but one.

The small red sun burns, giving light to one solitary planet and Jackson's home as it circles the lonely world.

There is one civilization on this planet. The first people Jackson had ever saved from the creeping darkness he has sworn his life to destroy.

With a labored breath he forces his way into Sigmund's room. The great obelisk that is the ancient computer stares, unfeeling, at the dying god.

"Thank you, Sigmund." Jackson collapses into a chair in front of the intelligence.

"Of course, sir." The voice comes from the walls themselves.

It is dignified, respectful. Not because Sigmund is any of these things, but only because that is the voice Jackson expected to hear the first time the two of them met.

"How long?" Jackson asks simply.

Sigmund knows him well enough to determine his meaning, "Twenty-four hours your time, sir. It will be six hours on UF-87."

"Any way to speed that up?"

Jackson wants to end this fight. He started it twenty years before. And after failing then, the bait he placed expecting this day has caught his prey. He does not want the rat to fight his way free now.

"Not if you wish to return at full power, sir. We can cut that time in half, but my data on Saban indicates you will need to be closer to full strength."

"He was afraid, Sigmund," Jackson says. "I could see it in his eyes. I can use that."

"He fears the Machine, sir. Not necessarily you."

"As far as he's concerned, I am the Machine," Jackson snarls through his pain.

"Of course, sir. Half strength then?"

"Do it." He closes his eyes as the light in the chamber changes to a deep green.

Soon, the god is asleep.

As he sleeps the intelligence that he calls Sigmund works to heal him. Energy is harvested from the burning sun and fed into the man. But not too much at once, for he is only a man, and if Sigmund is not careful the man will die.

He says he is a god, and he is, of a sort. But he was a man first. So Sigmund takes its time, methodically harvesting and sharing the power with Jackson.

Despite itself, Sigmund cares about this man. He is the longest lived deus Sigmund has ever served. Young, by the standards of the Machine, but old for one of his calling.

He is also first in centuries that the Machine has found worthy to give to Sigmund.

Sigmund, in the heartless way of a computer, hopes that the man will continue to live.

While filling Jackson with strength, Sigmund finds a tendril of a shadow crawling through the man's heart. This is not the first time it has seen this. It is a common thing for one of Jackson's calling.

Sigmund sears the shadow away with an extra burst from the healing sun.

One day, that darkness will envelop the young god. But today Sigmund removes it and prepares Jackson to be a hero once more.

Never *the* hero, Sigmund allows itself to muse. Never center stage as Jackson had once wanted. No, Jackson's place was in the background. His strength has always been in making others stronger.

The computer considers UF-87 and wonders if Jack Bloodfist is truly meant to be the hero of that story.

If it had shoulders it would shrug. What should it care? Its purpose is to keep this god alive for as long as possible. And, when it becomes necessary, to end him.

Ancient hardware moves silently as the intelligence heals its master and prepares him for his next battle.

NINETEEN

The eight of us sat in the broken, gore-filled, remains of the lodge's main room. Mo had finished cleaning and wrapping Denny's injury and was taking a look at Jack Goretusk, I'm gonna call him Jack Three. Four of us in one room is too many.

Anyway, she was wrapping Three's head while he made random, grunting comments. Luckily all in orcish, or she may not have been willing to help him. I almost crushed his throat with my foot after his comment about how good she looked in my wet shirt. It sounds worse in orcish, trust me.

Mike Jensen, despite his injuries looking much worse, sword through the chest and all, was going to be fine. Turns out he was a member of Kirk's little club. Kirk had helped the officer upstairs to put him to bed in one of the lodge's suites.

In the light, Kirk himself didn't look very good, but he claimed he was fine. At least he could still walk.

The two Jacks, One and Two respectively, seemed mostly fine. Each had a collection of new cuts and bruises, but they'd proven themselves pretty adequate in a fight.

Not surprising. They were about the same age as Luke and myself; all three of them had been alive before we stepped through the portal. That was back when the fist still tried to adhere to tradition. All of us had spent our free time for the first ten or so years training with Aunt Karen, the fist weapon master.

The neighbors had thought she was running a martial arts dojo in the trailer park. Even had a few parents try to sign their kids up for classes. When they offered to pay Karen had even accepted. Not really related, but if you ever get in a fight in a bar in Summervale, well, there are a few humans in town that will know how to hurt you.

"We really need to get these two to a hospital," Mo said.

Jack Three found that funny for some reason and started laughing.

"Yeah. Probably a good idea," I said.

I was sitting on the floor in front of Denny—I'd dragged the dead paladin out of the way. I was afraid to move because Denny had fallen asleep with her legs resting on my shoulders. She was using my suit jacket as a pillow as well, a line of drool pooling on the fabric.

There were apparently some very good painkillers in that first aid kit. Mo had already had to chase both Jack One and Two away from the bag when she had given one of the pills to Three.

"Plenty of cars outside." Kirk came down the stairs, cleaning the blood on his hands off with a white towel. "They even have sirens."

"I'll drive!" Jack Two sat up straight in his chair, voice excited.

"No." I jumped at the sound of Denny's voice. "Blood-fist drives. He's the least stupid of you." Her voice was groggy from the medication, but she seemed mostly aware of what she was saying. "Kirk, let Charles Slayinghand out of his cell. Leave everyone else locked up unless he says different."

"Yes, ma'am." He nodded respectfully, his eyes darting to the still-glowing silver stains on his furniture.

Kirk respects people; he's enough of a minority—native, gay, werewolf, all those things that are not the majority—that he always tries to treat everyone well, no matter who they are. That's the sense I've always got from him anyway.

So he'd always treated Denny well. I mean, strong, independent black woman? Of course he was going to be extra friendly. But the tone in his voice now was different. I guessed he had not known she was an elf. I didn't quite understand why that changed anything, but it did for some reason.

"Okay, dumbass." She kicked me in the back of the head. "You're gonna have to carry me."

I made sure the smile was gone from my face before I turned around and picked her up.

She pointed around me at Jack One, "You stay and help the handsome gay man."

Apparently the drugs really were working.

Kirk and One stood in the door and watched us as we made our slow way down the driveway.

"Dude, she thinks you're hot," Jack One said. "You should ask her out."

"You caught the gay part, right?"

"So?"

Jack Two and Mo helped Three climb inside the back of the front cruiser in the line and Mo climbed in after him.

I placed Denny in the final seat as gently as I could. Even with the painkillers the detective's face contorted into a pained snarl as she was forced to sit.

Mo gently guided Denny into a more horizontal position.

Jack and I climbed in the front. He eyed the steering wheel enviously as I turned the key in the ignition.

It took about ten minutes following the narrow, mostly dirt roads, to get to the freeway. From there it was a ten-minute drive back into town.

Or, at least, it would have been with traffic.

"How do I turn the lights on?" I asked.

"No, don't even think about it," Denny said from the back.

"Right here, cousin." I let out an excited laugh as Jack Two flipped the switch.

"Jackasses," Denny grumbled. I could still hear the pain in her voice. It cut through her normally angry tone like fire through a field of dry grass.

She was hurting, so I pressed the gas down as far and as hard as I could.

I'm pretty sure I gave at least one of the nurses or doctors a heart attack when I stormed into the emergency room, a dying elf cradled in my arms.

"I need David Terzi, right now!" I bellowed.

It was only after I had shouted that the atmosphere of the room hit me. People in scrubs and white jackets rushed around with the urgent air that is only ever possible in a hospital after some sort of major crisis.

I remembered my mother's warning and my fear reasserted itself. Beside me I could sense Mo acknowledging the feel of the room as I had.

The two Jacks wheeled up beside us, Three now in a wheelchair.

"Oh my God." A tired looking nurse stopped in front of us. "Are you okay?"

"I'm fine, not my blood." My bare chest was still covered in dried paladin blood.

I nodded my head to Denny, who had passed out halfway there. "Doctor Terzi. Get him, now."

"He's with another patient. Men in armor?" she asked. She only looked sad, not surprised, at my nod.

"Okay. I can look at her." She reached out to pull the bandage up but I snarled.

"I said, Terzi. Get him. NOW!" She flinched back, bumping into a passing doctor.

Her gaze went from me, my entire top half covered in gore, possibly brain matter, to Mo, wearing nothing but a muddy, still damp dress shirt, and finally the two Jacks. Two offered a charming, tusk-filled grin.

"Please?" Mo asked, giving the woman a pleading look. Her hand stroked my arm gently, trying to calm me down, I guessed.

The nurse swallowed then rushed off, I hoped, to get the only asshole in the area qualified to sew up a dying drow elf.

"Jack." Two and I spun at the sound of our name, Three managed a halfhearted, grunt.

Matt Fitzpatrick rushed over, hanging up on whatever phone call he'd been on.

"Matt. Thank God," I said. "We need David Terzi."

Matt stopped, eyes wide, before rushing over to us. "Den. Oh shit. Armored assholes? What am I saying? Of course it was. Come on."

He turned to lead us down the hallway before a familiar, asshole voice could be heard.

"This had better be damn important." Terzi marched into the hallway, the nurse following close behind with a gurney.

He stopped short when he saw Denny in my arms. "Oh." He turned to the nurse. "I'm going to need a private room for the detective. Hurry."

She rushed off as the doctor indicated I put Denny on the gurney.

"Are you hurt?" he asked me as he lifted the edge of the bandage Mogayne had wrapped around Denny's waist. A thin stream of silver blood leaked down onto the sheets.

"I'm fine. Head injury in the wheelchair, though."

Terzi spared a glance for the orc and nodded. "He's probably fine, but we'll bring him with."

I looked around the waiting room and took in all the uncomfortable, anxious faces as Matt and I helped Terzi with the gurney. I was less surprised than I should have been to see I wasn't the only one covered in blood. "What happened?"

Terzi looked up in surprise, "What do you mean? Weren't you at the station?"

I shook my head.

"Oh. Well I'm told men in armor marched into the police station. Started swinging swords around. A lot of dead. More wounded. Quite a few of your family here already. I was just with one of them. Hull Bloodfist?"

"Alright," Jack Two said, "I like that old bastard. Tells good stories."

"Have you seen Luke Goretusk? His family?" I asked.

Terzi shrugged. "Don't know. Maybe. Seen too many today." He guided the gurney into an empty room, the nurse stood outside the door waiting for us.

"You're going to have to wait out here," Terzi said to us.

I started to enter the room anyway but Matt stopped me. "I'll sit with her. They can't keep me out."

"She'll be fine, Jack," Terzi said. He pointed to the two

Jack's. "I'll get a nurse to look at your friend. Wait there. Someone I trust," he said to me, probably expecting me to argue.

"Fine," I said and turned to Matt. "You let me know the second she's awake, okay?"

The detective nodded as he let himself inside the room and Terzi closed the door.

"Now what?" I asked no one in particular.

"It's not over yet, Jack." Mogayne's hand rested on my forearm, the tips of her fingers digging into the skin. She still looked scared, but there was resolve there as well.

"Right. I think I need to call Ma."

"Mind if we swing by my apartment first?" she asked. "I'd really like to put on some real clothes."

"Sure." I said goodbye to the Jacks, giving Two a card just in case he didn't have my number.

Then we left. Left that building of sadness, death, and hope. God, I hate hospitals.

I sat at Mogayne's kitchen table while she took a shower. I would have sat on the couch, but I didn't want to stain the thing.

Her television was on and every station was the breaking news. All the talking heads had to talk about was the attack on the police station.

The numbers they reported were horrible. Almost thirty dead, even more wounded. Most of those cops, but a lot of civilians as well. More than a few of the survivors were in critical condition, some expected to pass before the day ended.

No names had been released yet, so I had no way of

knowing if Luke and Lise were okay. Luke hadn't been answering his phone, which had me in a little bit of a panic.

The reporters were blaming the attack on terrorists. Which I guess is actually accurate, though they did make sure to mention that no known groups had taken credit for the attack yet.

The nature of the attack had them pretty confused as well. Not every day someone walks into a police station with swords. It's definitely more newsworthy when they get away with it.

And, of course, nothing had been said about Kirk's club-house. I imagine the networks wouldn't have been able to handle the ratings, so it was for the best we hadn't said anything yet.

The city of Summervale had effectively been put into a police state. All of the surrounding cities had volunteered their own uniformed men and women to help, and every federal agency that had anything to do with this sort of thing had been called. Every major intersection in the city had law enforcement of one branch or another, local and federal, keeping an eye on things.

While not listening to the same reports and speculation from people that knew less about the situation than I did, I tried to make calls.

I rotated between calling Luke and Ma, both her apartment number and Jack's Place.

After the fifth time going through the list of numbers I let out an angry growl and forced myself to not slam my thin phone on the table.

The screen was already cracked from any number of heroic feats from the day and I really didn't want to destroy it completely.

Okay, I did. I really, really did. Breaking something would have been amazing right then, but I controlled myself. I settled for a string of artfully used profanities instead.

I stood up, no longer able to sit still, and paced the small apartment.

It only took my about ten steps from one end of the tiled kitchen to the window in her living room, and I made that walk several times before I decided to do what anyone would do. I inspected things.

It was my first time in Mo's apartment. Despite the fact that we'd sort of been dating for almost a year she'd never invited me over.

So I took advantage of this rare opportunity and looked at shit.

The apartment wasn't really what I had expected. I'd been picturing something sleeker, more of a modern aesthetic. Instead, it was full of furniture that had either been found antiquing or on the side of the road. Both her couch and the mismatched armchair looked like they were as old as the building, which meant they had been around for the better part of a century.

I'm not saying the apartment was bad or gross, or anything like that. It was functional. Everything had a purpose and was only there to fill that purpose.

There was only one picture on the wall—a landscape painting of the ocean, a rocky shoreline caressed by a green sea. That one made sense to me, now that I knew more about her. Still didn't know what she was, but water, that was a safe theme.

There were things missing that I had always pictured whenever I imagined her home. Family portraits, framed news stories. Basically anything that might prove the space belonged to Mogayne Thornhill was missing. Except the smell.

It definitely smelled like her. And it was a comfortable space. So, I liked it.

"You should wash up."

I jerked away from the painting to find Mo standing in the hallway drying her hair.

She was dressed in real clothes again and I found I kind of missed her in my nasty shirt. I wasn't going to say that though.

"I don't have anything to change into," I said.

"I could throw your stuff in the wash?" she offered, her bare feet pacing across the kitchen and opening what I had thought was the pantry to reveal an old washing machine and its ancient counterpart.

"I think the pants might be dry clean only." I wasn't sure. I'd always just assumed they were. I looked down at myself and considered them. Blood and who knows what else covered them. "I don't know if that even matters anymore," I said.

Mo grimaced. "I'm gonna try anyway. Get in there."

"I still haven't heard from Ma..." I started.

"I'll answer your phone if anyone calls. Leave your pants outside the bathroom door. I left a towel in there for you."

I did as the attractive woman commanded and squeezed down the narrow hallway and into the small bathroom.

I remember hearing once that the average height of the modern human has increased over the years. I bring this up because Mo's building was old. And I don't think the bathroom had been updated recently.

I looked down at the shower head as it sent a stream of warm water down my bottom half. I tried to bend over to wet my head, but in the end I just sat down in the tub and let the water get all of me.

Up to that point in my life, that shower was the most amazing thing to ever happen to me.

I, self-consciously stepped back out into the hallway smelling of roses and cucumber lime, a blessedly large towel wrapped around my waist. I tentatively poked my head out into the front room. The dryer was loudly trying to walk itself out of the closet.

The contents of my pants sat on the kitchen table. The orc bard Danyl had given me stood guard over the few stained business cards and my wallet.

"Feel better?" Mo asked from her old couch.

"So much better." I considered sitting down but remembered that I was basically naked and instead just stood awkwardly in the kitchen, eyes darting from the still working dryer to the cute redhead that was studying me.

"You can sit down, Jack," she said with a smile. "I promise I won't peek."

"Um, okay." I settled into the overstuffed armchair facing the TV. After a few seconds of anxiously staring at the talking heads I shot a quick glance at Mo.

She was still smiling, and very obviously breaking her promise of not looking.

"Yes?" I asked.

"Almost a loincloth." Her grin widened into something wicked and inviting.

I snorted. "Yeah. Now you're just missing the fur bikini."

"Orcs wear fur bikinis?" she asked, voice low and full of mock horror.

"Probably."

She laughed as she stretched out on the couch, closing

her eyes and covering her face with an arm. The laugh cracked a little at the end, but she kept the semblance of a smile.

"Jack?" she asked, eyes still closed. "What do you think we're doing?"

"What do you mean?"

"I mean us. Not this whole fighting guys with swords."

"Oh, *that* us." I studied her. "Well, I was always taught that the woman gets to decide that."

She opened her eyes and stared at me. "What?"

I shrugged. "Orcs and goblins are matriarchal. Sort of. I mean, I've always hoped that this us you speak of would go somewhere serious. But that was always your call."

"You're an idiot." She pushed herself to her feet and took the two steps to the armchair slowly.

"Huh?" I countered.

"A year. A whole damn year and neither of us bring this up." She shook her head as she threw a leg over me and sat down in my lap.

My body knew what was happening before I did and I started to blush slightly; Mo's wicked grin grew wider even as her cheeks grew darker.

"It's been a long day, Jack Bloodfist," she said, her forehead resting on my own.

I wanted to watch what her hands were doing. I could tell they were doing interesting things with the buttons of her shirt.

"Yeah, really long," I agreed, lost in the deep green of her eyes.

She tossed her shirt onto the couch behind her, followed closely by another, much smaller, article of clothing.

I stared as she stood to shimmy out of her jeans. Staring was all I could do.

Her pale skin was occasionally broken with thin, silver scars, some straight, some curved at strange angles. I wanted nothing more than to touch her.

Mogayne Thornhill is a beautiful woman. She is the most beautiful creature I have ever seen, clothed or otherwise. Some might argue with me, but they would be wrong.

She returned my stare, her face flushing slightly as I took all of her in.

"Well?" she asked, voice nervous.

I stood, letting the towel drop, and embraced her, bending down and pulling her mouth to my own. She moaned at the kiss, and I pressed closer against her.

She lay down on the soft carpet of her living room and pulled me down on top of her.

We both moved urgently, the stress of the day and our own desires, denied for so long, driving us forward.

And that is all I'm going to say about that.

A perfectly reasonable amount of time later I was slipping back into my clean but irreparably stained pants and possibly still okay shirt.

Mo sat on her couch, already dressed, and watched me as she ran a brush through her hair.

My phone began to ring from the couch and she answered it before I could object.

"Hello? Oh, hi, Mrs. Bloodfist," she said, grinning at the look of horror on my face. "Sure, he's right here, hang on." She tossed the phone the short distance to the dryer and I caught it.

"Ma?" I said, practically slamming the phone to my ear. "Where the hell have you been?"

"Jack boy, are you okay?" She ignored my question.

"I'm fine. What about you?"

"Jack, we have a problem."

"Besides the angry, murderous knights, right?"

"Don't take that tone with me. I am still your mother!"

I sighed. "Fine. Where are you? I'll come get you."

"Jack's Place. But meet me at the apartment. They're planning on meeting here soon."

"Who?" I asked.

"I'll explain when you get here. Then you can tell me why you've been keeping this girl secret from me. Is she pretty?"

"Ma. Not the time. I'll be there soon." I hung up.

"I have to go and pick up Ma. Are you going to be okay?" I asked trying to wrap my tie around my neck.

She was across the room before I looked up. "I'm coming with you."

"Mo, you don't have to. It's probably safer here."

She shook her head. "Jack," her voice was low, scared. "I really don't want to be alone right now. Not today. Please?"

I have never been able to say no to a pretty girl. Well, I probably have, but never Mo. She has a way of making me do whatever the hell she wants. I think it's her eyes. Stupid, sexy Thornhill.

Of course I took her with.

TWENTY

We took Mo's car, a sporty little thing, only a few years old. Made my now undrivable junk heap look even more like the pile of shit it was.

We hit a few of the police checkpoints as we went, but none of them kept us for very long. Mo did a great job of spinning our sob story.

She didn't lie. Not really. I was actually worried about my family. Mo promised them that as soon as we made it there we would stay inside and they graciously let us pass. I can guarantee that wouldn't have worked if I'd been driving.

Goblin Burrows seemed pretty active as we pulled into the lot. Goblins were rushing in and out of the building. Those leaving pulled their families behind them, urgently shouting as they tried to carry everything they owned.

One younger goblin tripped and sent a game console and a small TV sliding across the sidewalk. She cursed loudly in goblin, ignoring Mo and me as we passed.

A lot of them had noticed us by that point, and they all eyed me with a mix of apprehension and unmasked fear. Those exiting the building walked on the grass to avoid me.

Mrs. Zaretsky, one of the few non-goblins still in the building, greeted me at the entrance. "Hi, Jack. Are you coming to help your mother move? I was so surprised to hear everyone was leaving. Did Marty finally kick them out?"

"I don't think so, Mrs. Zaretsky," I shouted over my shoulder as we marched inside, "but maybe you should go visit your daughter today."

The old woman waved at us as we turned to head up the stairs, and shakily turned back to the front doors to watch the activity.

Several goblins swore at us as I pushed a path through the steady stream to get to the third floor. Those that recognized me cursed more loudly. Some even scrambled over the railing and went straight down the wall.

I did my best to ignore them. From the little Ma had told me I suspected that if I stopped to ask what they were doing I'd either get no answer, or one that pissed me off.

The third-floor hallway was a mess. Apartment doors stood open as goblins tossed their belongings onto the worn carpet of the hall. Some sifted through the junk, collecting whatever was theirs, or whatever looked worth taking, and shouted instructions to whoever was unloading the rooms.

"You check under the sink? I think I hid something under there a few months ago."

"Hang on, I'll check."

"Where's my Batman shirt? It was under my bed. Did someone take it already?"

"How the hell was I supposed to know to check under the beds? Do it yourself, you little shit!"

Most of them were too preoccupied to notice us as we made our way to Ma's apartment.

None of them even looked up as I stomped through

their piles of crap. Mo was more considerate and weaved around the clumps of scavenging goblins.

Ma's door was the only one in the hallway still closed. I tried to open it, but it was locked. I smashed my fist against it several times and shouted, "Ma, we're here! Let us in."

I tried a few more times, adding a colorful word or two every time.

I felt something tug at my sleeve and I looked at Mo who was studying the rest of the hallway.

My shout had got the attention of the rest of the floor's occupants. Many had rushed inside their own rooms and slammed the doors, but some stood and glared at me, not even trying to hide their anger.

My initial confusion at the anger in their eyes was replaced very quickly by anger. "You have a problem with me?" I demanded in goblin, turning from Ma's door and striding toward them.

They all flinched back, but the anger stayed. "You'll bring him here. Leave!" one said, finding his voice before the others.

I laughed. "You think my being here makes a difference? He wants us all dead, little cousin."

"No. The magician bought us our safety. But you ruin that."

I blinked at that. Bought their safety? I studied the piles of belongings on the floor. "Is this safety why you're all leaving?"

He looked away from me, face twisted by something—shame, maybe.

"It's a precaution, Jack," another said, slightly less angry, "but you should leave. If only for your mother's sake."

"Where is she?" I asked.

A few of them looked at each other nervously, and the

slightly friendlier goblin answered, "Well, last I heard, Terry had her and your grandfather at the diner. Sorry, Jack. The paladin wanted all Bloodfists dead."

"You bastards," I snarled as I barreled past them, running for the stairs.

I'd almost forgotten about Mo until she caught up with me at the front door. "What's going on?" She asked.

I didn't stop moving as I explained. We rushed across the road to the diner.

The parking lot of Jack's Place was empty except for the little hatchback that Ma and Gramps used when they needed to run into town for something. The lights inside were off and I saw no movement through the dirty windows.

"Do you think we're too late?" Mo asked.

"I don't know." I reached under my jacket and pulled my ax out. The rough wood felt good in my hand. Reassuring.

The front door of the building was unlocked and Mogayne and I let ourselves in.

The dining room was empty and silent. "Ma?" I shouted into the empty restaurant.

We were in the middle of the room when I heard them.

I spun at the sound of the goblins climbing down the walls behind us. They dropped down in front of the glass doors and locked them.

Terry jeered up at me, his face smug. "Thanks for coming, frog." His tone was even nastier than the last time I'd seen him, if that were possible.

"What are you doing, Terry?" I asked, putting myself between Mo and the goblins.

"Protecting my clan." He puffed out his slight, self-important chest.

"From what? Me?" I demanded.

"From you and all your kind. You orcs brought this on us. If it hadn't been for your father we never would have had to run. Saban never would have looked for us if it hadn't been for you. But he's promised me forgiveness. If we give you to him, we'll be safe."

"Give us to him?" I was slowly catching up again. "You betrayed the fist. After everything my father did for you?" I took a step toward him but two other goblins jumped between us, short, sharp blades reflecting the setting sun as it filtered through the dust of the windows.

I froze in place. I had always considered these creatures my family. Called them cousin even when there was no blood to tie us. They didn't trust me, and they had been willing to kill me and my father's family to protect themselves. But I still couldn't bring myself to hurt them. Not yet.

"Pynwids." I said it softly, the pain in my chest from the betrayal preventing me from screaming like I wanted.

"No, frog. I'm sorry." Terry almost did sound sorry as he signaled someone behind me.

I turned to the kitchen to find half of the diner now filled with goblins. Several more came out of the kitchen leading my mother and Gramps. Both of them were tied and gagged.

I met Ma's eyes, and the anger I saw there fueled my own.

"All of you?" I asked, my voice rising. I turned in a slow circle. None of them would meet my gaze.

"*All* of you?" I shouted it this time as I raised Ukufa.

I pointed the spearhead tip around the room, making sure I focused on every one of them. "You assholes," I hissed. "You pathetic pieces of shit. How dare you?"

I stopped my circle, facing Terry through his body-guards. He was the only one who didn't look away.

The little bastard had the balls to grin. "After Saban takes you, he will let us go."

"No he won't." I promised, "You're all dead."

I could feel the warmth of Mogayne at my side, and glancing over my shoulder I noted that the goblins were moving to circle us. I wrapped my free hand around her and pulled her close.

I met her eyes—her beautiful, terrified eyes—and mouthed, "Stay close."

She nodded, jaw clenched against her fear.

The look of shock on Terry's face as we charged him was incredibly satisfying.

The two knife-wielding goblins were too surprised to move.

I caught the first one with a kick under the chin. Being well over twice his size meant that kick sent the idiot flying. Terry dove out of the way as his guard smashed into the door.

I brought Ukufa's handle down on the top of the second's head and he dropped.

None of the other goblin's moved. They just watched as I stepped over the unconscious body and unlocked the door.

"Now," I said, turning to face the room, but the words froze in my throat as Mo screamed.

"Jack!" Half a dozen goblins leaped on her, dragging her to her hands and knees.

She struggled against them, trying to crawl toward me, but the rest of the room swarmed her, small hands finding hold and dragging her back into the mass of them.

"Leave her alone!" They all froze at my roar.

Every face in the room considered me as I strode

forward. "Leave. Her. Alone." I stepped into the horde and raised my ax. They scattered.

Some scrambled up tables, others hid behind the bar, and, as they all moved, Mo came into sight.

She lay curled in the fetal position on the floor, a hand clasped over her side with a small river of red blood pouring from between her fingers.

My breath caught in my throat as I knelt down and touched the warmth of the blood.

"Mogayne?" I asked.

She looked up at me, expression fierce. "I'll be okay."

I felt the knife bite into the meat of my shoulder as Terry latched himself on for the second time that day.

His warm, stale breath came in sharp gusts as he hissed in my ear, "I can't let you leave, frog. If none of them will kill you, I will. I will give your ears to Saban as payment for their safety."

I did the exact same thing as that morning. I brought my hand up and wrapped a fist around his head.

Somehow he even managed to sound surprised as I threw him across the room.

He hit a window, the pane cracking from the force of my throw.

Any goblins that had been near the window shuffled back out of my way as I stalked across the room.

I placed a foot on Terry's chest and stepped down. Hard. His small hands scratched uselessly at the cotton of my stained pants.

"I only do this to protect my clan," I snarled, pouring every ounce of sarcasm I could spare into the statement.

It didn't matter that it was partly true, because right then, I only did it because I was angry. Because he had hurt me. Had betrayed me and convinced others to do the same.

Because he had caused a woman I cared for, one I knew I could grow to love, to be hurt. Had made her bleed.

I reached over my shoulder and pulled out his knife, wincing as it slid out.

Terry's eye's opened wide as he watched the blade. He tried to jerk out of the way as I dropped it beside him.

Then, for the second time that day, Ukufa carved through skull.

I only swung once. Terry broke easily. The crack brought to mind stepping on a pine cone in the fall.

"Untie them," I said, without looking up from Terry's corpse.

"Jack?" I jerked at Mo's touch.

She stood next to me, almost doubled over in pain.

"Mo?" I pulled her close, gently, trying not to touch her side.

"You all just watch as he kills your own?" I had never heard that voice before, but I recognized it instantly.

Standing in the doorway, red cape resting on the ground, was Saban. Eight paladins flanked him, four to a side. Every one of them had hands on weapons.

"I suppose I should have heeded Arthur's warning and not trusted the little magician." He studied me as he spoke to his men. "Kill them all."

"No." I stepped away from Terry's corpse, still holding Mo to my side. I did my best to put myself between the knights and the rest of the room.

The paladins were not impressed with my show of bravery, and instead continued to march inside the diner.

"Don't just stand there," I said, keeping my eyes on the paladins, but directing my shouts to the goblins, "run, you motherfucking idiots!"

My voice seemed to shake them out of whatever paralysis they'd been experiencing. The dining room filled with the sounds of dozens of goblins fleeing.

I was ready to die, but Mo at my side made that decision seem really stupid. So I readied myself to run as well.

Once the goblins had started moving the paladins had increased their own speed. One tried to run past me toward the back of the restaurant, where ma and the others had retreated.

I threw my ax at his head and it connected with his helmet. He staggered to the side, his legs catching on a rogue bar stool, and collapsed.

I ducked under the swing of another's sword and pushed him away with the hand not wrapped around Mo.

With the little bit of space I had given myself I turned to Mo and pulled her up in both arms.

She let out a cry of pain from my less than gentle attempts to save her life.

I cradled her to my chest and turned to run.

Goblins move fast, and in the few seconds I had bought them, they had emptied the building. I was relieved that at least one of them had been kind enough to untie Ma and Gramps. It made me feel better about running away.

I rushed through the opening that led behind the counter and into the kitchen.

A few skinny goblins were still forcing their way out the back door as I barreled into the room.

A gauntleted hand brushed my back and I only just stepped fast enough to stay ahead of its owner. I instinctively dove forward as the inevitable sword cut the air where I'd been standing.

I rolled in the air so I landed on my back, still tightly holding Mogayne. She let out another cry of pain, or fear, or a combination of the two.

She pulled herself off me and started to half crawl, half stagger toward the open door.

"Hurry, Jack," she urged as she pulled herself up.

I did a backward crab crawl as the paladin swung his sword down toward me again. More of the knights were marching into the small kitchen behind the first.

A large metal table took up the center of the room, leaving only enough space for them to stand in single file, so I really only had to worry about the first man through the door. Even that wasn't ideal, though.

I tried to climb to my feet and hurry outside, grabbing the counter that rang along the wall.

I jerked my hand back quickly. I'd grabbed the side of the kitchens deep fryer. Some idiot had left it on.

Before I could use the table to pull myself up a booted foot pushed me back down. I thought of Uncle Terry as the paladin raised his sword over his head. I guessed I probably deserved what was coming. I still wasn't happy about it, but I could appreciate the symmetry of the whole thing.

I let out a cry of fear and anger as the sword began to fall. Then a confused grunt as it was knocked off course by a metal fry basket.

Mogayne stood over me, her breathing heavy and ragged, blood still oozing from her side, metal basket held like a sword.

The distraction provided just enough time for me to pull myself up and grab the man's sword arm.

The guy behind him tried to stab at me from around his friend, but in the close quarters I actually had the advantage and was able to dodge.

Using the hand not wrapped around a steel-covered arm I grabbed at the front knight's helmet, fingertips gripping the narrow eye slits. I jerked his head back and forth a few times before he did that flame-on routine they were all so fond of.

The quick burst of cold fire convinced me to release him by shoving him back toward his partner. The two stumbled back together, in turn knocking those behind them back further.

I pressed my attack and rammed the front man with my shoulder. The momentum pushed everyone but the front two back out the kitchen door. The speed of my tackle hadn't allowed his fire to catch at all.

While he was disoriented I followed Mo's lead and grabbed the second basket from the deep fryer and smashed the mesh over the paladin's head. It bounced uselessly off the helmet.

Adjusting my plan, I flipped the basket over and repeated the motion. This time the basket rested neatly over the knight's helmet. It felt like catching a troll with a butterfly net.

With the lip of the basket resting at the base of his neck I jerked him forward violently. He stumbled forward and I used the momentum to turn him toward the fryer.

He smacked into the metal duct of the fan above the unit, but when I jerked again I pulled him down and he missed.

He screamed as his face was submerged in the black, rancid oil.

I released the basket and hurried away from him as he fell away from fryer. The flames around him had just as much red as blue now, though the oil on his armor burned away quickly.

"Let's go," I shouted to Mo.

I turned, expecting to find her right behind me, but she was gone. I looked up and found her standing at the kitchen's large sink. It was one of those industrial sinks with the hose that hangs over it. Perfect for cleaning dishes. And for spraying water across the room into a boiling vat of oil.

I dove away from the fryer as Mo turned on the water.

The stream hit the oil, and the air above the fryer filled with white steam, and as the oil in the air met with the flames around the knight there was a column of orange and black fire.

The hungry inferno climbed up the first knight, replacing his head with a ball of orange as the oil that still coated him caught in earnest.

The knights behind him turned to run, but the front man fell backward, catching the knight closest.

Flame continued to stream from the fryer, lapping up the walls and along the thrashing forms of the knights.

Every surface the fire touched caught alight. What did I tell you about goblin food?

I swept Mogayne up in my arms again and rushed out the back door.

We were greeted by Saban and his still-impressive army of surviving knights.

TWENTY-ONE

Saban stood in front of the five rows of armored men. The knights stood in a loose formation, studying the smoke that was now billowing out of the kitchen behind me. The screams inside were growing louder. All of the knights in front of us burned that bright blue I'd come to hate.

"Where did you get this, orc?" Saban asked, turning my ax in his hand.

He didn't seem concerned with the pained cries of the men cooking alive. He just studied the ax, his face impassive.

I remained silent, forcing myself to stay put despite the heat of the fire that demanded I move forward.

I glanced around the parking lot and was relieved to see no dead goblins on the asphalt. In the growing darkness of the evening they had apparently all been able to escape.

Mo let out a quiet whimper and her grip tightened on my shirt. I could feel her heart beating, fast and hard. I forced myself to hum, as much for her benefit as my own, and her grip loosened slightly.

I'd always felt it, but never really figured it out before.

But whenever I hummed I managed to find confidence, a lack of fear. I'd always assumed it was just the power of music, that I was just distracting myself from the fear with the song, but as I looked down into Mo's eyes, I started to suspect it was something else.

"Did Jackson give it to you?" Saban continued, not at all put off by my silence. "Do you know what Jackson is? Do you serve him?" His tone changed slightly the more he spoke about Jackson. I wanted to say it was fear, but I recognized it as anger.

He had his reasons, I supposed. The wizard had defiled his temple all those years ago. That still seemed like a stupid reason to kill so many people. But gods are fickle, aren't they?

He finally looked up from the ax and considered me. He blinked in what looked like surprise. "How are you doing that?" he demanded.

I glanced around, looking at all the nothing I'd done. I wondered if maybe he meant the fire, but there was no way Ukufa was interesting enough that he hadn't noticed.

I considered him as he looked at his men. They all seemed restless. Some of them shifted their weight from leg to leg and others were nervously wringing at sword hilts. I couldn't see their faces, but I got the feeling they were nervous.

I idly wondered why some of them had turned their fires off. Hadn't they all just been on?

Mogayne gently tapped my arm and I lowered her feet to the ground. She seemed remarkably calm considering we were most likely about to die. I felt strangely at peace as well.

I kept humming, thrilling in the courage it seemed to be giving us both.

"Stop it," Saban growled, taking a step forward.

His men eyed each other, as though trying to decide if they should follow.

"I SAID *STOP*!" The god charged us.

Mogayne shoved me to the side, getting my feet moving and she dove the other way, just dodging Saban's frighteningly fast swing.

"Sing, Jack!" Mo shouted at me.

Her push had startled me and I'd stopped humming as I'd avoided the ax blow.

I realized the parking lot was brighter than it had been seconds before. The paladins were lit up again, their blue flames almost matching the orange in intensity.

Things started making sense at that point. I started to hum again, trying to recall the feeling of power and confidence I had found earlier.

Saban turned on me and I dodged again. Behind us the blue fires dulled.

I was lucky that the knights seemed content to just watch the fight. I suspected they were not used to having their powers taken. And I knew that's what was happening. The more I hummed, the stronger I felt. I found I was able to dodge the god's swings more effectively than I probably had a right to.

Mo had said to sing. The thought was an idle one, but I thought it might be a good idea. If humming did this, what could the actual song do?

As I opened my mouth to sing, the cavalry arrived.

The channeled thunder of a single gunshot drowned out the rushing crackle of the fire for just a heartbeat.

Saban staggered forward a step, sparks flying from the plate over his back.

He spun with an angry snarl, a jagged hole where the

bullet had hit the steel. His skin was unbroken, and the sight froze me in place, stuck any song in my throat.

The shot had broken whatever spell had the paladins stuck in place and the knights burst back into flame and movement.

Luckily they weren't the only people moving. Gunshots began to ring from all around the parking lot. Men dressed in black tactical vests marched out of the trees that surrounded the lot, shotguns and rifles firing.

There were almost as many of these newcomers as there were knights, and they all moved like they knew what they were doing. The way they walked, guns to shoulder, sweeping the area, they looked professional. That's the word for them.

The first shooter fired again, and I realized they were firing from across the street, most likely from the roof of one of the apartment buildings.

Saban didn't budge as the shot struck him in the chest. His eyes only narrowed as he glared at the building across from us.

The knights all had their fires turned up to high as they waited in formation for the shooters. None of the shots from this new force could get through the shields. Blue shock waves appeared in the air all around them and slugs ricocheted into the asphalt of the parking lot.

My new friend Vladik walked at the front of the new arrivals, dressed in the same SWAT get up and firing a massive shotgun from the hip.

I really wanted to watch what was happening, but instinct warned against that.

I looked back at Saban in time to see the ax coming and fell back out of the way.

More sparks flew from his back, but he ignored them as he raised my ax again.

You know how humans have a flight or fight response? Orcs don't have that. We only have a fight response. Sure, we'll run if we manage to stave of the berserker rage long enough to decide survival is a good idea. But usually, it's fight.

My adrenaline had worked its way to that point and I decided that taking on a god head-on was the best idea ever. I leaped inside Saban's range and tried to tackle him. In retrospect, it was the worst idea ever. I mean, he was just shrugging off bullets.

But I got close enough that instead of using the ax he just hit me with a rushed backhand. That sent me flying across the parking lot.

I crushed the passenger door of Ma's car with the force of my impact. It hurt like hell.

Once all four wheels were back on the ground the car released me and I slid to the ground. My chest hurt and I wasn't sure I could breathe.

An arm darted out from under the car and warm, soft fingers wrapped around my own limp hand.

"Hey," I managed to croak to Mo before I passed out.

Jackson wakes. For half a day, as he senses time, he has slept. As he slept, the computer, Sigmund, has worked to heal him. Has worked in an attempt to return the god's power.

Jackson rises from his seat, opening and closing his hands experimentally. He can feel the power there. It is not as much as he had on that hillside fighting the beastmen. It is far less than he had the last time he was forced to fight anyone nearing Saban's strength. But it is more than he had the last time he faced the god of justice and his knights.

"What have I missed?" he asks Sigmund.

"Saban is currently engaged with the wizard and her people. He is losing men faster than I would have expected."

"Good. Guess we both underestimated them. Are they all together?"

"The paladin, Arthur Shield, and several of his compatriots are currently unaccounted for. But I believe if you manage to defeat Saban, any of his men remaining will effectively be removed as threats."

"Do you know where they are?"

"No, sir. It seems Saban has found a way to prevent me from scanning the world properly. It is only his nature as a former Deus that has allowed me to find him."

"Show me."

Sigmund's ancient gears turn and a wall fills with an image.

For that moment, Jackson enters the same field of time as the battling warriors.

Jack Bloodfist is thrown across the small, pothole-filled parking lot and strikes the only parked car, collapsing to the ground, broken.

The Russian moves across the parking lot, firing his shotgun at a paladin who stands motionless, all energy focused on keeping his shield up. Vladik loads the gun as quickly as Jackson has ever seen, there are no breaks between shots. Pump, fire, load. He shows no concern at the nature of his opponents' shields.

Jackson grins at the prowess of Leonora's soldiers. They have learned from their last battle with these knights.

Vladik fires one last shot and steps through the blue light that encircles the paladin. He throws the empty gun aside and draws a longsword from a sheath at his waist.

He is as large as the armored man, and it quickly becomes plain that he is stronger.

Around Vladik and his foe there are dozens of others in the same black gear, all firing at shields, swords on hips or backs ready to draw when close enough.

"Clever girl." Jackson's grin widens. He is always happy when others prove him right.

Every world has its heroes, and he is happy to know that several of that world's stand together this day.

From across the street, on top of a building, Umanand fires round after round into the battle.

Saban turns away from the sniper, ignoring any stray shots that break his armor. He strides with purpose toward his servants, ready to turn the tide in his favor.

Jackson holds up a hand and the image slows to a crawl. He has returned to the time of his world. The minutes tick much faster in his plane.

"Let's give them a show, Sigmund." He removes the blood-stained jeans and t-shirt he is wearing and marches through the halls of his home.

As he approaches the doorway he needs to confront Saban he holds up the small cloth that holds his armory. Its surface writes itself with words understood in only one world within the Machine.

He touches a line of flowing text and the surface changes. He touches another and the black ink lights from within.

Around him the air shimmers with a glittering blue. The lights coalesce into armor. Black as the starless skies outside his home, the segmented plates fit perfectly and he moves as freely as if he were still naked. His own strength is augmented by the gifts of this steel.

This is the armor of a god. A Deus. Given to him by the Machine. Around his neck hangs a long, red scarf, the deep red fabric a subtle symbol of his station.

He will be wearing this when he defeats Saban. Despite his treachery, Saban deserves no less.

He clenches his jaw as he places a gauntleted fist on the necessary door. It slides open to reveal a great expanse of nothing.

"Draw from the sun, Sigmund. I need to get right there."

"Of course, sir. I assume you want a flashy entrance."

"I said to give them a show, didn't I?"

He steps through the door.

TWENTY-TWO

At the edge of my senses I could hear her crying, pleading with me.

The words were unclear, but I heard my name, repeated again and again. "Please, Jack, wake up."

I opened my eyes with a groan to find Mogayne huddled over me.

Her eyes were red-rimmed and her face was puffy from crying. Some women manage to look pretty while crying. Mo is not one of those.

"Jack!" She wiped her arm across her nose before grabbing my face with both hands and kissing me.

"Mmf," I said around her mouth.

"I thought you were dead," she said after finally letting me breathe.

"How long was I out?" I asked. Every hair of my beard screamed in pain.

She shook her head. "Not long, but you stopped breathing for a second."

"The fight?"

In answer she looked out across the parking lot. I

followed her eyes. Only after I saw the fighting did the sound rush back in.

The knights and the special ops guys were going at it the old-fashioned way. They'd given up on guns and were fighting with the medieval weaponry that they'd brought with them.

Unfortunately the fight seemed rather one-sided. Saban had waded into the mess and was swinging his fists around, sending men and women flying with vicious hits. Every so often he swung my ax and took off a limb.

Even the knights that didn't have the direct support of their god were doing disappointingly well. A few of the good guys went down with a stab through the gut, or by losing a limb. One of them scratched uselessly at the armored fist wrapped around her throat, right before her face lit up like a gas-soaked campfire.

A single gunshot fired, and I recognized it as the same rifle that had been peppering Saban earlier.

The god threw a hand over his shoulder as though swatting a fly. A small flattened disk of lead fell to the ground.

"Enough!" he bellowed.

His voice carried enough authority that everyone stopped fighting. Paladins and soldiers backed away cautiously.

Saban's voice was still reverberating as he turned toward Goblin Burrows, and whoever had been firing on him. His eyes narrowed and he held up his hand, palm out.

I felt the explosion more than I heard it. My body screamed in protest as Mo and I scrambled to the edge of the car so we could peer across the street.

The building was missing an apartment-sized chunk from the top floor.

We both turned again to see what Saban was planning to do next.

He was aiming his bomb-launching palm at Vladik. The paladin that had been fighting the Russian just moments before looked very nervous. Even wearing his helmet it was obvious.

"I am tired of this. I only came to punish those who desecrated my temple. But this world chose its side. For that, you all have to die."

He turned a hate filled glare on his knights. "And you, you are all weak. I will count it no great loss if you all die here today. It will allow me to ensure my next world has stronger guardians."

No one was able to find the will to move. Saban's voice didn't seem to allow it.

Then the very fabric of the world shook. Even the air vibrated from the force of it.

If you've ever heard the sound of reality tearing, of one world forcing itself into another, you'll understand.

I had been asleep the first time I would have seen this, but I know for a fact it hadn't been this loud. There couldn't have been that much fire.

All eyes were drawn up. Even Saban stared, hands slowly lowering as his mouth fell open.

I followed everyone's gaze, pulling myself up to peer over the car at the sky.

In the fading light of the setting sun it was impossible to miss.

The hole in the sky was closing fast, but I could still see through it. I could see the red sun, the shadow of the world that orbited it.

The red light filtered through the opening, brightening

the city around us. I saw no other stars with that sun. I don't know why I noticed that, but it scared me.

Then the sky sealed closed and I was left with just the memory of it.

And the sight of the black figure falling through the sky. It was burning, like a rocket reentering the atmosphere.

As it fell farther I could see it was human, or at least human-shaped, wearing black armor, now red on the underside from the speed of its fall. A red strip of something flew behind it like a banner.

It fell head first right toward our small battleground. The figure tucked itself forward and rolled so its feet were aimed downward, and it hit the ground.

The shock wave of the landing knocked everyone, except Saban, off their feet.

Glass shattered and flames flared. The car flipped over, with Mogayne and me thrown back to land on top of it.

The black armor rose slowly from its crouch, steam rising from the softly glowing metal and from the cracks of the bus-sized crater. The long, red scarf fluttered in the breeze, though I felt no wind.

Despite my pain I couldn't look away. I forced my eyes to stay open.

The black helmet's visor opened itself down the middle and the two halves folded back around the side of the head.

Jackson Smith scanned the parking lot, his face emotionless. He spotted me, sprawled out painfully on top of the flipped car, and smiled. I almost thought I saw relief in his eyes.

From a childhood of watching melodramatic action cartoons, I expected a speech of some kind. I mean, Goku always got one, but the real world doesn't always allow for that.

Saban jumped from his position halfway across the parking lot and tackled Jackson.

The two of them flew across the remainder of the lot and hit the ground where the road started. Their momentum carved a deep path through the asphalt, only stopping in the thin strip of grass that fronted Goblin Burrows.

With Jackson on the bottom, the two began to punch each other. Armored fists swung, and each hit sounded like boulders falling from a cliff.

Saban swung my ax at Jackson's head, but the wizard deftly dodged it, catching the god's forearm. He got his legs up and between the two of them, and kicked Saban back over his head.

The silver armor shot through the wall of the apartment building and the black rushed in through the hole after.

I pushed myself up, straining to see across the street. I was able to make out the flash of movement before the fight moved away from the hole in the wall.

Behind me I could hear the fight between the comparatively normal people start again.

I briefly thought about joining in before I collapsed on my back with a pained grunt.

"You okay?" I asked Mo.

"Been worse. I think."

"Cool."

The two of us stared up at the sky as it slowly turned black. I was distracted from my stargazing by the sound of tires crunching on the parking lot.

I turned my head to see three trucks parking around us. The beds of all of them were filled with orcs. The crudely drawn logo of Slaying Construction plastered on the doors.

I grunted again as I pushed myself to my elbows and studied the newcomers.

Jack One jumped out of the passenger seat of the first truck, Charles Slayinghand from the driver's.

"Hey, cousin," Jack said, a large sledgehammer resting on his shoulder. "Need a hand?"

I started to laugh as I slid off the car and forced myself to a standing position. Mo was at my side almost instantly, and the two of us supported each other as we waited for my family to circle us.

Charles was watching the fight between the humans intently. He rested his pickax against the upside down car as he rolled up his shirtsleeves. "I'm assuming the men in black are friendly."

"Enough."

"Good. Alright, let's go everyone."

"Hang on, boy," a voice shouted from behind him.

Charles turned to consider the elderly orc that pushed her way forward.

"No offense meant. But I've only ever fought under a Bloodfist. Slayinghands are great for running a fist, but a battle needs a Bloodfist at the head. What do you say, Garack? You feel up to it?" Twenty sets of orc eyes turned to consider me.

I shrugged, and it hurt more than any shrug has a right to. "First time for everything."

"You learned the songs yet?" she asked.

I blinked. "I think so." I knew one song. And I was sure it wasn't the one she had in mind. But I had the sense the words didn't matter. It was what I did with them.

"Good. Always better when a warcrier is giving the orders."

Charles sighed. "Fine. What are our orders, Jack?"

"If it needs a can opener, kill it."

That was enough for them. Mo and I helped each other turn as the orcs streamed past us. They jostled us in their excitement, huge shoulders almost knocking us back to the ground.

"How original," Charles said as he hefted his weapon and joined the others.

They all carried tools of some kind. Hammers, picks. One even waved a shovel over his head.

"You should probably sing," Mo said.

"Yeah." I started with the hum; I figured I'd go with what I knew worked.

The knights were ready for the orcs, and managed to have a second front ready to intercept. But now they were surrounded.

When I could feel the confidence growing in my chest I started to sing. The same song as always.

As the fight continued, my song grew louder. In the same way I'd considered Mo when humming, I tried to think of my cousins as they fought.

I could feel the power flowing through me, and I tried to share it. Before long, both Mo and I were standing straighter; my back didn't ache as much, and I thought I might be able to walk without help.

The blue fires around the knights were dimming again, and it may have been my imagination, but it seemed that a few orcs had red halos around their makeshift weapons.

Jack One had somehow fought his way through the ranks of paladins and was fighting side by side with Vladik. The big Russian blocked a sword, and Jack smashed the knight in the knees with his sledgehammer. As the paladin fell, Jack hit him again on the back of the head, and the armored figure collapsed on its face.

Vladik casually slid his sword between helm and backplate.

"*I have read a fiery gospel writ in burnished rows of steel. As ye deal with my contemners, so with you my grace shall deal. Let the hero, born of woman, crush the serpent with his heel, since God is marching on.*"

Before I could start the chorus again, there was the sound of smashing brick.

Jackson's black armor flew from the top story of the apartment building and he sped across the street like a meteor, crashing through the burning roof of Jack's Place.

I followed his path back to the building and found Saban framed in the new hole in the wall.

Saban bent his knees, and without the benefit of a running start, jumped from the hole. He flew higher than Jackson, but the destination was the same.

The flames licking up the walls of Jack's Place flared as the silver armor smashed through the roof.

Jackson rolls away as Saban's form smashes through the ceiling above.

The god's plate-covered knee shatters the already broken ground.

Jackson rises just fast enough to dodge the swing of the ax.

He curses the orc for losing the weapon, though, he knows that if Saban dropped the weapon it would be found again. It is impossible to lose. Unless someone is stupid enough to leave it where it can be found by a new wielder.

He manages to dodge the next swing, though only by fractions of an inch.

He is not able to dodge the kick. It sends him flying through another burning wall.

A heavy foot plants itself on his chest and he looks up into Saban's eyes.

The god is sweating, his face red from the heat of the fire.

"What did you hope to do, Deus?" Saban demands, pushing down hard with his boot.

Jackson wills his visor open. The sudden heat of the flames makes him gasp, but he forces himself to answer. "Send you to the Plain, Saban. You're a deserter. You must have known this was coming."

"I thought it might. But I had chosen a world so insignificant, I thought..." he shrugs, apparently not feeling his explanation is worth the effort. "Why you? You cannot be that old. Why not Kreiger?"

"He offered, but everyone thought it best someone impartial be sent."

"And the green-skinned monsters? Why force them into our little game?"

Jackson strains against the leg that holds him down, but Saban snarls, pushing down harder, raising the ax.

"Answer me, little Deus."

"You invaded their world. Raised yourself up as a god, you took that gear's rightful guardian and forced him to serve you. You'd corrupted everything with your presence. The monsters were the only ones who could do it."

Saban lowers the ax, his expression thoughtful. "I had not considered that gear worthy of its own guardian. Who?"

Jackson sneers. "I'll give you one guess." At his side he holds his fist, the faint blue outline of a sword barely visible in the smoky air of the burning building.

"I suppose it doesn't matter. I am done with that world. Maybe this one will offer more?"

"No. Not for you." Jackson swings his arm up, the spell already leaving his lips. "Zen so!"

Saban's eyes open wide as he throws his arms up to intercept the blow. The invisible blade cuts through his armor. The cut stops at his flesh, but the force throws him back off Jackson.

The ax, Ukufa, spins in the air and lands in a column of hungry flames.

"You'll never take this world. Not with its guardian right outside." Jackson stalks through the smoke and flame toward the prone god.

"What? That orc? You think just because his song can steal a little of my strength that he can protect anything from me?" Saban pushes himself to his knees, red face angry. "He can do nothing."

"Not Jack. He's not from this world. It would never accept him as its guardian. Maybe, if you hadn't interfered, he might have been the next guardian of his home. But you're wrong. His song can end you. That's why I brought the orcs into our little game."

"Ha." Saban barks a humorless laugh as he pushes himself to his feet.

The two men eye each other from across the inferno-walled room.

"He would burn to nothing before taking a fraction of my strength. Let me show you the real power of a god."

Saban's eyes fill with a blue that eclipses the amber flames with its light.

Jackson charges, hoping to stop whatever power Saban is preparing. His visor closes just in time to catch the punch.

The force of the blow kills the flames right around the

two men and sends Jackson flying through the wall that separates them from the battle outside.

After hours of hunting, of avoiding police and government agents, Arthur Shield has found the orc.

After the success of their attack on the police station, most of his brothers returned to Saban's side. But Shield refused. He'd made a promise to Shakill Goretusk. Promised he would kill her son, his wife and child. And now... now he is close.

He can smell the orc's corruption as he stalks the building.

Arthur has followed the van Luke left in for the better part of the evening. Hid behind buildings and cars, from the cover of trees, as the police transport dropped off its passengers one by one.

He'd noted the well-appointed home where Luke Goretusk left his wife and daughter, and he plans to visit them very soon. He ignored any safe house where humans were unloaded. Made plans and silent promises to visit any of the locations an orc was left. He would prove the promise of safety the officers made to be worthless.

But Luke was first. He had promised.

Goretusk and several other orcs had asked to be taken to a warehouse just outside of town. The officer had seemed reluctant to leave them alone, but something Luke had said had convinced the man to leave.

Then more orcs had come. Almost two dozen of the monsters.

Shield would have once thought his chances of killing

that many to be very good, but now, in his old age, he second-guesses himself.

The orcs left, piling into trucks, all carrying tools. The weapons of peasants in revolt. Shield trusts his god to kill them.

But he has not seen Luke leave. Of all he marked in the building, that orc alone remains.

All of Arthur's instincts warn him. The orc knows he is there. Is waiting inside.

And finally, after waiting, letting the green-skinned barbarian sweat, Arthur Shield enters the building.

He sneers at the crudely drawn image over the door— the orc and its spear.

There will be slaying, however. With that he agrees.

The whole building reeks of them, shows signs of their constant inhabitation of this place. Walls are punched in by large fists, words are scrawled over the brick of the building. Profane words in his native tongue.

There is no light, save what he creates. He considers, for a moment, turning off the light. Removing himself as a target. But ranged attacks will do nothing against his shield.

He decides to let the orc know. Let him quake in whichever hole he cowers.

His head snaps up at the sound of something coming to life.

Luke Goretusk roars his defiance as he drops from his hiding place in the warehouse racking. In his hands a saw blade spins hungrily.

Shield pulls up his broken sword to meet the spinning wheel of blades.

The momentum of the orc's fall knocks the blade down in a shower of sparks, but Arthur steps back quickly, dodging the second attack.

Luke throws the saw up and forward, the spinning blades just missing the plate steel of the knight's armor. At the top of the swing, he pulls back down and to the side, stepping forward as he does so.

Shield walks back, away from the surprisingly fast swings of the bulky power saw. When he needs to, he flicks his wrist and diverts the saw's path.

"I'll kill you," Luke snarls, every swing more urgent. "I'll kill you for what you did."

"No you won't, boy." Arthur swings his sword again, aiming for the grip on top of the improvised weapon. The glowing blade slices through three of Luke's fingers and the handle.

Luke roars in pain as he drops the tool. It clatters to the ground, running a few more squealing rotations of the blade, then it falls silent.

But the orc does not. He grasps his partial hand in the other and curses. But only for a little while.

Then he throws his head back and laughs. He runs the stubs of his three fingers over his face, leaving three lines of red down the green skin, and then he charges the knight.

Arthur throws his weapon to the ground and accepts the orc's tackle. He wraps Luke in his burning arms and picks him up.

With a twist of his hip he throws the orc over a shoulder and Luke twists away into the darkness, his shirt and the skin beneath catching alight.

Arthur follows the low light of burning flesh and finds Luke sitting against a metal beam.

The orc's eyes narrow, but he makes no other move. "Do it, then," he says, voice filled with pain.

"Of course."

Arthur raises a palm toward the orc, ready to push it through the chest, to squeeze all breath from the lungs.

The fire burning the orc blinks out, then the fire that covers the knight's body flickers and dies.

"No."

Arthur turns in the direction he knows his god lies. Something is very wrong.

I heard the sound of steel on steel before the sound of the burning wall smashing outward.

Jackson hit the pitted asphalt and slid to a stop, another trench of ripped-up pavement behind him.

I'd apparently stolen enough strength from the power rangers that I was able to turn and watch Jackson's progress without my entire body exploding in pain. Just a slight twinge in my lower back.

The part of me that wasn't caught up in the death and destruction around me found immense satisfaction in my new found abilities. Especially the apparent healing factor. I was like Rogue stealing from Wolverine.

In the time it took me to turn around, Saban had cleared the distance between himself and Jackson and had wrapped a now ax-less hand around the wizard's throat. He pulled Jackson off the ground and started to smash his visored face with a glowing fist.

I kept singing, trying to focus on Saban. Willing myself to take all his strength, but the god only started to glow brighter. For the first time he had his own aura of blue fire to match his men.

I watched, terrified of what was obviously going to happen.

Saban screamed in Jackson's face, each word punctuated by a ground shaking punch. "I... will... never... go... back! I am done with fighting its war."

He stopped punching Jackson long enough for an answer. They were close enough that I could just hear the weak reply. "If you won't go, then I have to kill you."

Saban threw his head back and laughed. There was no humor in that laugh. It was the sound of a man who had long ago given up on being human. I don't know why, but at that moment I realized that Saban *was* human.

The fear, the anger. Only a man could wear those emotions the way Saban did.

Jackson looked down from the laughing face of the god and focused on me. Even through the visor I could feel the intensity of his stare.

I understood, instantly, what had to be done.

Saban began another relentless beating of Jackson's limp form. The wizard offered no defense, just flinched and curled with every blow.

I pushed myself off of Mogayne's shoulder and ran. She shouted for me to stop, but it was too late. I was in motion.

I couldn't sing as I ran, and Saban's flames erupted, enveloping ten feet of parking lot around him.

"Sing, Warcrier!" Jackson's voice echoed out of his helmet.

I was just feet away from the two of them. Saban turned toward me, his eyes wide in surprise and anger.

I opened my mouth and sang.

One single, long note.

Directly in my path was a section of turned-up asphalt, and instead of going around I stepped on it and vaulted up into the air.

The whole time I screamed my song. My chest

thrummed with the power of it. At that moment, I knew what a warcrier was. What we could do. What *I* could do. I understood the pride in my father's voice every time he'd told me I had warcrier lungs.

I began to burn from the inside. I felt that at any moment my flesh would erupt into flames, that my muscles would disintegrate, bones shatter.

Saban seemed to sag, as though his armor weighed too much. His movements were sluggish as he raised an arm to defend himself. His eyes filled with fear as the arc of my jump became obvious.

In midair, I idly wished I still had Ukufa, and I brought both hands above my head, as though I still did.

Saban's strength continued to burn inside. I could feel it as my song took it all. Feel it in my arms, my hands. In my ax.

I brought Ukufa down with a wet thud and ended my song.

It turns out gods bleed. And they bleed red.

TWENTY-THREE

I stood over Saban's body, my hands shaking and muscles aching. My breath burned as it escaped my chest.

Somehow, I wasn't surprised to see my ax sticking out of the broken remains of the former god's skull. It had felt right that it be there when I needed it.

With their god dead, the paladins seemed to have lost all their power, and many of them had lost the will to fight.

My family and Vladik and his friends, however, had not.

I turned to watch; the killing didn't stop. Some of the knights put up a valiant front, but they were outnumbered now. Outnumbered and without that extra something Saban had given them.

I watched as Charles Slayinghand sent his pickax through the helmet of one knight that had thrown his sword down and dropped to his knees.

Jack One was relentlessly swinging his hammer against a paladin that had fallen to the ground, face pressed against the pavement.

Over the sound of the killing and dying I could hear the

moans and wails of mourning. I heard what it sounds like when a god dies.

The only thing left when a god dies is the faithful.

I won't say it was guilt, but something convinced me it had to stop.

"ENOUGH!" I shouted.

The swinging weapons stopped. Several orcs, and more than a few humans, blinked and seemed to realize what they had been doing.

They stepped away from the now docile knights.

The sound of a helicopter brought my head up, and I looked up at the craft.

I recognized the logo from one of the bigger news networks. I realized after a minute of staring at the thing that this was the first type of spectator I'd seen since arriving at Jack's Place.

There had been no one cowering behind cars, or peeking out of windows. I hadn't even seen anyone on the streets running in terror when Jackson had made his entrance.

I didn't have that long to think about that before a fleet of unmarked black SUVs pulled into the parking lot and filled the street around us. Those were followed by a small fleet of ambulances and sedans with flashing lights.

I heard a cough at my feet and looked down to find Jackson grinning up at me from his black helmet.

I helped him up from the ground and he grunted a thank you as he stretched his neck.

"Good work, Garack." He sounded like he meant it.

"What just happened?" I asked him.

A stream of medics from the ambulances rushed past us, ignoring the standing for the sake of those in worse condition.

"What do you mean? Weren't you watching?"

"You know what I mean."

"You just killed a god." He eyed the corpse behind me. "A dangerous god."

"I get the feeling there's more to it than that."

He met my eyes. "You're smarter than you look. Just like your father. He was too smart for his own good."

Around us the men in black were in motion. Vladik and some of his buddies were helping the medics sort through the wounded. Several of the black vehicles unloaded their passengers, men and women in suits who began to pace the battlefield as though it were a board room and shouted instructions to whoever would listen.

I half watched the activity around us while I spoke with Jackson. "I don't think anyone's ever accused me of being too smart."

"They will."

I forced what I hoped was a convincing smile. "Why don't you explain it to me anyway. What was Saban talking about?"

Jackson looked around the lot, paying particular attention to the suits. "Alright, twenty years ago I was in your world looking for Saban."

I nodded, Karen had told me as much, "Why?"

"I was given an assignment by the Machine to..." he paused, looking for the right word. "...retire him."

"The Machine?" I'd heard the capital M in the word. He said it with, if not reverence, then severe respect.

"Yeah. Don't worry about that too much. You're a smart guy. I'm sure you'll figure it out."

"Fine, whatever. Retire him from what? And since when do wizards get to retire gods?"

"Does that really matter?"

"It does to me."

"I'm not a wizard, Jack. I kind of hoped you'd get that part on your own."

"Then what are you?"

"I'm a deus. A god."

"A god that works for some machine?" Something at the back of my mind was working, but I couldn't quite figure out what dots it was connecting.

"Yeah. Anyway, as I'm sure you know, my plan to take care of Saban failed. Your family was put in danger. So I brought you here."

"Why here? I always wanted to know."

He shrugged. "This world doesn't matter. As far as the Machine is concerned it has absolutely no value. On the off chance that Saban followed, which I was kind of counting on, the collateral would be well within acceptable parameters."

"No value?" I snarled.

I thought of Denny, of Mo, of all my friends who had been hurt, who could at that moment be lying dead on the pavement. I was slowly growing less impressed with my childhood hero.

He just shrugged again. "Strategically, yes. There are plenty of other worlds that are worth more." His eyes drifted past me. "At least, that's what I thought."

I followed his eyes and found the distraction. Leonora was speaking with Charles. Her right arm was in a sling, but other than that she was dressed in the same tactical gear as everyone else, minus any bloodstains.

She noticed us staring and said something to Charles, apparently to excuse herself, and started toward us.

"Thank you, Jack," Jackson said again. "Seriously. If it hadn't been for your power as a warsinger—"

"Warcrier," I corrected automatically.

"Yeah, if it hadn't been for that, I'd be paste."

I turned to look at him again and found him studying me. His eyes were surprisingly cold. Calculating. He was studying a chessboard, and I had the feeling I had been promoted from pawn to knight.

"One day, I'll tell you the whole story. But for now, I need to speak with our mutual friend."

Leonora stepped up to us, her eyes locked on Jackson. She spared me an approving nod as she brushed past, but other than that I didn't exist.

"I'm not done." I grabbed Leonora's shoulder and pulled her back behind me. "I expect answers next time we talk, wizard."

He smiled at the title and nodded. "Fine, orc. Next time we meet, I'll answer any question you have."

"Good." I spared them an angry glare as I stalked away.

I could feel their eyes drilling into my back, but I refused to look over my shoulder. I had better things to do.

In the chaos of the parking lot it took me a while to find what I was looking for. Every orc I passed, whether they were being treated by a medic or carousing with other survivors, raised a hand and cheered, or gave me a respectful nod. From the older orcs that nod was a serious compliment.

I returned their greetings with a halfhearted wave as my eyes scanned the crowds.

Finally I found her.

Mo was sitting on the back of one of the ambulances, her shirt folded next to her, as an EMT inspected the cuts that covered her torso.

Anger at the goblins flared up again as I approached. There were far more cuts on her body than I had noticed before. Most shallow, just the one in her side apparently serious. But I was sure they all hurt.

I would be making some house calls later. Even if they had all packed up and left town, I would find them.

I sat down next to Mo, trying to avoid staring.

She shifted slightly, putting her back toward me.

"How you holding up?" I asked.

"Hurting a little. You?"

"A little sore. Pissed, mostly."

I found myself staring at Jackson and Leonora. They were ignoring everyone else now, heads close together, completely absorbed in their conversation.

I forced my eyes away and down to my hands. They were still shaking, and I realized I had no energy left. Whatever Saban had left me when he'd died had barely lasted my short hike across the lot.

"Are you Mr. Bloodfist?" a voice asked.

I looked up to find a large man in a very expensive suit.

"Who's asking?"

"My name is Barrie Lester. I work for the Dongli Conglomerate."

"The what-now?"

He smiled a patient smile. "Forgive me. I thought you knew. We are..." he waved a hand around, indicating the parking lot and all its activity. "We handle situations like this." He gave me a meaningful look that I didn't have the energy to interpret.

"Okay? So you're the guys that use murderers and wizards to do your dirty work?" I glanced at Leonora again, remembering some of what she'd told us earlier in the day.

His smile broadened. "That's right. You met Leonora and her squad, good. Yes, that's one aspect of our company." He didn't seem ashamed at all.

"Okay. What can I do for you?" I didn't have the strength to care, but I kept talking anyway.

"Well, I just wanted to thank you for your assistance in today's events. And of course, we were wondering if there was anything we could do to compensate you for your time."

I narrowed my eyes. "You want to pay me?"

"You did manage to eliminate several serious risks to national security. It's sort of the thing we're usually paid for. Very well, I should add. We thought it only fair to give you a commission."

My mouth opened but nothing came out.

I jumped as Mo stuck a hand under my ass and inside my back pocket. I shifted my weight to allow her access and she pulled her hand out holding a creased, sweat-dampened business card.

"You can send the check to that address," she said as she handed Barrie the card.

He accepted the card, not seeming to mind the condition it was in.

He smiled as he read it. "Fixer. I like it." He slipped the card into a breast pocket and turned away. "We'll be in touch, Mr. Bloodfist."

I watched him until he blended into the crowd. "What the hell is going on?" I asked.

"I dunno," Mo said as she threw half her blanket around my shoulders and leaned against me, "but I think I like it more than whatever was happening."

In the darkness of the warehouse Luke Goretusk watches as Arthur Shield falls to his knees and cries.

The old man rips off his helmet and unabashedly wails into the dark, tears streaming from his eyes and matting his beard.

Luke tries to rise, to move, but the pain of his charred chest is too much, and he settles back in his seat, a hissed breath all he can manage.

He decides it will be easier to wait for the knight to recover, to finish what he started. The pain is too much to do otherwise.

Before Shield does recover the building is swarmed by men and women in black tactical vests. The lights flicker on and the armed newcomers surround Arthur, guns leveled at the crying old man.

A stern middle-aged woman with her arm in a sling pushes through the crowd and stands in front of Shield. "Come on, Arthur. You're better than this. Act like the warrior I know you are."

"Leave me be, Leonora," the man sobs. "My lord has died. Let me have my grief."

"Yeah, he is dead. His skull was split open by Jack Bloodfist. How does that make you feel?"

Arthur's sob turns into a snarl of rage as he jumps toward the woman, hands open to break her neck.

But now he is just an old man again.

She easily sidesteps him, and her uninjured arm swings, driving a glowing fist into his face.

The man collapses. When he tries to push himself back up half a dozen boots are pressed on his back, pushing him back to the ground.

"Take care of this, Vladik," Leonora says to the big Russian.

"Yes, ma'am." The large man pulls a dagger from a

sheath and kneels to cut away the leather straps of the paladin's armor.

Leonora steps next to Luke and squats down to eye level. "You wouldn't by chance be Luke Goretusk, would you?"

"I am." The words hurt far more than just breathing, which has been almost unbearable.

"Good, your cousin was worried about you. Told me to make you call your wife. She's worried too."

She pulls out a phone and stretches it toward Luke.

The orc tries to lift his arms, but, with a grimace, gives up.

"Mind dialing for me?"

She nods and enters the numbers he instructs. She holds the phone to his ear as it rings.

"Hello?" Lise's voice is the most beautiful thing he's ever heard.

"Hey, babe." This time the pain is as sweet as it is crippling.

"Luke? Oh, thank God. Are you okay?"

"Yeah. Never been better. How's Mik?"

"She's right here. Miki, come talk to your dad."

"Daddy!" His gorgeous daughter's loud voice almost deafens him.

He grins.

He is lifted and placed on a stretcher, and as they wheel him out of the building he talks to his wife and daughter.

Leonora follows closely, face a patient mask as she holds the phone to the orc's ear.

Across town, in her hospital bed, Denelle Halldorson watches the live news report as the helicopter circles the parking lot of Jack's Place.

Fire engines are parked around the burning building,

doing their best to contain the blaze. All around the inferno men in suits and uniforms intermingle with large people Denelle knows to be orcs.

All over the potted and cracked asphalt men are removed from their armor and cuffed and manacled. They are herded into armored prisoner transport vehicles, each unmarked vehicle attended by a man or woman in a suit.

"Good job, boys," Halldorson says to no one in particular.

"What's that, Den?" Matt Fitzpatrick rises from his seat in the corner, surprised that his partner is awake after the drugs that have been pumped into her.

He finds her asleep, an uncharacteristic smile on her face.

TWENTY-FOUR

All things considered, I think everything turned out pretty well.

I mean, except for the depressingly large number of dead people.

Before sending her to rescue Luke I was able to get a few answers from Leonora. Turns out that after Mo and I had left them in the woods, she'd started tracking me again.

I guess she knew that eventually I'd be targeted, so once Saban and his flunkies had made their appearance, Dongli had done their thing and secured the area. Which was pretty lucky for everyone in the surrounding area.

They somehow managed to evacuate two entire city blocks around the diner without the paladins noticing. They also had a pretty decent perimeter set up. They'd let the orcs through on Leonora's orders; she'd had a hunch they'd be of use. And they also captured and detained any of my goblin relatives that had escaped.

They'd released them all back into the wild without much fuss after Saban was dead and all the knights were rounded up

The next day, Barrie Lester hand-delivered my check himself.

I stood in my doorway in slack jawed wonder at the number of zeroes.

"You're sure this is right?" I asked.

"Afraid so. Leonora pushed for more, but a first-time fee tends to be smaller than we'd like sometimes. We also took a little out to cover damages. Your grandfather will be receiving that check shortly."

"Oh, uh, of course." I did my best to pretend that I thought the check was too small instead of more than I'd make in two years of solid work.

"The next one will be better. I promise." He pulled out a card and handed it to me. "I'll be in touch, Mr. Bloodfist."

"Wait." I stopped him before he finished turning to leave. "What about Arthur Shield? You found him with my cousin, what's going to happen to him?"

Barrie's face went serious for a moment. "He's been taken care of. You'll never see Arthur again."

"Okay. Good." I stretched out my hand and Barrie accepted it with a firm shake.

"Have a good day, Jack."

"You too."

Over the course of the next week I did my best to make sure any loose ends were tied up. I started by using some of the money from my nice big check to buy myself a new suit.

Mo drove me to an unremarkable brick-faced building flanked by even more unremarkable brick faced buildings. Inside was very remarkable.

"I didn't even know this place existed," I said as I paced the line of displayed suits.

"That's because you only wear off the rack," she said with a playful grin. "Today, you're getting a real suit."

The tailor gave me a doubtful look as he instructed me to stand in front of some mirrors. "And what would the gentleman like today?" I wasn't even offended when he directed the question at Mo.

"Let's start with wool," I said. "I was thinking gray." Mo gave me an approving nod in the mirror.

"Of course."

From there I selected the fabric and the cut. Mo vetoed a few of my choices, but in the end I think we made the best choice.

Just so I wouldn't feel under-dressed for the rest of the things I needed to do, I also grabbed an off-the-rack suit. Turned out that Charles used this tailor, so they had some big and tall available.

Mo picked out a red silk tie for me. It was a little thinner than I was used to, but damn, did I look good.

From there we went to a car lot. Again, not one I would have stepped foot on without that extra nice check.

The suit makes the man. That saying is true. Where before I would have had a really hard time even getting a salesman to pay attention to me, now I was being pulled in three different directions.

"That one," I said, interrupting the three salespeople trying to get my attention.

One of them won their staring contest and led me to the Cadillac.

It was a deep red. That year's model of my dearly departed POS. What can I say, brand loyalty. The leather seats felt like heaven, and the wood-inlaid wheel felt perfect in my oversized fists.

"We'll just run your credit score and see about getting you a loan," the salesman said.

"Nah. I'll pay cash."

His eyes bulged a little, but in the end I drove it off the lot.

My visit with Charles Slayinghand was much more painless than I'd expected.

"I understand. Honestly, the fist should be at a place now where we don't need you to do every little thing for us. Though, I will miss you covering for some of the boys."

"Well, I'm sure I can still be convinced to help. You guys are still family. The issue is, it turns out I have not been charging enough for what I do."

Charles smiled. "I think we all hoped you'd never figure that out. Well, if you're not against it, I'd like to keep you on retainer. How much do you think that would cost me?"

"Tell you what: I'll do my normal duties for the next few months, no charge, *if* you rebuild Jack's Place. For cheap."

"Deal."

The next meeting went just as well as expected. Now that I was officially a freelancer, I needed work. Preferably something I was good at. Being ready for violence chief among my skills, I was the perfect choice for Kirk.

"So you want to work security, Jackie?" Kirk asked from behind his desk at the *Phases* office.

"Yup."

"Alright. You'll be working nights. Usually once, but sometimes two or three times a month. I'll email you the schedule."

"Great. Hey, how's Mike doing?"

"Oh, Officer Jensen will be fine. Sword through the heart doesn't take too long for a werewolf to heal. He just needs a lot of rare steaks and plenty of fluids."

"Good. I don't know if the city can afford to be short so many officers for so long."

"We'll find out."

"So, what are you doing about repairs on the clubhouse?"

"Basement's untouched. Figured I'd worry about it next month."

I pulled Charles Slayinghand's card out of my pocket and handed it to him. "Tell him you want Luke Goretusk to oversee the project."

I visited with Kirk for a little longer before leaving his office. Mo was at her desk and turned to face me.

I waited for her to say something but she just stared at me. "Not going to ask how it went?"

She snorted in the most ladylike fashion. "Please, I know how it went."

Before I could retort with something clever, my phone rang.

"Hey, Matt," I said.

"Hey, Jack. David says she should wake up today," Fitzpatrick told me. The man sounded tired.

I could understand that. I'd stopped by the hospital a few times in the last few days, but the detective had been asleep every time I showed up. As far as I knew, Fitzpatrick hadn't left the hospital in all that time. I'm not sure what his wife thought of that.

Mo joined me for the trip and we walked in on a fully conscious Denny sitting up in her bed.

"Jack, Mogayne." She looked up from her computer long enough to give each of us a curt nod of her head, and then she went back to work.

"Hey, Denny," I said as I took the seat Fitzpatrick offered me right next to the bed.

"Detective," she corrected, but it didn't carry the venom her corrections usually did.

We sat in silence for a long time as Denny worked on her reports for the events of the week.

"Should you be working like that?" Mogayne asked, obviously not as comfortable with the silence as the rest of us were.

Denny shrugged and continued writing.

"Elves heal fast, Miss Thornhill." David Terzi pushed his way into the room carrying a tray of food.

Denny eyed the tray warily as the doctor placed it on the table next to her laptop.

"Oh, it's fine. Got it from the staff kitchen. Much better than the stuff we give most patients."

"If you say so." Denny ignored the food and continued typing her report.

Terzi patted her arm fondly and turned to leave.

"Terzi," I said, straining to keep my voice civil. "Thank you."

"Of course, Jack." He closed the door behind him.

Denny pointed at Fitzpatrick without looking up, then at the tray of food. "Eat, Matt. Sally would be furious with me if I didn't make sure you ate."

Matt didn't even argue as he slid the tray off the table and onto his lap.

"Jack," Denny said, "that was good work the other day. If you ever consider a career change, I'd be able to get you into the academy without much issue."

"Thanks, Den, but I think I'm okay."

"If you say so. Nice suit, by the way."

My most painful visit of the week was my stop at Goblin Burrows.

I sat in Ma and Gramps's cramped living room, the shelves of knick-knacks kept staring at me with judging eyes for what I had come to say.

Outside was the sound of construction as crews of orcs from Slaying Construction worked to rebuild the missing apartment.

"Jack boy—" Ma started after I explained myself.

"Don't, Ma," I said. "I'm resigning. The clan can handle themselves without me. Obviously the two of you will always have my help, but I can't forgive the rest of the clan after what they did. Do you really think I could work for any of them after what they did to Mogayne? They almost killed her!" I didn't think it worth mentioning that they'd tied up the two of them as well as tried to hand me over to a group of vengeful zealots.

"We tried, Garack. Tried to stop them." Ma was as close to tears as I'd ever seen her.

I shook my head. "I know, Ma. But you didn't. And I want nothing to do with them. Ever again. So when you see them next, you give them a message from me." I rose from my seat, readjusting my new suit.

"What's that, Jack boy?" Gramps asked.

"You tell them I say, *fuck you.*"

Honestly, I didn't hold it against any of them. But I wasn't going to risk the greasy little bastards risking my, or Mo's, life again.

"By the way, I talked to Charles Slayinghand. The orcs will take care of the repairs of Jack's Place. You'll be getting a check from Dongli Conglomerate to pay for the damages."

It felt good to leave them on at least a slightly positive note.

My cousin Luke only had to stay in the hospital a few days. I made sure to visit him as often as I could. At first it hurt him to even talk, so I just sat there with him, and with Lise on the other side of the bed, Miki rotating between laps to sit in. I hummed quietly the whole time.

When Terzi finally said Luke was ready to go home, they took him to Lise's parents' place. None of them were ready to go back to their own home yet.

Lise planned a small, celebratory dinner to mark Luke's release from the hospital. I was invited, and Mo joined me. It was our first official evening as a couple.

The evening was nice. Lise's father grills a mean steak.

We all sat around the back yard, drinking and eating and filling the air with quiet, friendly chatter.

Early on in the evening Luke struggled to his feet, his face a mask of pain. He pushed Lise's hand away gently as she tried to help him. Once on his feet he raised his can of beer. "For the dead," he said, his voice still coarse.

"For the dead," we all echoed and poured our drinks onto the grass.

Miki sat in uncharacteristic silence as she studied the adults. Finally she stood up on her little chair and raised her glass of milk. "For Gramma." She poured the milk into the grass and I think almost everyone teared up a little.

Of course the orcs didn't. We're pretty good at not crying.

TWENTY-FIVE

Jackson stares out one of the many windows in his home. He studies the empty sky that fills with the image of his world, half in shadow, half lit by the light of the solitary red sun.

He wonders if he should have given the full story to Jack Bloodfist. Answered all his questions. He considers calling the orc.

But no. He isn't ready for that yet. One day he will be. Maybe one day soon. But not today.

He has made what arrangements he can for the orc's future. He has asked the wizard Leonora to watch him. The orc has magic in him, an inherent power that no one else in his current world shares.

Jackson has told Leonora of that power, and instructed her on how to prepare him. How to make him stronger.

"You're sure, Sigmund?" he asks the silent computer.

"With a ninety-seven percent certainty," Sigmund answers.

"Hm." Jackson watches clouds skim across the face of his world. "That's interesting."

"It does seem unprecedented, sir."

"When will it happen?"

"That I cannot say. Too many variables to predict accurately."

"Can you guess his calling?" Jackson asks, though he has his own suspicions.

"Again, sir, too many variables. There are any number of Deus ready and willing to step down. He could fill many of those roles."

Jackson feels a stirring within himself. Is it anger? Jealousy? Why must Sigmund lie to him? To *Him*?

He closes his eyes and probes inward. His senses touch the tendril of darkness within his heart.

With jaws firmly clenched he burns it away with a flash of his power.

He is not ready yet. He knows how every one before him has ended their calling. But he refuses. He has already lasted longer than any of his predecessors. He will do what none of them could. He will win.

Sigmund believes Jackson is unaware of the darkness that is slowly eating away at his heart. He lets the computer believe that. It doesn't matter too much. The Machine has a contingency. It always does.

For decades Jackson has fought, afraid to allow himself to fall to the evil that so desperately wants him. Afraid that maybe, just maybe, the Machine doesn't have anyone ready to replace him. That there will be no one there to kill him when it needs to be done.

Now he knows. Knows that in an insignificant world there lives a warcrier. An orc that will one day, if and when it becomes necessary, become a god.

Jackson is scared.

- - -

From the outside the building looks like any of the other skyscrapers in the city. Maybe a little more modern, definitely more expensive.

Halfway up the generous floor count of the Dongli Conglomerate's world headquarters are cells.

Cells that hold some of the most dangerous men and women in this world and others.

In one of these cells is a man. He is not kneeling.

The spartan chamber holds him, a cot, a stainless steel toilet, and a camera that watches his every movement.

His name is Arthur Shield. And his god is dead. Throughout this building are his former brothers. Their god is dead, too.

Within their hearts burn anger and hate. Some stronger than others, but all feel the pain of their god's death.

Higher floors hold the offices of some of the most powerful people on the planet. From their desks decisions are made that change the course of history. They deal in the currency of life.

These decisions are of no concern to the Machine.

Hundreds of miles away, in a small trailer, exactly like all the others, perhaps less modern, much less expensive, there lives an orc.

He does not yet have the power to deal in the currency of life. He is poor by the standards of this world. But his decisions are marked by the Machine. They matter.

"You never did tell me what you are," Jack Bloodfist says to the woman in his bed.

She stretches as she looks at him. He could look at any inch of her, but he focuses on the sea green of her eyes as she smiles.

"Really want to know?" she asks.

"I want to say, wereotter. But that feels wrong."

"That's because it is." Her voice is as lazy as the hand drawing circles on his chest. "I'm a selkie."

"I have no idea what that is," he says, always honest with her.

"I know." She rolls over and presses her back against his chest. "Does it really matter?"

"Not one bit." He holds her. Tightly.

They move together now, and, for this night at least, both are happy.

EPILOGUE

And now, I'm here. Beneath the dual sky. I try to stay to the side that is full.

Full of life, death. Love and hate. Full of everything that ever was and ever might hope to be.

But no matter how far in that direction I march over the dry, red ground, through the rough, dying grass, I can always see that other sky. Full of nothing. A nothing that seems to writhe, and reach. I can feel the hungry mouths that no one has ever seen. They strain towards me through the infinite expanse of nothing.

And now I'm here. Standing alone in the red sand, a soft white glow lighting the ground that is lacking in any clear path.

Many have come here before me. Every god that has failed at their task has been sent here. Sent to continue the fight.

This is where Jackson always intended to send Saban before I killed him. Before I marked myself. Before the Machine decided I was needed.

None have ever left. But I will.

A lot has happened between then and now. Please forgive me if I don't share it all right away. This story will take a little time. And right now, I would rather think of that happy moment I shared with Mogayne Thornhill.

I can hear the footfalls in the sand now. I know what they are. I have to run. I will share more when it's safe to do so.

I will leave you with this promise: I will leave this place. If I have to, I will pull myself, hand over hand, up the pillar that holds all Creation.

I will climb to the top of infinity, past nothing, through the hungry mouths of ancient, rejected evil.

I will do anything just to see those green eyes again.

End of Book 1

Thank you for reading *Jack Bloodfist: Fixer*, if you enjoyed it, please consider leaving a review.

Jack Bloodfist returns in: *Freelancer*
Available Now

jamesjakins.com